Because of Her

Copyright © 2023 Chrystal Murphy

All rights reserved. This book or any portion thereof may not be reproduced or used in any manner whatsoever without the express written permission of the publisher, except for the use of brief quotations in a book review.

First Printing, 2023

ISBN: 979-8-9878140-0-0

www.chrystalmurphy.com

For my Cookie.

Without you, none of this would be possible.

Prologue

It's one of the most frightening yet beautiful things I have ever seen. The irresistible orange and red flames flickering in the night sky are intoxicating. All I can do now is watch and wait. It's too late to try and put the fire out or to help anyone that might still be inside the building, but at least I got out in time.

I wanted to breathe them in. It's as if the flames were hypnotizing me, but every time I tried, I started to choke from the smoke emanating from them. I wanted to know what the flame felt like when the fire started to overtake the living room, but the pain from the intense heat warned me away very quickly. The flames burned my skin 'til it bubbled and blistered.

I didn't mean to start a fire like this, but what else was I supposed to do? I tried to put it out. I didn't want it to get so out of control. I only wanted to burn the bad parts. The emotions and feelings that I had locked away for so long—the ones that had been controlling my life for years. But love can force you to make bad choices.

It's one of the most dangerous things you can put yourself in front of, even more dangerous than fire. It creeps up inside of you, twisting itself tightly around all your organs, absorbing into your system until you have no self-control anymore. You can't breathe or eat unless it allows you to. It flutters all around your chest and stomach, tickling at first then wrenching everything out of place violently. When it's over it's ripped away from you, clawing and screeching and leaving scars that never heal.

I know that I need to leave before the firefighters and the police get here. I don't want anyone to know that I was here tonight, but the way the smoke is marking the tan building with black charcoal is beautiful in a strange way. The city lights in the background give it a mysterious presence. I can't stop staring at it; it's mesmerizing.

At least it's all over now. I won't have to worry about it anymore. I can put all these painful feelings behind me.

I can hear the sirens in the background. They are still faint, so I have a little more time to watch it all burn.

1
Emily

"Okay, you can open your eyes now," Christina says.

I gasp when I open my eyes and look in front of me. The building that she brought me to see today is absolutely gorgeous. She said it was beautiful, but I am a little taken aback by how truly beautiful it is. It takes my breath away for a moment.

The ornate Victorian building at 322 Plum Street stands three stories tall. It is light brown, closer to the color of sand, and looks freshly painted. It seems to be made from some sort of stone architecture, perhaps limestone or sandstone. It has a steep gabled roof and lots of detailed gothic curlicue trim above each of its tall, thin windows. Some of the curlicues are shaped in patterns that look like flowers and leaves and others are large sunbursts that explode out of the building.

"Wow, it's like a dollhouse," I say breathlessly.

"I know, right! Just like we had when we were little girls."

I wish I had had a dollhouse like this when I was little. I didn't know that girls even had this kind of thing in real life. I have seen them in their bedrooms on television, but I never knew anyone that had one.

Christina turns to me with a huge smile on her face. "Do you like it?"

"I mean, of course I like it. It's beautiful, but I...." I trail off. "I just don't know how to feel about this yet. It's all so sudden."

"Emily, this has your name written all over it. The bottom floor is a commercial rental, and the top two floors are apartments. This retail space would be perfect for your business. Look at this street. This part of town is such a trendy spot for the artistic type."

I take some time to look up and down the street as she is talking.

"There is a custom jewelry store; a handmade soap store; a yoga studio; add in more eclectic shops, boutiques spas, and an art studio right next door. Not to mention so many cute little coffee shops, cafés, and restaurants all around here. The East Fourth Street district is highly sought after for store rentals right now."

The streets of downtown Cincinnati are busy today. There is a good deal of people walking around, carrying shopping bags, going in and out of the stores and cafés. Everyone looks carefree, enjoying the last day of summer. Tomorrow is the fall equinox, and the leaves here in the city have already started to turn various shades of oranges and yellows, but the weather has stayed fairly warm, with today being in the mid-'70s.

A lot of the shoppers are sipping out of blue paper and plastic cups. They must be from a coffee shop nearby. I make a note in my phone to check that out. I keep a list of all the things that I want to try from the city in an app on my phone. I have only been living here in the Cincinnati area for eight months now, and I want to experience everything.

Most of the stores seem to be small independent businesses. Christina is probably right; my furniture business would fit in well here.

I have a small business upcycling and restoring old furniture. I find old pieces at various places—thrift shops, antique stores, and garage sales—but my favorite place to find pieces is estate sales. People never know what they are getting rid of. It's usually a family that has lost a loved one, and they just want to clean out the house and get rid of all the junk. Half of the time, though, it's not junk; it's something that can be repurposed into something new and can be worth quite a bit of money.

I started this business first as a hobby when I was in high school, then slowly began using my skills to make some extra money after I graduated. After I moved to Cincinnati, I started my own business out of my home. Since then, I have built a huge following selling what I make out of my workshop.

I have been selling things online through Facebook Marketplace and Craigslist and have been doing really well, but business has been so insanely busy lately that I can hardly keep up with the demand.

I can take most old furniture that I find and make it look like new again, in a more modern and stylish way. You can show me a picture or a design that you like, and I can make a used piece of furniture look just like it at a fraction of the price.

Just last month, a lady showed me a dresser that she wanted from an *Anthropologie* magazine. It was $2,000, which is absolutely ridiculous. I found a similar dresser at an estate sale for fifty bucks. After stripping all the old varnish off, I sanded it, repaired some damage to the wood, and then cleaned it well. It was like a freshly built dresser again. I painted it the same matte black as the *Anthropologie* dresser and added some wood details, gold hardware and legs, and, *poof!* almost the same dresser.

My client was extremely happy, and so was I. Not only did I make a pretty good profit off that piece, but then seven other people contacted me from her referrals. The increased referral business, on top of the dozens of other people already waiting for pieces, means it's time to make a change.

My choice is to either scale back my clientele and reduce my inventory or rent retail space and hire some more employees. It is apparent that I can no longer keep up with the demand. I have a couple of guys that work for a moving company that come and help me move the pieces that I get around town, but that's all the help I have right now.

This is where Christina comes in. She is my real estate agent, but if I'm being honest, she is now more than that. She has become a good friend. She helped me find the house that I live in now and is super good at her job. All I had to do was tell her what I was looking for and she automatically knew which house I would love. The first place she took me to see I fell in love with and made an offer that day.

All I had to do was simply mention this morning over coffee that I might be interested in retail space, and before I knew it, she was dragging me down to Plum Street with my eyes closed.

"When you said you wanted to rent retail space, I knew this was kismet," Christina says.

"I said I was thinking about *renting* retail space," I correct her.

She ignores my correction and goes on talking. "I just found out they were putting this building on the market a few days ago. No one even knows about it yet. I found out from my friend Brandi who works for the Alexander Group; she's the owner's personal assistant. They own this building and a bunch of other properties.

"She told me that they were going to be using this building to start a new division of their company, but that all went downhill pretty fast. It is all quite scandalous."

"Scandalous?" I raise my eyebrows. "What does that have to do with opening up a new division?"

Christina gets that wicked smile on her face when she is about to tell me some juicy gossip. I have seen this often. She loves to talk about things that go on in the real estate industry.

"The owner's wife was going to open an interior design business here and use the apartments at showrooms, but they are getting divorced now."

"What's so scandalous about divorce?" I ask.

"There was something else that happened. I am going to get all the details about it from Brandi over drinks on Friday," she squeals.

I love Christina so much. I am so lucky she chose me to be one of her hundreds of friends. She is the type of woman that is always on the go, living the fantasy life I am sure most women her age would dream of. At thirty-five, she could easily pass for her mid-twenties, living downtown and making a ton of money in the real estate industry. She is not tied down with a husband or any kids. She has a boyfriend from what I can tell, but he doesn't seem to control what she does. She is always traveling around the world with him or one of her many, many friends. I am not entirely sure how she knows so many people, but there are always tons of pictures of them on her social media pages.

"So, this is your lucky day, Emily. I could get this for you."

"I don't know, I still need to think it over," I tell her hesitantly.

"Well, you'd better think quickly because when this goes on the market it will get snatched up lightning fast. Like I said, this is a very sought-after part of town," she warns me.

I look up and down the street again, my mind running a mile a minute.

"What are you so scared of?" she asks.

I am scared of a lot of things. What if I fail? What if I screw it all up and have to go back to where I was before? Things have been going so well lately. I still cannot believe how drastically things have changed since I moved here. Before, my life was a catastrophe, but I pulled it together, and this year has been the best year of my life so far.

I think of what my mother would have said about this. She would say, "Close your eyes and make a wish." We would do this often when I was growing up while lying in bed together at night. Lying in the one and only bed we had in our tiny studio apartment, usually after she came home from being with one of her many boyfriends—battered, bruised, or heartbroken. There was always some asshole treating her like crap. We would make up all kinds of stories about things we were going to do, places we were going to see. We would create whole new versions of ourselves, with new names and appearances, and then wish for it all to come true. She would be so proud of how far I have come in life.

"Can we look inside?" I ask.

"Not yet. They still have some things to tie up after all the renovations, but you will be amazed when you see inside this place. Brandi showed me some pictures of what they have done with the space. It is 1,200 square feet, has twelve-foot ceilings, open brick walls, natural hardwood floors…so many upgrades from before. It has a break room with a kitchenette and a storage area in the basement. There is an entrance in the alley that has wide double doors so you can easily move furniture in and out."

"What used to be here?" I ask her.

"If I can remember properly, it was some shop, but that was a year ago, so I'm not exactly sure."

"Will they want to move their business back in?"

"No, I am sure after the fire they would not want to do that. There was a lot of damage done to this place."

"Um, excuse me? Did you say fire!?" I say incredulously.

"No need to worry. I know what you are thinking. It was not a big deal. There were just minor injuries, and everyone was fine. The emergency crews managed to rescue everyone from the building. No deaths here!" she says with a nervous laugh.

She is reassuring me because the house that I bought had a history of deaths. So, for her to show me yet another property with such tragedies would be morbid.

"How did the fire happen?" I ask.

"I am not sure what happened. The fire started on the second floor, and it was deemed an accident. But since then, they have fireproofed the whole building and installed all new fire escapes."

I look at the black, iron fire escape stairs leading down from the top floor and think how hideous they look against the beautiful sandy building.

She looks at her watch. "Oh shoot, I have an appointment to get to. Sorry love, I've got to run." She turns to me and grabs both of my arms a little too tightly. "Please, Emily, think about this. It is an amazing opportunity. I would not have told you about it first if I didn't think you deserved it more than anyone else."

I promise her that I will let her know as soon as possible and watch her walk up the street.

I look back at the building and wonder what it looks like inside. If it's anything like the outside, it must be incredible. I try to imagine what open brick walls and twelve-foot ceilings must look like.

I walk up to the front of the building. There are two black doors set apart from each other, with small windows on the top of them. In between them are two large sets of black-framed windows. All of the windows are covered with brown paper except the door to the left. I walk to the door and peek through the small window. To the left, there is a narrow stairway leading upstairs and a hallway to the right leading to the back of the building. This must be the door to the apartment entrance. I try it and it's locked. There is a keypad on the wall where you can enter a passcode from the number pad, and underneath is six buttons that must connect to the unoccupied apartments. I push them all just in case someone might be in there that could let me in. I wait for a minute and hear nothing back.

I walk to the door located on the right and try the handle, but it's locked as well. I try to peek in between all the brown paper on the windows, but they have it taped up from the inside pretty well, so I can't see anything.

I remember the alley doors that Christina mentioned and walk down to the end of the block and find a space in between the buildings that leads back to the alley. When I get there, I walk back up past the other buildings toward number 322. I find the double doors hidden in an alcove with the correct numbers written on them.

There is no one in the alley, so I walk up a few steps through the alcove to the black-framed glass doors to try the handle. Just as I am reaching for it, an alarm starts blaring loudly. I am startled by the ear-piercing sound. I step back out into the alley and look around. I see that it's coming from a car parked about two hundred feet away

The rhythmic beeping of the car alarm echoes down the entire alley, bouncing off the walls of the buildings, making it sound way louder than it should. I watch carefully to see if anyone will come out to check on their car.

Instead, I hear a woman yell from one of the windows, "God dammit, get your car alarm fixed already." Then a few seconds later, a louder double beep from a key fob signals to turn it off. They must have done that from inside one of the buildings because I still don't see anyone in the alley.

I compose myself and walk back up to the door and try the handle. Of course, it's locked as well. I cup my hands around my eyes and look in through the windowpanes. It's dark inside but not completely blacked out; the brown paper from the front windows allows some light to come though. From what I can tell, it's completely empty. I don't see anyone in there.

I step back out of the alcove and turn to stare at the building, feeling disappointed. I sigh. I guess I can wait for Christina to get me inside.

I start to walk away and see a pile of old red bricks stacked up by the building next door. Suddenly, the car alarm goes off again, and before I even have a moment to think about what I am doing, I see the glass from the double-paned window shatter from the brick I barely even remember grabbing and throwing.

I only hear a faint sound of glass shattering because the sound from the car alarm is too loud. The double beep from the fob disengages the alarm again. I poise myself ready to run in case anyone could have possibly heard the glass breaking. I am fairly certain that no one could hear it over that alarm, but I wait to make sure. I count to ten slowly, then to fifty. The only thing I hear is the faint sound of traffic coming from the other side of the alley.

I walk the few steps again and reach my arm in through the broken glass on the door, taking care not to cut myself on any of the shards. I reach down deep into the doorframe and turn the lock from the inside until it clicks. I turn the handle and it opens right up. I wait a second to see if there will be another alarm coming from the inside of the building, but nothing happens. That must be something the business will have to install when they rent this place.

I walk in and close the door behind me so no one knows I am inside. Which is pretty useless, considering all of the broken glass around the door. I probably should not have broken the glass, but when I turn the light switch on and look at the room, I think it is worth it.

There is a short hallway leading into a much larger room. I walk a few steps in and to the left is the break room with a refrigerator, sink, some counter space, and cabinets. The hallway offers plenty of space to haul furniture through, even if some of the pieces are large. I can smell fresh paint and new wood in the air. I pass the break room and head further into the space. A large, magnificent showroom opens up when I get out of the hallway. The ceilings are so tall it makes the room seem much larger than 1200 square feet. So, this is what twelve-foot ceilings are like. It's nice. The brick walls are whitewashed to look modern. The wood floors appear to be oak, and there isn't a single scuff on them. They are shiny, as if someone recently polished them. I don't see any remnants of a fire or smell any smoke.

I am standing in the room, staring in awe at how nice it is, when the car alarm goes off in the alley again. This time I hear the same woman scream out of the window, "Move your fucking car or I'm coming down there with a baseball bat!"

I feel like that's my cue to leave before anyone comes out into the alley. I go out quickly through the shattered door and head back the way I came. I walk with a sense of something new taking hold in my life, a feeling like just maybe I can make this happen.

2

Victoria

A huge wave of relief rolls over my body as I settle into my seat on the plane. The flight from Los Angeles to Cincinnati won't be long, just over four hours, but I need every minute of that to settle my nerves and collect myself from the chaos that happened here.

There is a bustle of people walking past me to the back of the plane, looking for their seats in coach. This airline boasted luxury, spacious seating for first-class passengers, but there isn't enough space to prevent some of them from bumping into me with their luggage as they pass.

My irritation rises when the traffic stops and a chubby man in a business suit stares at me with a sly smile on his face. He is trying his hardest to make eye contact with me, but I refuse to give him anything but a glare from the corner of my eye. He brushes my arm with his fingers when the line of people starts moving again, and a wave of annoyance runs through me. I look around frantically for the flight attendant. I desperately need a drink.

I will be able to calm down as soon as the flight takes off, speeding far away from this place and home to my family and friends. I will completely reset my life and forget about everything that has happened here in LA. I will forget about Brent and our marriage that didn't even last a year, the Alexander Group, and all the people within it. No one will ever know what I have done.

I know that's wishful thinking, though. There is a chance that Brent will change his mind and tell everyone what has happened. He has promised that if I make the divorce easy on him, he won't speak about it to my family or his. Everyone would be so angry with me. Our families have been friends for years. Our fathers have known each other since they were in college, but even if that weren't the case, they would still think what I did was wrong.

An elderly lady bangs her carry-on case into my arm and does not apologize. Why do they have priority boarding for first-class passengers, forcing us to get on the plane first? They should allow time for first class to board *after* everyone else has boarded. I should have just sat in my seat in the terminal until they almost closed the gates.

Where in the hell is the flight attendant?

I close my eyes and try to drown out the people all around me. My thoughts go right to everyone back home in Cincinnati. I can't wait to see them all again. My parents, Katie, my sister Evelyn, but especially Hudson, my brother. He is my rock, the one I will be able to turn to for help. I will tell him about the divorce, but not the real reason for it unless I absolutely have to. Hudson and Brent have been friends for a long time so he will probably be a little upset that we have ended things, but I know that I am more important to him.

My sister Evelyn and my parents are a different story, though. They will all be immensely disappointed in me. I can only imagine the look on my father's face when he finds out. Then will come the lectures about needing to get my life into order and about all the bad choices I make in life. My father is not one to accept failure, especially not when it causes him shame.

Finally, the overly cheery flight attendant comes by and greets me with a fake smile plastered across her face.

"It's about time," I say, irritated.

"I'm so sorry, ma'am, we are a little short-staffed today, but I will take care of whatever you need right now. Would you like a glass of wine or some water before we take off?" she asks me with the same over-rehearsed tone of voice she uses with all the passengers.

I stare at her incredulously. I need something much stronger than wine.

"Vodka on the rocks, make it a double."

She nods and heads straight to the gally, her high ponytail swinging back and forth.

I steady myself while I wait, twisting the silver bracelet on my arm, touching each of the charms as I turn it around my wrist. My mother gave it to me a long time ago, and it gives me comfort when I need it.

The pilot comes over the loudspeaker as the other flight attendants start to close and lock the doors of the plane.

"Welcome to Delta flight 881 from Los Angeles to Cincinnati. Today should be an easy flight. We have good weather the entire way there and are third in line for takeoff. We have a good headwind, so we will be arriving in Cincinnati a bit earlier than scheduled. The flight time is four hours and twenty-three minutes."

The perky flight attendant comes back and sets my drink on my tray table. I don't even look up at her. I grab the drink, pull it to my lips and take a large gulp. I feel the vodka burn as it runs down my throat and, soon after, the welcoming numbing effect the alcohol has on my body.

I watch out the window as the landscape of Los Angeles starts to fade away, and I know that everything is going to be alright.

3

Emily

I awake early from sleep that never really came. Which isn't surprising. It never really does, but last night I tossed and turned much more than usual. My mind would just not shut off. I couldn't stop thinking about what Christina said, about how this rental would be a great opportunity for me.

The building was so gorgeous inside and out. I imagined myself walking in and flipping over the open sign, greeting all my customers as they come in. Getting to know the other business owners on the block, maybe making some friends. I also imagined no one showing up, making a mockery of myself, and failing. I just don't know if I am ready to take such a huge step. It's really scary for me to put myself out there like that when so many things could go wrong.

I know I shouldn't feel this way. So many positive things have happened since I moved here, but I am worried that at any moment everything will come crashing down. That all this luck I have been having will come to an end. But is it really luck? Or is it that I finally have gotten rid of all the toxicity in my life and worked hard to get where I am today?

I look at the clock on my nightstand. It says 6:13 a.m. I sigh and tiredly swing my legs out of bed.

I look around my bedroom to make sure it is the same bedroom that I currently live in, something I have done every morning since moving here. I make sure that the walls are the same dusty lavender that I painted them six months ago. That the floors have the new plush beige carpet I had installed right after I moved in, and the art on the walls are the flowers that I took pictures of myself and had made into canvases. I do this because, after all this time, I still can't get used to this being all mine. I am a lot better since I first moved in, though. I don't think I slept more than three hours a night for the first several months I was here. I would wake up in the middle of the night covered in sweat, worried about where I was, thinking I might be back in that place I ran far away from.

I head into the bathroom and stand in front of the mirror, looking at my reflection. The person staring back is someone that I barely recognize. I was so broken down by everything that life had thrown at me at such a young age. Now I'm someone new, and I am not going to let anything break me like that ever again.

I take a deep breath and hold it in as long as I can, then slowly let it out. I do this three times in a row. I learned to do this in situations to bring myself into focus or when I need to calm myself down. I used to have a lot more anxiety. I have been able to manage it better now, but I still do this every morning so I can remember to stay focused.

I splash water on my face and brush my teeth to get ready for the day. I am not one to wear makeup or style my hair. I just run a brush through my long brown strands and tie it back into a ponytail for the day.

I have my yoga class this morning. I go to the Yoga Loft every Tuesday and Thursday religiously. It's another way to help center myself.

One benefit of waking up this early is that I can get in a run before my class starts. Running has become a passion of mine since I moved here. A fresh start for me meant picking up new hobbies and learning new things that make me a better person. It was also a good way to lose the weight that had taken over my life. It was hard at first; I didn't realize that you actually had to learn to run. The first time I tried to go for a run, I thought I was going into cardiac arrest from the pain shooting through my body and the lack of breath. Now I can easily run miles without breaking a sweat.

I put on my matching leggings, sports bra, and jacket that I bought from an expensive store in the mall, one that proclaims their "athletic wear will navigate you on your journey with confidence and poise." A ridiculous statement, really, but that tiny little logo they put on the back of their clothing somehow makes me feel empowered. It's something I would never have worn or cared about before, and I certainly would not have been able to afford it on my own, but things have dramatically changed for me.

Growing up, it was just me and my mother, and we were poor, to say the least. She worked at a crappy diner and didn't make very much money. The money that she did make barely paid for the rent on the tiny studio apartment we lived in.

She was a beautiful woman with long brown hair, huge blue eyes, and could always pass for my big sister—mostly because she was so young when she had me—but she had an innocence about her, an innocence that most people took for granted. She could have gotten a much better job, but her self-esteem was too low. It was so low that she worked at that diner for years and allowed man after man to treat her like dirt, and she kept going back for more.

One night after work she came home and told me to put on my pretty dress, the only one I had ever owned. I was fourteen at the time and that pretty dress barely fit me anymore. She spent an hour doing her hair, putting on her makeup, and she put on a black dress that I had never seen before.

When we walked outside our apartment, there was a very handsome man standing out there waiting for us. He was dressed nicely in a jacket with a tie. He opened the car doors for us to his shiny BMW. When inside, he turned around and told me his name was Brooks and he was going to be my new father.

This was so unlike any situation my mother had ever put me in before. She had lots and lots of boyfriends, I'm sure some of them with money, but I never saw any of them in person. Sometimes she would show me photos, or I would hear their voices talking to her over the phone late at night, but never did she bring any of them to our apartment or take me out with any of them.

We went to a nice restaurant with cloth napkins and fancy food. I had never been to a place like that before, and I sat there eating dinner, watching them talk and laugh. My mother was smiling and had a new presence about her. She seemed happy for the first time ever in my entire life.

After dinner he drove us home, and the next day we were packing our things and moving into his house. He had a huge expensive house outside the city in the suburbs. It was the biggest and most beautiful house I had ever been in, and I was given my own room—my very first room all to myself—and I was in heaven.

Shortly after we moved in, they married by the justice of the peace. It was me, my mom, Brooks, and his mother. She was an old, scary lady who scowled at us the entire time. Shortly after that, he adopted me officially as his daughter. I never knew my real dad, so this was all very exciting for me.

We were all happy until two years later when my mother was diagnosed with cancer. She held on for quite a long time, but the cancer eventually consumed her, and she died just a few weeks after my nineteenth birthday. That was the first heartbreak in my life, one of three to come in just a few short years.

Brooks had a good job working in the city at some sort of security company, but he didn't make a lot of money, and he didn't give me much other than that amazing bedroom all to myself, which was enough for me. The house we lived in was owned by his mother, and the BMW he drove was also owned by her. Since I had to stay home and take care of my mother for years, I never had a real job, just the furniture I would flip occasionally to make a little money. Something I could do at home to be close to my mother.

A few months after she died, so did Brooks, and I was left with no one. His mother wanted nothing to do with me even though he had adopted me, and I had lived in his home for five years as his daughter. After his death she made me leave, telling me that she never wanted to see me again.

I thought for sure I was going back to having nothing and being poor again until I learned that he had a life insurance policy for quite a bit of money through the company he worked at. He had not willed it to anyone and didn't have a beneficiary, so since I was the next of kin due to the fact he had adopted me, I received the money. Which I am sure he would have never approved of; he just had never thought to have a proper beneficiary. His mother was so mad when she found out I was getting this money. She was never aware he had this policy, which was very satisfying for me because of the way she treated me in the end. It took a while, but I received the money just before moving here to Cincinnati.

Now I can buy whatever I want, all on my own… Well, within means. It's not a huge sum of money, not so much that it will take care of me for a lifetime, but it was way more than enough to get me started with a house, a workshop, and a large truck to haul furniture around with.

I tie up my tennis shoes and head out the back door. The morning light is just coming up over the horizon of my property. I stand there in awe, looking at how beautiful it is. The yellow and pink from the sun spread across the fields behind my house. I love this place so much. I am so glad that it is mine. I used to think I was in heaven to have that bedroom in Brooks' house. This is way better.

When I told Christina that I wanted something remote that had plenty of privacy and a large separate area to work out of, like a garage or barn, she brought me here to see this house. It couldn't have been more perfect. Instead of a garage or a barn, it had a large workshop set up by the previous owners with tiled floors, full electricity, heat, A/C, and lots of windows to let the light in. The perfect place to get started on my own furniture business, and the land that came with it was a bonus.

This house is about thirty minutes from downtown Cincinnati on five acres of land. It was built in the '60s by a couple that owned a small country store nearby in the small town called Aurora. From what I heard from talking to some people in town after I bought the house, their country store had been pretty popular amongst the locals, and it drew in a lot of shoppers from the city. They sold all sorts of specialty items, from local meats and dairy to fresh produce, flowers, and plants, some of which grew on this very property.

The orchard behind the house had once been lush and vast but it has mostly died and dried up since the house went up for sale. I found some old photo albums stuffed in a closet in the house that were full of pictures of the couple that lived here. Most were of the orchard and gardens when it was in its prime. It was full of all sorts of plants, flowers, and tons of apple trees, shades of red and green. I tried to maintain what I could, but the property had already begun to become overgrown long before I bought it. There was way too much work to do and no way for me to keep it up. I'm sure they had many workers cultivating the property when they owned it. They couldn't have done it on their own.

The couple died a year before I bought the place. They had no children to carry on their legacy. The house and store were both inherited by a sister who put them both up for sale immediately after the tragedy. The grocery store was bought quickly and turned into one of those organic grocery stores, but the house had been on the market for quite some time, continuing to put the orchard in ruins. It had been looked at by several people, but they always declined a sale due to the nature of what had happened.

To me, it didn't matter that the couple had died inside the home. The tub that the man had drowned his wife in had long been removed and replaced with a beautiful vintage claw tub, and the blood that had been spattered on the wall from the self-inflicted, fatal gunshot wound had been cleaned and the walls had been repainted. What mattered is that this home was going to be mine, all mine. The first real thing I have ever owned.

Christina told me that there had been several families that came and looked at the property knowing what had happened and were able to overlook the incident, mostly because the price was well below market value, but when they saw the ravine behind the orchard, they always declined to make an offer.

Behind the gardens and the orchard is a vast ravine that edges the back of the property line, stretching over a mile. In most places it's more of a gully that you could easily walk down into, but directly behind the apple trees in the orchard, there is an extreme drop-off of about a hundred feet that made any interested buyers decline. They all had said it was too dangerous for their children or animals.

I had no interest in having any children or animals, so none of that bothered me. Christina asked me once if I was bothered by their deaths or the ghosts that might be in the home, but it doesn't at all. The entire earth has had someone die on every part of it at some point in time, so we're always surrounded by ghosts. Besides, I have plenty of ghosts in my life and have had no hauntings yet.

After I bought the house and property, I tried to contact the sister to give her the photo album that I found and to get some more information about the couple that owned it. I wanted to know some of their stories. They must have been so happy here. She would not respond to any of my attempts to speak with her, so I gave up. I assumed it was just too hard for her. I had some of the photos blown up to put in the living room. I wanted to honor that couple and all they had achieved.

The land now is mostly overgrown by weeds that have overtaken most of the apple trees and the other plants, but I was able to keep a small portion of the crops maintained. After I spent the spring fertilizing, pruning, and trying to keep the wild animals away, some of the trees, tomato plants, and cabbage grew fruitfully. There are even some zinnias, begonias, and daylilies that managed to hold on.

Now it's officially fall and everything is starting to die and wilt, which makes me a little sad. Some of the trees are still growing healthy apples. From what I have learned, this type of apple might still grow until November.

Tending to the garden has been therapeutic and also a great workout, plus I have an amazing tan from being in the sunshine all summer. I am sad to see that it is all coming to an end, but there is always next year, and I have other plans for this winter.

After my run, I head back inside the house and eat a healthy breakfast, as I do every morning now. I used to stuff my face with pancakes, french toast, sausage, whatever you could think of, but now it's mostly egg whites and spinach for me. It's one of the things that helped me lose the extra weight I was carrying. I would love to be able to eat a large steaming hot plate of pancakes with lots of butter and syrup, but the new me would rather be healthier and skinnier.

I grab my truck keys to head out to my yoga class. The truck was another purchase I was able to make all on my own after moving here. It's an older Dodge Ram 1500. Perfect for hauling around furniture. It was either that or a creepy white van. I think I definitely made the right choice.

I jingle the keys between my fingers. I do this every time I handle them just to make sure they are real. I have never owned my own vehicle before. I don't even have a driver's license. I know that is not very smart. I could get pulled over, and without a driver's license or any way to get car insurance, I could end up in a lot of trouble. I plan on getting it soon, it just hasn't been that important. You don't need one to buy a vehicle in the first place or to buy a house or a business, just a state-issued ID card, which I have. I run my finger along the edges of the keys and then squeeze them so tightly in my palm that they create indentations in my skin. Another way I prove to myself that this is all real.

I arrive at the Yoga Loft a little before the class starts. It's full of mostly the regular Tuesday morning crowd, all spreading out their yoga mats and starting their meditation poses. Shiva, the instructor, is talking to a girl I have never seen before. As soon as she spots me, she grabs the new girl's hand and pulls her in my direction.

"Emily darling, this is Harper," she introduces the girl to me, saying her name with a long-exaggerated R in the middle. She always speaks in an overly eccentric tone of voice. "Harrrrper is new to the class. She is the one I was telling you about who performs magical feats with my hair. Emily here is my star student. You should have seen her when she first came to me; you would hardly recognize her to look at her now." She pauses to look me up and down with admiration as if she molded me from clay herself. "She is some of my finest work, I would have to say."

I give the new girl a tiny wave, slightly embarrassed.

"Harper works at this amazing salon called Fringe over on Butler Street downtown. She is the only one who knows what my real hair color actually is." Shiva looks at me with a serious expression. "I mean, I don't even know," she laughs wickedly.

I force a smile on my face only to be polite to this new girl. Shiva does this every time a new person comes to class. Just because I have lost quite a bit of weight since starting here, she thinks it's all due to her magical powers. When really, it's the hundreds of hours I have spent running and the low-calorie diet I have tortured myself with.

The Yoga Loft is in Oakley. It's a trendy part of Cincinnati that is between my house and downtown. I found this place after I went to my first estate sale here. I loaded up with a ton of great pieces, and as I was driving back home, I passed this place. I saw a very tall woman with the brightest red hair I had ever seen in real life walking out of a place called Yoga Loft. Right then and there, I knew that I had to give yoga a chance. It looked like a fun place. That woman turned out to be the owner, Shiva, with her red hair the color of strawberries. She welcomed me with open arms, and even though she can be a little over the top and demanding, I still love it here.

We all stand there for a moment staring awkwardly at each other before Shiva gets distracted. She waves to the woman walking in the front door.

"Brenda, sweetheart, you weren't here all last week. My goodness, I was so worried."

She forgets all about her conversation with us and rushes over to Brenda, who looks embarrassed to be caught. Shiva always harps on the students who miss class.

I break the awkward silence with Harper by walking to my usual spot and laying down my mat. She follows me and sets hers down next to mine.

"She can be a bit much," I say to Harper, "but she is a really great instructor."

"Oh, believe me, I know." She looks over at Shiva to make sure she is out of earshot, but she is still lecturing poor Brenda about why it is important to be here every week. "She is the same way when she comes into my salon. I am actually the owner of Fringe, but she always calls me one of the employees." Harper rolls her eyes. "She has been trying to get me to come to this class forever. She tells me all the time that she can alter my body and that this class will transform me into the beautiful soul I was meant to be." We both laugh at this. "I am getting married in six weeks and need to drop a few pounds to fit into my dress, so I finally took her up on that promise." I glance down at her ring finger and see a huge sparkling rock that looks to be a very expensive diamond.

"Between you and me," I say, leaning in close to her, "Shiva is not even her real name. It's Glenda, like the good witch from *The Wizard of Oz*." We both laugh hysterically at this and begin our yoga stretches while we wait for Shiva (or Glenda) to start the class.

"So, how much weight did you lose?" she asks me.

"Just a few pounds, but she makes it seem more dramatic than it actually is," I lie to her.

The truth is, it's a lot more than just a few pounds. I have lost eighty-five pounds since I moved here. I knew I needed to get rid of the weight quickly, so that's when I started running, doing yoga, and basically starving myself.

I wasn't always overweight, though. I was very thin when I was growing up. Being so poor, we didn't have much food besides the one meal my mother brought home after her shift at the diner, and we didn't have a car, so I had to walk everywhere. After we moved in with Brooks, that all changed. I didn't do much of anything besides go to school and stay in the house watching movies and TV shows. At first it was mostly because the kids at school were really mean, and I didn't have any friends, but later it was because I stayed home to take care of my mother after she got sick.

The fridge was always stocked with whatever I wanted. Foods that I had never tasted before. I stuffed myself day after day with the various concoctions that I would come up with. After a few years of eating like that, it finally started to catch up with me, but at that time, I didn't care what I looked like. Now I do care—I care a lot. I don't want to be that chubby girl that no one liked before.

Harper startles when Shiva rings the ridiculous gong she has on a pedestal in front of the class. She mouths *What the fuck* and I giggle at her.

"That's what she does when she wants to start the class," I tell her quietly. The room goes silent, and we begin with our poses.

After we finish our last child's pose and Shiva excuses us, I am rolling up my mat when Harper asks me if I want to grab a smoothie across the street with her. I am thrilled at the opportunity to make a new friend, but I try not to seem too eager. I can come off as awkward in most social situations, so I just say, "Sure, sounds great."

The only other friend I have is Christina. She is the first friend I have had as an adult, which I know is pretty ridiculous. I had friends at my first school when it was just me and my mom in the city, but after we moved in with Brooks to the suburbs, I had to switch schools. I was in high school by then, and being the new kid was not so great. I had nothing in common with any of the kids. They had all grown up with lots of money. I didn't, and they all thought I was weird. So, I just kept to myself. The girls tried to bully me at first, but they got bored and gave up after a while.

We get to the smoothie shop, and I order a small lite strawberry smoothie from the menu, and Harper orders a chocolate, peanut butter, and banana smoothie. I get a pang of jealousy because that sounds really good compared to mine.

We get our drinks and take a seat. I am trying to think of what to say when she takes the clip out of her hair that has been holding it on top of her head and shakes her head back and forth to release her long golden-blonde locks. They fall perfectly around her shoulders as if she just styled them to look that way.

"Your hair is really pretty," I say, admiring it. "Do you do it yourself?"

"If you mean the blowout, then yes, but the color and cut, most definitely not," she laughs, and I feel stupid for making such a dumb comment. I had no idea if that was her natural hair or not, and it's not like she could have gotten to the back of her head to cut or color it.

"Another girl at my salon does it. I have some pretty great talent working for me," she says proudly.

"It must be fun to own your own salon. I know nothing about hair or about anything in the beauty industry, for that matter." I touch my hair self-consciously. It's still in my usual ponytail and sweaty from my run this morning. "I have only trimmed my hair a handful of times but never cut off any real length, and I definitely have never changed the color of it," I admit to her while looking at the strands of my hair.

"Virgin hair!"

Her expression brightens, and now I feel even more embarrassed. I'm a twenty-two-year-old girl who has never been to a beauty salon, but I don't tell her this. She would definitely think that was weird.

"Well, if you ever want a change, you should come in sometime. I don't take any new clients, but like I said, there is lots of talent at Fringe." She says the name of her business with such love and affection it makes me smile. I call my online store Modern Resale, but if I open a brick-and-mortar store, I would give it a much better name. Something that would make me smile the way Harper is about her place.

I zone out and wonder what I would look like with hair more like hers. Mine is a mousy shade of brown, all one length and very boring. When I take it out of my ponytail it falls down to my hips. Her hair has all sorts of layers that give it a healthy, bouncy look. I try to imagine my hair shorter and a different color. I realize I am staring creepily at her and look away. I can be so awkward in social situations.

We spend quite a while at the smoothie shop. She asks me questions about my business and how I learned to do it.

"I watched the home channel a lot when I was in high school. I was so impressed with the shows where people flipped furniture. The things they could do with old stuff amazed me. My mother would take me to the Goodwill in town when she could, and I would pick out one thing to try and flip on my own. It turned out I was pretty good at it. I used the money I would make selling it online to buy more supplies and learn to do more intricate things."

I pull out my phone and show her pictures of pieces that I have sold from my Modern Resale Facebook page.

"Wow, you are amazing, and furniture flipping is so trendy right now."

"Thanks. It really has started to take off over the last couple of months. It keeps me very busy."

"Are you from this area?" she asks me.

"No, I moved here at the beginning of the year. Back in February."

"Oh, cool. I have always lived here in Ohio. What made you leave and come to Cincy?"

"There was just nothing there for me anymore, and I needed a big change."

"Boyfriend?" she asks.

"No, not anymore. I was dating this guy back home and I broke it off right before I moved here. Let's just say it was a very bad relationship and things did not end well."

"Yikes, that sounds serious. You will have to tell me all about it sometime, but I have to go now. I have a client starting at one today. It's been really fun hanging out with you."

We exchange numbers before she walks down the street. I feel so happy that I have made a friend. She seems really nice, and it would be great to have someone to go do something with. I really hope that we see each other again.

4

Victoria

I head straight to Katie's house after I get off the plane. She has been my best friend since we were in kindergarten, and I would trust her with my life. She has always been an amazingly loyal friend and has never judged me for anything I have ever done. I have always told her everything—well, not everything…but most things.

    I was so thankful that she and her boyfriend recently broke up and that he moved out. It makes it much easier for me to come and stay here with her for a little bit while I transition back to Cincinnati. She has the swankiest apartment downtown on a penthouse floor that overlooks the city, and it's walking distance to all the best bars and clubs in town.

    We are getting ready to head out for the evening when I explode into detail about everything that happened while I was in Los Angeles. It pours out of me like word vomit. I tell her all about the divorce and what I did to Brent.

    "I am never getting married again, ever. This was the worst mistake of my life. Honestly, what was I thinking in the first place? It's Brent Alexander. He's like not even attractive at all, and he's short. Remember in high school we always made fun of him because it seemed like he would never grow? Did you know that I couldn't even wear my heels because then I would be taller than him? I don't want to be taller than my husband. I want him to tower over me, to be masculine and strong. I want to feel small next to him. When I was standing next to Brent, all I felt was like a sasquatch!"

When I am finished with my rant, I turn from the mirror, and Katie's mouth has dropped to the floor.

"Wow, Victoria, why don't you tell me how you really feel," she says sarcastically. "You are not a sasquatch."

"I know, but standing next to the Keebler Elf, I was."

"You are really bitter about this divorce," she says, clearly thrown by my comments.

"I'm not bitter. I am just over all of this. I want this divorce to be done and over with. To move on and forget about Brent and everyone at the stupid Alexander Group."

"Have you told your family that you're back yet?"

"Nope, no one knows I'm here."

"Not even Hudson?" She raises her eyebrows.

"No, Katie, not even Hudson. And when they find out I'm back, you can't tell them anything I have told you. Brent has sworn that if I give him a quick and easy divorce and don't take anything from his company, then he won't tell anyone what happened."

"Okay fine, I won't say a word—on one condition." She pauses dramatically.

"What?"

"You hurry up and finish putting your makeup on so that we can go out already. I have been sitting here listening to your tirade for almost two hours now and I'm ready to go party with my best friend that I haven't seen in almost a year. We need to get out there and find you another husband."

"Shut up!" I punch her lightly on the arm.

She laughs. "Fine, let's go find a husband for me then, or at least a boyfriend, or maybe just a hot guy to give me some attention. After Brian left, I haven't been able to meet any decent guys. I have been on all the dating apps, and it's nothing but losers."

"Okay, okay, you're right. Let's get the hell out of here and go have some fun."

The next morning, I wake up with the worst hangover ever. I reach out to the side table in Katie's guest room for some water. Thankfully there is a half-drunk bottle I left there last night. I chug it down in two gulps, but it doesn't come close to quenching my thirst. I need a gallon of water to hydrate me after all the alcohol I drank last night. How many shots did we take? I have no idea. It's all a complete blur.

I sit up and stretch out my body. Sleeping in Katie's guest room is like sleeping in a five-star hotel. The views of the downtown skyline are gorgeous and her bed feels like fluffy clouds, but all that luxury still doesn't wash away the hangover.

Katie walks into the room looking worse than I feel. "Water," she says in a croaky voice holding a couple of bottles for us.

"I am never leaving this bed," I say as she chucks one of the bottles at me directly into my lap.

She comes over and crawls in next to me. "Seriously though, Victoria, what are you going to do?"

I take in a deep breath and sigh loudly. "I am going to call Hudson today. I will tell him what is going on—not everything, but I will let him know that I'm back and he and I can figure out my next move together."

"You know Hudson is totally going to understand if you explain everything. He's the last person that would be judgmental about this kind of thing. He is the biggest player, and I can't imagine him supporting anyone getting married. He won't care about what you did or that you are getting divorced. He will probably congratulate you."

"Under different circumstances, you are probably right, but Brent is a good friend of our family. Our dads have known each other for like forty years or something. Hudson will be pissed if I upset our parents again. I did too much of that last year. I wish I could tell him, though. He is the only person I can talk to."

"Um...excuse me?" she says, annoyed.

"Except you, of course! I meant in my family." I scoot over, wrap my arm around hers, and lay my head on her shoulder. "I am so thankful that I have you, Katie. You have no idea. I would have been a mess coming back here without you."

"You'd better not forget that." She pushes me up to sit and looks me in the eye. "You've got this, Victoria. You're only twenty-eight. You're fucking gorgeous, smart as hell, and you have your whole life ahead of you. Soon enough, Brent will just be a distant memory."

"You're right, as usual. I will get my shit together soon. Can I stay here for a few more days in your horrible guest room?"

She rolls her eyes at me. "Of course, you can stay here as long as you need to. But call Hudson today."

"Okay, I will call him right now."

Katie goes back into her bedroom to give me some privacy. I pick up my phone and call Hudson.

"Hey, little bro," I say in my fakest, happiest tone of voice. I fiddle with the charms of my bracelet nervously. I am worried about what he is going to say.

"Well, hello there, stranger. You don't call, you don't write," he says jokingly.

"Oh stop, you know how I am, horrible at keeping in touch. But guess what, I'm back in town."

"That's awesome. What are you doing here in Cincinnati? I thought you weren't coming back 'til the holidays?"

"Yeah, well LA is way too busy, and the traffic is horrible, so here I am." I laugh nervously into the phone. "Actually, I just missed you so much I just had to come back sooner."

"Of course you did. I mean, I am the greatest little brother ever. Where are you? Did you and Brent just get in?"

"It's just me here, and I'm at Katie's. I got in a few days ago, actually. The two of us have been busy running around, so I am sorry I'm just now getting around to calling you."

"Oh, I see how it is. Katie is more important than me," he teases. "What kind of running around have you two troublemakers been doing?"

"Katie just went through this horrible breakup and needed a friend, so we have just been going out around the city."

"Didn't Katie and Brian break up months ago?" he asks.

"Yes, but you know how fragile she is. I just really missed all of you. I haven't been able to make any good connections with people in LA. They are so fake out there."

"Ah, well, who needs friends when you're a newlywed living in marital bliss? I am sure the two of you never leave the house."

"Well, we have a lot to talk about," I quietly mumble.

"I thought that you might pop up soon. There has been a lot of activity next door at 322. Brandi has been in and out of there a lot over the last couple of days. It looks like they are wrapping up all the renovations. So, you can get moved in soon, which I am so pumped about. I can't wait for us to be neighbors. I thought you had said you guys weren't moving in until the first of the year."

Yuck, just hearing Brandi's name sends ice through my veins. She is Brent's personal assistant and a raging bitch. She has always hated me and is probably extremely happy that me and Brent are done. She has always had a thing for him. I am not sure what exactly she knows about the divorce, but she knows everything that goes on at the Alexander Group. God, I hope that she doesn't know the truth. I'm sure she would love to tell everyone what I did.

"Did you talk to Brandi about anything?" I ask him.

"Yeah, she stopped in yesterday, actually, and asked me if you were back in town."

"Oh?" I say curiously.

"She mentioned something about a brick being thrown through the alley doors and alluded to the idea that you maybe had done it. But you know how she is. She has never liked you. I think she has a hard-on for your husband," he laughs. "Wait, you were here this week, so it probably was you!" He laughs harder, entertaining himself.

"What? I would never!"

"I'm kidding, dork. Why would you throw a brick inside your own building? It was probably just some homeless person."

"Did she say anything else to you?"

"Just her strange sort of flirting that she always does with me. She wants to come and take a personal art class with me here at the studio."

"Are you offering private classes there now?"

"Yes, but not for her. I'm sure she wants more than just art lessons."

"I'm sure she does. Stay away from her. She's crazy. What are you up to today? Can you get away for drinks this afternoon?"

"Not today, but I can meet you Thursday at lunch. Let's meet at this new Irish bar that just opened on Vine Street at noon."

"Can't wait," I tell him and hang up the phone. I let out a long sigh of relief. At least I got that part out of the way.

5

Emily

I am picking up some furniture I purchased from an estate sale in the Market district downtown, which just happens to be near 322 Plum Street. I pull up my map app and see that it's only a fifteen-minute walk away, so I decide to leave my truck and take a stroll through the streets to go check out the building again.

I haven't spent much time getting to know this area of the city. Most of the places I get furniture from are on the outskirts of town, mostly out in the suburbs, but not so much in the downtown area. If I'm going to possibly open a store down here, then I need to get to know it better.

Before I came here, I would have never thought it would be a nice place to live. I had originally thought of going to Florida. The idea of hot weather year-round was something I had dreamed about since I was a little girl. I wanted to be surrounded by palm trees and beaches and never have to wear a heavy winter coat.

I had stopped in Cincinnati to see if I could find my biological father. My mother told me that he took off shortly after I was born, and she never knew why. According to my birth certificate, his name was Shane Patrick, and his birthplace was Ohio. Before my mom died, she said that he had mentioned the city of Cincinnati a few times, so I decided to come here and try to find him.

I am not sure what I expected to find. After all, he is the one who just took off and left us, and that doesn't sit well with me, but I was in a bad place at that time. After the death of my mom, my stepdad, and the awful breakup with the first and only boyfriend I had ever had, I thought finding a connection with someone would be good for me. I spent a few weeks looking and was never able to find anyone with that name that knew me or my mother. So, I just decided that probably wasn't his real name; he may have just forged it on my birth certificate. After all, why put down your real name if you don't plan on sticking around? He was only in my mom's life for a short time, and given her track record with men, that was probably what had happened.

What I did find, though, was how much I liked it here. There was just something special about this city. Then I met Christina, and when she showed me my dream house, I decided to stay. I can always visit Florida.

The walk is nice. I have always liked autumn. There is a faint scent of fall that the new crisp air brings. Some of the plants and trees are making their last big change before winter comes and they lose their color. There is something in that air that does something to the blood that runs through my veins, making me feel alive. Maybe a big change will be happening for me too.

I make notes in my phone of all the bars and restaurants I pass along the way that I want to come back and try. I eat healthy most of the time, but I love to splurge every now and then, and going out to eat at a new restaurant I have never been to is my favorite thing to do. I have noticed that Cincinnati has quite the eclectic restaurant and bar scene.

I am not paying much attention to where I am walking, spending too much time looking at the buildings, when I crash right into a girl standing in the middle of the sidewalk, my phone dropping on the concrete with a thud.

"Damnit!" I yell out and quickly reach down to pick up my phone. She doesn't even register me or notice that I nearly knocked her over. She is too busy staring at a building. Her posture is as stiff as a board, and she is hyper-focused on the place in front of her, eyes darting from one window to the next as if she is waiting for someone or something to appear in one of them.

I examine my phone for damage. It seems to be fine. Then I stare at her, trying to figure out what state of mind she is in. She seems to be angry, or maybe sad…or just plain crazy.

I look at the building that she is examining. I think that it might be someone's home, but it's hard to tell down here. The buildings are mixed together, with some as residences and some as businesses. It could be a store, or where someone lives, or maybe it's a restaurant, or maybe both. I don't see any signs advertising a business, so it must be a home. The buildings on each side of it appear to be homes as well.

It's charming, very similar to the Victorian-style building on Plum Street. It's two stories and is light gray with cream trim and a maroon-colored front door. The windows are all tall and thin, with ledges for flowerpots below each of them. There is a small, well-maintained flower garden out front surrounded by a wrought iron gate.

It takes her several minutes to realize I'm standing next to her. She finally snaps out of her window trance and startles when she looks at me as if I just appeared out of thin air. Her posture softens and she puts a smile on her face. In an instant she has turned into a completely different girl. It's freaking me out a little bit.

"Hi there," she says to me in a chipper tone of voice as if nothing had happened.

"Are you okay?" I take a step back from her in case she is, in fact, crazy. I don't need to be attacked today.

I get a better look at her and see that she is very pretty. She has medium-length blonde hair, the color of honey, bright blue eyes lined with black eyeliner, and long full eyelashes that make her look like a cat. Her eyes look more angry than sad now that I can see them. She is a little shorter than me, standing at about 5'4". She's thin, and her skin is very pale.

She has the type of look that I think I would like to look like myself. Maybe not so pale, though. I like the way I look with a tan, but her hair is gorgeous, and her makeup is perfect. I wonder if her eyelashes are real? They are so long and full, like tiny spiders.

She is much thinner than I would like to be. I am comfortable with the weight I have gotten down to. I originally thought I needed to get to 110 pounds, but when I hit 130, I realized that I loved the curves that were revealed after losing all the unnecessary fat.

I wonder what I would look like if I changed my hair to look more like hers or Harper's and put a little makeup on my face. I wouldn't even know how to apply my makeup like this girl. I could use mascara, but she has a winged look that must have taken a very steady hand.

"Do you know Hudson?" she asks without answering my question.

"No, I don't know any Hudson. I was just walking by, and there you were, standing in the middle of the sidewalk. I asked you if you were okay?" She doesn't let me finish talking; she takes off hastily down the sidewalk. I watch her until she disappears, confused by the exchange we just had. I look curiously back at the building she was staring at.

I am looking down at my phone and scrolling through the screens to make sure it's still working properly when I hear a door creak open. It's the door to the building she was staring at. It surprises me. I didn't think anyone was in there, and I almost drop my phone on the concrete again.

I look up and see a man's head pop out through a small crack in the door. He looks both ways up and down the street several times before he decides that it's safe and then opens the door further. He slings a gray backpack over his shoulder and walks out of the building.

The first thing I notice is how hot this guy is. I don't just mean good-looking hot; I mean cover-of-a-magazine hot. Like *GQ* or *Esquire*. He has medium brown hair that's long and tousled and kind of messy but looks like he meant it to be styled that way. His eyes flash a bright color that is either blue or green, with thick bushy eyebrows. He's tall. He must be like 6'3" or maybe even taller. He has olive skin and a little stubble on his chin and above his lips.

I realize quickly that I am standing in front of this building, staring just as awkwardly as that girl was, so I quickly bend down and pretend to tie my shoes. I must look stupid trying to tie my shoes with a cell phone in my hand, so I stand up. Thankfully he is on the move down the street without even noticing me.

He is walking the same way I was heading, so I decide to follow him. There aren't a lot of people walking on this street right now, but enough for me to not seem like I'm purposely following him.

He's wearing a fitted white button-up shirt and black pants with a black belt and oxford gray shoes. The whole outfit looks like it was tailored specifically to hug his body. It's just tight enough to show his muscles underneath. He's so tall and has long legs, and his strides are fast and confident, so it is hard for me to keep up with him.

Suddenly, he stops at a bus stop where several other people are waiting. I walk past him, staring at him from the corner of my eye until he's out of my periphery. I can understand why that girl was waiting for him. I have only seen guys that look like him in movies.

I forget all about him and the blonde girl when I get to Plum Street. There it is, the beautiful building with the curlicue starbursts. The sunlight is shining across the top of the opposite building, and this time of day it bounces off the windows, making it even prettier than the first time I saw it. I feel like it calls to me the moment it sees me. Like it was waiting for me all along.

I decide right then and there that I want this place. I text Christina immediately: *You were right, I want it. Will you be able to get it for me?*

She texts back quickly, *That's not a problem at all, but don't you want to see inside first?*

6
Emily

Harper is at the Yoga Loft again today. When I walk up, she is by the front door waiting for me. I'm thrilled that she came back.

"Hey there," she calls out enthusiastically.

"I am so glad to see you came back."

"I don't think Shiva would have ever let me live it down if I only came to one class. I have to admit it was pretty fun."

We walk in, lay our mats in the same spot and sit there chatting until we see Shiva walk in. She's always here first before anyone else arrives, but today she is almost ten minutes late.

We both stop mid-sentence and stare, waiting for her to speak to us. The entire class goes silent. She doesn't seem to be her usual jovial self today. She doesn't greet the class or offer any reason for being late. She just rolls out her mat in the front of the class without saying a word. She looks rough. Her bright red hair is a mess, and it looks like she didn't sleep much. Our mats are so close to her that I can smell last night's booze and cigarette smoke oozing off her. Harper and I look at each other dubiously, both wide-eyed and gaping, as if we have a secret language.

Shiva starts the class and, at the same time, Harper and I both notice it. A giant hickey on her neck. It's not just a little blemish but a full-on love bite. We both collapse onto our mats from downward dog and start laughing hysterically. Shiva barely notices our hysterics. Before, we would have had a lecture from her about taking the class seriously, but today she doesn't seem to care.

We finally compose ourselves and finish through our poses, making sucking faces at each other the entire time.

When the class is over, we linger around outside the studio, hoping that Shiva will come and speak with us after class. We want to get some of the details on what she was up to last night, but she hurries out of the studio, locking the door quickly, and heads to her Prius in the parking lot.

"That is so weird," I tell Harper. "I have never seen her like that before. She is always all about having a clean body and soul. I can't even imagine her going out and getting drunk and showing up to class hungover like that."

"Well, I guess everyone has their secrets," Harper says.

We start walking to our vehicles and I get up the courage to ask her if she wants to hang out again.

"Would you be interested in checking out this coffee shop with me? It's downtown in the Fourth Street district. I always see everyone carrying around these blue cups from there, so it must be good."

"Yeah, I would love to. My salon is close to that area, so I can head to work afterwards."

We get to the coffee shop and order our drinks, me a black coffee with one package of Stevia, and her a caramel macchiato with extra whipped cream. We grab a seat outside on the patio. I stare longingly at her drink. How does she drink such high-caloric drinks and still look like she does? She's only about ten pounds heavier than I am, plus she's a few inches taller.

"This place is so adorable," she squeals, "and we can still sit outside. The weather is gorgeous today."

"The summer temperatures seem to be holding out really well. Or is it always like this in the fall here?"

"You never know with Ohio. Just wait five minutes and the weather will change."

"Well, I'm not complaining. It's really nice."

"I should have brought Monkey here with me today," she says, pointing at the huge dog bowl filled with water at the corner of the patio. "Must be a dog-friendly place if they leave the water bowl out like that."

"Monkey?" I say, confused.

"He's my second greatest love, other than Ethan, of course." I furrow my brow in confusion. "Sorry! My puppy, he's a labradoodle. Ethan and I just got him three months ago; he's our practice baby for when we finally get to have one of our own," she says animatedly.

Something I have noticed so far about Harper is she always seems to be so enthusiastic about everything.

"Ethan is your fiancé?"

"Yes!" She flings her hand up in the air and flashes me that huge diamond. "We got engaged over the summer. He proposed to me at Joshua Tree National Park, and we are going to have our wedding there too. Have you been out there?"

"Nope, I have never been to California. I would love to go there someday."

"You would not believe how romantic it is there. The park is gorgeous, and the weather will be perfect in November. Ethan has been an avid hiker his whole life. His family has been taking hiking trips together since he was two years old. It was during the first time he took me to Joshua Tree with his whole family that I realized that I was deeply in love with him. It's a really special place for us."

"My stepdad used to be really into hiking too. He would go on trips all over the place, hiking for days at a time."

"Did you ever go with him?"

"No, he never took me to do anything like that. We didn't have a very close relationship."

"Does any of your family live here in Ohio?"

"No, my mom and my stepdad both died a few years ago. I have no siblings, and I never knew my real father. So, it's just me here."

Harper looks like she is going to cry. "That's so sad. How did they die?"

"They both died from cancer just a few months apart from each other. It was just one of those freak things that happen, but don't be sad. I have moved past it and I'm doing just fine."

I quickly change the subject, feeling uncomfortable talking about my past.

"I want to know all about your wedding plans."

She goes on to tell me all about how they met, the proposal, and all the wedding details. I sip my coffee while she tells me everything about Ethan and the wedding. I am happy for her. She seemed to have found one of those great romances that you only see in the movies. I watched a lot of TV as a teenager, especially the Hallmark channel. I always dreamed of having a whirlwind love affair the way they did in the movies on that channel, but after the one relationship that I did have, I realized that there is no such thing, which is just fine with me. I am much happier as an independent single girl anyway.

"We are already starting to train Monkey to be the ring bearer. They have these dog collars that you can attach the ring box to. It will be so adorable," she says excitedly.

I think about a dog walking down the aisle with thousands of dollars of jewelry attached to its collar and can't imagine how that is a good idea.

She stops talking for a moment and looks around the patio of the coffee shop again.

"This place is just darling. I have never been here before. The bridal shop where I bought my dress is just a few blocks away from here." Her face lights up. "Hey, I have a great idea." I think that she is going to ask me to come and look at her dress, but I almost spit out my coffee when she asks me to come to her wedding in California. "I mean, you would have to get out to Joshua Tree, but we have rented out a bunch of Airbnb's that sleep dozens of people each. So, there is room for everyone."

I sit there amazed, thinking about going to Harper's wedding. I have never been to a wedding. I have seen hundreds of them on TV, and that would be so much fun, but I have something else going on soon.

"That is very sweet of you, and I would love to, but I might have some other plans around that time. Can I show you something? It's just a block away from here."

"Of course," she says and hops out of her seat.

We walk around the corner and up one block until we are standing in front of the stone Victorian building.

"Wow, what a pretty building," she exclaims.

"I know it's so gorgeous, right? I have the opportunity to bring my furniture business here. It's going to be available for rent soon. My friend is a real estate agent, so she can get me a contract if I decide to take it."

The squeal from Harper is so loud it startles me. She starts hopping up and down, and her voice goes up about five octaves.

"Emily, oh my god, you have to take it, you just have to. When I bought my salon, it was the best thing that ever happened to me. It changed my whole life, and we would be working close to each other. We would be able to have lunch dates and coffee dates and happy hours." She hugs me so tight it almost crushes my lungs.

After some more gushing over how much fun we will have working downtown together, I ask her if I could also come in and get my hair done sometime. I tell her that I am ready for a really big change. There is more squealing and hopping and hugging before we finally part ways.

I get in my truck to head home. I really should get some more work done; after all, I will need to fill an entire store soon. But I don't want to go home just yet. I am on such a high today.

I pull out my phone and look at the list of bars that I put in it the other day. I would love to have a good beer right now. I see the name of an Irish bar that I typed in and remember the delicious smells coming from the front door. That's perfect. I could totally go for a good Irish beer.

Killarney's Irish Pub has a nice setup. There are quite a few tables on each side of the large room, with a long community table running down the middle and a large half-moon-shaped bar with plenty of seating. The place is packed for lunchtime. The bar area is completely full of people that look like they came from work and are here to enjoy the lunch hour specials, still dressed in their button-up shirts, ties, and dresses. This place must have some really good food for it to be this busy.

"Sit anywhere you want!" the man pouring beer behind the bar calls out to me.

I find an open table, have a seat, and open the menu. The waitress comes by, and I order a Smithwick's Irish Ale and a mini shepherd's pie appetizer.

I pull out my phone and start answering some emails when I hear a man's voice call out in front of me, "There she is!" he says, walking toward me.

I look up, and there he is—the tall, gorgeous man from the other day. What was his name again? Harrison? He keeps walking towards me, and my body tenses up. Is he talking to me? It seems like he is looking right at me. Did he see me in front of his building? I nervously try to compose myself before he arrives at my table. I must look like a deer caught in headlights because I can't seem to move my body.

"I am so happy that you are here." His voice is deep and husky, and he is right in front of my table now, so I mumble something unintelligible like "Um, hi there," and start to stand up right before he bumps into me with the same gray backpack he was wearing before and pushes me back into my seat.

"I'm so sorry," he stops briefly and says to me, putting his hand on my shoulder. Then he walks right past me.

I realize then that he was talking to whoever is seated at the table behind me. I can't see them, but I know that it's a female when she says, "I am so happy to see you too."

My face burns with embarrassment, and I wonder if he heard what I had mumbled or if anyone in the pub did, for that matter. I cautiously look around to see if anyone had noticed the debacle.

The couple is close enough to me that I can hear bits and pieces of what they are saying, but the restaurant is very busy, and the other voices are loud and make hearing conversations difficult. This must be a date or something like that because they really seem to be happy to see each other. I wonder if this is the blonde girl from the street. I don't dare turn around and look. If it is her, she might recognize me and say something. That would make this even more embarrassing.

My beer and appetizer arrive. I eat and drink while pretending to be still checking my emails, but I am intently trying to listen to their conversation. There is some talk about her husband and about their sister. So, I guess they are not dating. They must be siblings.

Then I hear him say the words Plum Street. Oh my god, did I hear that right? Are they talking about the same Plum Street? I shift myself to a better position to hear them more clearly. I almost shush the group of men sitting at the long table in the middle of the room, but that would obviously draw unwanted attention.

Because of Her

I am so frustrated that I can't hear what they are saying. I can only make out a few words here and there. I swear it keeps getting louder and louder in here.

He doesn't stay long. I'm not even sure if she stayed long enough to finish one drink. I hear his chair scoot out, and then he is right next to me, saying his goodbyes to the woman. I get a whiff of his cologne. It smells amazing. What is that scent? Oranges? Sandalwood?

He starts walking toward the door when he suddenly turns around. "Oh, I forgot to give this to you." He unslings his backpack from his shoulder, reaches inside, and takes out a purple flyer. He walks past me and hands it to the woman he was with.

"Oh my, it's very purple," she says sarcastically as he walks out.

I quickly switch my seat to the one across the table from me so that I can see who the girl is. Now that he has left, I don't care if it is the blonde from the other day or if she sees me.

It's not the same girl from the sidewalk. It's an even more striking girl with raven hair, dark brown eyes, pale skin like a ceramic doll, and high cheekbones. She is wearing bright red lipstick, lots of pink blush, and has dark, perfectly trimmed eyebrows. She looks like a Hollywood actress from the 1940s. This guy sure does know a bunch of gorgeous women. I guess that happens when you look like he does.

Her phone rings, and she answers it. She raises her voice to the person on the phone. "Hold on, Katie, let me go to the lady's room to talk. I can barely hear you."

She gets up and walks to the back of the pub. She is tall, like a model. Maybe 5'9" or 5'10" and slender like one as well.

I see a trifold purple flyer sitting on her table. I quickly throw a twenty-dollar bill on my table and grab my things. I stand up and take a quick look around to see if anyone is watching, and when I am satisfied that no one is, I grab the flyer and quickly leave the pub.

I walk as fast as I can away from there until I know that I have put enough distance between us. I open the flyer and scour the contents. It's an advertisement for a painting class called Highball Painting with Hudson Berman. Oh, Hudson was his name, not Harrison. The class is on the last Saturday of the month, which is coming up this weekend. I am astonished when I see where it is located: 320 Plum Street, right next door to my store.

I have to go to this class. What a great opportunity to get to be a part of the neighborhood. There must be all sorts of people that own businesses and live in that area that go to things like this. Maybe Christina will want to go? Or Harper? I feel bad asking on such short notice, but there is no way I am going alone.

7

Victoria

I head over early to the Irish pub Hudson told me to meet him at. I need to have a drink before he gets there to calm my nerves. We have a lot to talk about today. I am going to have to tell him about the divorce. I am sure it will all be fine. Hudson is my little brother and he's like a best friend to me. We have been through so much together. He's going to help me come up with a plan of what to do next and how to tell the rest of the family. I won't tell him everything, of course, but just enough so that he will be on my side.

Killarney's is a little hole-in-the-wall place that I have never been to before. That's not surprising, though. These last few days since being back in town, I have noticed that a lot of new places have sprung up. Cincinnati really seems to be thriving. The pub is busy and extremely loud. The menu serves lots of greasy food and beer on tap. Not the type of place I would have chosen, but it's just the type of place Hudson would like.

I see him walk through the front door and immediately feel at ease. All of my nerves and worry wash away as he walks toward me. He is just as handsome as always, with a big ear-to-ear smile. He is so excited to see me that he practically knocks over the girl at the table in front of me with his backpack.

"I can't believe you still carry around that backpack. Earth to Hudson, you aren't in college anymore," I tease him. "I am so glad to see you. Tell me all about what's been going on with you lately. I have barely spoken to you for months."

"Well, you're the one who never calls or comes back to visit."

"I know, I'm awful. I have just been so busy. You know how it is."

"Yeah, I bet you are *really* busy—busy with your husband."

I gather up my courage at that comment. No need to delay this. "About that, Hudson, that's why I needed to speak with you—"

He interrupts me abruptly, "Hey, have you talked to Evelyn since you've been back?"

"What?" I say, caught off guard.

"You know, our sister," he says.

I roll my eyes at him. "No, I haven't had a chance yet, but I will."

"Well, you better call her ASAP. She will be upset if she knows you have been here all week and haven't reached out. We have family brunch on Sunday."

"Are Mom and Dad going to be there?" I ask, worried.

"No, they are still in Greece. They were supposed to be back last week, but Mom is having the time of her life. She extended their trip another three weeks. I don't think that Dad is too happy about it, but you know, whatever makes her happy, he does. They will be back well before Halloween and Evelyn's birthday."

I look at him with confusion.

"You didn't know they were in Greece?" he asks.

"I did. Now I remember Mom telling me something about it. I just didn't know they were staying longer."

"They probably wouldn't have stayed so long if they would have known you were coming to town. No one has seen you in a long time, Victoria."

"I know, but I am here now."

"So anyway, me and you together on Plum Street. I can't wait to come and help you set up your interior design studio. How many showrooms will you have?"

The waitress comes to our table, and I am thankful for the interruption. I order another drink, and Hudson orders a beer. He's right. I haven't been back to Ohio since the end of last year. I was trying to get my life in order after all the craziness that had happened. I just wanted to leave Cincinnati and have a break from it all. After the holidays, I was supposed to come back here and start setting up my own interior design studio with six showrooms at 322 Plum Street. The Alexander Group has been doing all the renovations there just for me. Obviously, none of that is going to happen now.

"How is it going with the art studio? What do you actually do there? Sell supplies or something? Or is it just a place to give private lessons to pretty girls?" I say playfully.

He glares at me. "I don't need to hear any crap from you. I already hear it enough from Dad. You guys know that art is my passion and opening up this studio has always been a dream of mine. I am still working at the brewery, just not as much as before. Matt has really taken things over and is killing it. It has freed up some time for me to pursue this, but yes, I do sell supplies, and I paint in there. You should come and see it."

"Do we really want Matt to be taking over our family's business?"

He furrows his brow. "Vicky, he is part of our family just as much as the rest of us. He's been married to Evelyn for ten years, and they have four kids together. I seriously doubt he is going to screw the family over. He is doing amazing. Even Dad has let him do what he wants."

The waitress finally brings our drinks. Mine has been empty for a while.

"I started a painting class at the studio. It's once a month on the last Saturday. Have you ever been to those Painting with a Twist classes? The ones where you bring your own wine or cocktails and have a private instructor for a group of adults?"

"I think I have heard of it."

"It's a spin on that. It's called Highball Painting with Hudson."

"You're joking, right? That's what you're calling it?" I wait for him to get to the punchline.

"Yes, it's the perfect name. Every month there is a new theme. This Saturday is Tequila Sunrise. We are going to be painting a sunrise, and I am bringing in some tequila. It's as simple as that. Nothing but fun and amusement. It's this weekend. You have got to come."

"As much as I would love to do boozy painting," I say sarcastically, "I can't. Me and Katie have plans, but listen, I really need to talk to you about something."

He looks annoyed with me. "Right, you wanted to talk about something, and we will, but I have to get to the studio early today. I have a group of kids from the Art Academy coming in at two o'clock." He stands up to leave, and before I can argue with him, he says, "If I don't see you on Saturday, then I will see you on Sunday at family brunch," and then starts walking toward the door.

I am devastated that he is leaving so unexpectedly. He barely even touched his beer. I had thought we would spend the rest of the day together, and he would help me figure everything out, then we would go out and see some of our old spots like we used to before I left.

He stops abruptly and turns around, and I sigh with relief. He must have come to his senses about leaving. He hands me a flyer to his silly painting class and then turns around and walks away for real, this time out the front door. I don't even look at it. I throw it on the table, dismayed.

I sink down in my seat and grasp my bracelet. I twist the little charms in between my fingers, trying to calm myself down. I reminisce about how close Hudson and I were before I left to move to LA with Brent. We used to tear this town up. Going to clubs, dancing, staying out 'til the early morning. I remember all the nights we stayed up late talking.

My phone starts ringing, bringing me out of my reverie. I see that it's Katie. This bar is so damn loud. There is an obnoxious group of men sitting at a long table in the middle of the pub. They are talking so incredibly loud to each other that I can barely hear her, so I have to take her call in the lady's room.

"Sorry, I know you are out with Hudson right now, but I wanted to know if we were going to do something later or if you were out with Hudson all night. This guy from one of the dating apps that I have been waiting for weeks to ask me out just called and wants to meet up tonight," Katie says.

"No. Me and Hudson are not hanging out tonight," I say, disappointed. "He totally just bailed on me, and I am so bummed. You can't go out tonight, Katie, I need you. Let's go to the Reagan Room. That will cheer me up."

She agrees to stay with me. I knew she would. She is the best friend ever.

I hang up and head out of the bathroom to pay and leave this disgusting bar. The obnoxious men are still being loud in the middle of the pub. They all must be really drunk. A few of them are eyeing me like candy and I want to grab my drink and throw it in their faces. Instead, I grab it and finish it in one gulp. I look at the table to make sure I have gotten everything and notice that

Hudson's flyer is not where I left it. I look all around the table and at the floor. It's nowhere to be found. I'm infuriated that one of these drunk idiots probably stole it. I hold myself back from yelling at them. I can just ask Hudson for another flyer.

8
Emily

Harper calls me early Friday morning and tells me that if I have the time today, I can come into Fringe and get my hair done. She said that one of her stylists had a client cancel an appointment last minute and that it was a six-hour block of time so I could get whatever I wanted done. I wondered what they were doing to a person's hair that they had six hours blocked off for.

    I gladly accept her offer and rush down to her salon.

    Harper's salon is gorgeous and intimidating when I first walk in. There is already a full salon of people sitting in the chairs and the stylists have already gotten to work. It's just what I would have imagined her salon to look like. Everything is modern with black trim and large gold mirrors, but also girly with bright pink neon signs that say things like *Hello Gorgeous* and pink chairs. Some of the walls are covered with damask wallpaper, which also gives it a vintage feel.

    She introduces me to the stylist named Olivia that will be doing my hair. Olivia has very long, thick brown hair with dramatic blonde highlights and lots of curls. It must have taken her several hours to do that with her hair.

    She sits me in a chair and covers me with a shiny black cape that has pink letters on it spelling out *Fringe*. She pulls the hair tie out of my hair and gasps.

"What's wrong?" I say, startled.

"Oh sorry, nothing's wrong. I just didn't know how long your hair was. Harper didn't tell me."

I blush with embarrassment and remember what Harper said about my hair the other day: *It's virgin hair.*

The stylist seems really excited about that. "That's awesome. Most women don't have virgin hair anymore. What do you want to do today? Since Charlotte canceled, I am free almost the entire day."

"What were you going to do with Charlotte's hair?" I ask.

"She gets a full head of highlights, a root smudge, toner, and a haircut with lots of layering."

"That takes almost the whole day?" I ask curiously.

"Oh yeah, it's a lot of work. She likes to be platinum."

I have spent so much time trying to imagine what blonde, shorter hair would look like on me, and I haven't been able to wrap my mind around it. So, I decide to just go for it.

"What the hell, let's do that then," I tell Olivia.

She looks shocked. "You want me to cut all this hair off and make you a platinum blonde?"

"Yup, let's go for it. I am ready for a big change. Something dramatic. I was thinking maybe a shoulder-length cut, and if I don't like it, then it will just grow back out."

"Or if you don't like it, you can just get extensions like these," she says, shaking her head back and forth. "Okay then, I am going to put your hair into pigtails, and you show me exactly how short you want it cut."

She brushes out my hair, splits it in half, and wraps two hair bands around each side. I show her where I want it to land, right below my shoulder blades.

"That's a lot of hair that we can send to this place here in Cincinnati that makes wigs for people," she tells me.

"What?" I ask worriedly.

"Since you have healthy virgin hair, they would be thrilled to get it. You will make someone very happy."

I know what she is talking about. When I was taking care of my mother in the hospital, they talked about people donating their hair for cancer patients to have wigs made. I just don't like the idea of someone else wearing my hair. I never considered that they would donate it from a salon like this, but then again, where else would they get the hair from?

"I can't get you platinum blonde in just one visit, but I can do a darker shade of blonde." She shows me a chart of different shades of blonde and tells me to choose one. I had no idea there were so many different options.

I think about the blonde girl I ran into on the street with a honey color of blonde and tell Olivia that's what I would like.

Even though her scissors look like they are razor sharp, it still takes several slices to cut one of the ponytails off. When she gets them both cut off, she holds them up to me with a worried smile on her face like I might freak out.

I shrug my shoulders and give her a genuine smile. I am glad that all that hair is gone. I shake my head back and forth and am amazed at how light my head feels. She puts the hair into a green bag and sets it on her table.

We spend the next several hours with various chemicals on my hair that burn my scalp and smell horrible. I wonder about my safety numerous times while my eyes feel like they are burning out of my head.

The salon is lively. It really seems like a place that Harper would own. Everyone is so upbeat and cheerful. The stylists and the customers are all chatting with each other. Harper comes over throughout the day to see how I am doing in between her clients. I am so proud that she owns something like this. She definitely is the type of person that deserves it.

I occupy the time by listening to the multitude of stories that the women in the salon are telling. These women talk about some really personal stuff at the salon. I hear things like "My husband's penis doesn't work like it used to" and a story about a lady wanting to poison her neighbor's dog for barking too loud. It's quite entertaining. I can imagine if you did this for a job, it would never get boring.

I ask Harper and Olivia if they have ever been to a painting and drinking class. Harper responds in her overly enthusiastic way, "I love those types of things. They have all sorts of different classes you can take just like that with painting and drinking. They have one where you can carve things on wood and drinking, mold your own pottery and drinking."

I laugh at her because she is so cute when she gets excited about things.

"I went to a painting-with-a-twist class a couple of months ago on the East side with my boyfriend," Olivia says. "They had us paint farm animals. I chose a goat. My painting ended up looking like a goat that had been run over and mangled by a car. We threw them away when we got home, they were so hideous. I can be an artist here in the salon, but not on canvas, and especially not while I am drinking alcohol."

"I got a flyer for one yesterday. It's right next to the rental I showed you," I say to Harper.

"No way!" she exclaims. "We should totally go. When is it?"

"It's tomorrow night. It's such short notice, and I am sure you already have Saturday night plans."

"Actually, Ethan is going to watch football at his brother's house. I normally go, but I am so tired of football already this year, and it only just started. I was going to just stay home and watch movies with Monkey, but that sounds like so much fun. After the class we can grab dinner and some drinks. I know some great places to go around there."

I can imagine her on the couch with her dog, possibly both wearing matching pajamas. I bet they make something like that you can order online.

"It's a date, then," I say.

Harper claps happily and heads back to her clients. I breathe in a deep breath, feeling like things could not possibly get better for me here in Cincinnati. A new business, new house, new friends. Everything is just so perfect.

"This cut and color is going to be so hot on you. You have the perfect face shape to pull it off. I am going to put in a ton of layers and then we will put it up in rollers. When we take it out, it will look like bombshell hair," Olivia tells me.

I have no idea what that means, but it sounds great. "I'm so excited. This is my first time having anything like this done."

After the final rinse of my hair and a lot more scissor work, Olivia blow-dries my strands with several different sizes of brushes and puts them up in curlers. While it's setting, she brings over a rolling cart filled with all sorts of different makeup. It looks like she has everything you could need from the makeup aisle.

"You're in luck today because since I like you, you are getting a makeup application as well. You are going to look so hot when I am done with you."

I am so excited that she is going to do makeup too. "Do you know how to do this thing that looks like winged eyeliner, and really long lashes?"

"Sure do," she says.

Finally, after everything has been done, the rollers have been taken out, the scissors put away, and the curling iron has been put down, Harper and Olivia are standing in front of me. Olivia is smiling, looking proudly, and Harper looks like she is going to explode, her face turning bright red.

They turn me around to face the mirror, and my jaw drops. If I thought I looked like a different girl in the mirror before, then now I look like a foreign being from another planet. I do not recognize myself whatsoever, and for a second I think that I might actually cry a little. Which is ridiculous because I don't cry…ever.

I pull myself together while Harper's explosion unleashes.

"This is so insanely gorgeous, Olivia. I just can't believe how different you look right now, Emily. You are going to turn some heads tomorrow night at the painting class."

I have to admit she is right. I do look amazing. I can hardly believe that simply changing your hair and putting on some makeup can make you look and feel so good.

I tell Olivia to wrap up every product that she used today. Everything for my hair and my makeup.

We go over everything from contouring and blending to how I use the rollers and apply the lashes. She is tremendously patient while showing me all the details of what she was doing, considering it's all so new to me. I pay close attention since I don't wear any makeup and have no clue how to apply any of it.

When I get to the register, I get the total of how much everything has cost. Harper is definitely in the right field of work. She tries to give me a discount, but I won't allow it. I make sure I give Olivia a very good tip, and she gives me a bunch of cards to give to anyone that might want to come in and see her.

As I am leaving and we are saying our goodbyes, I see the green bag that my hair is in on Olivia's table. I tell them that I left my phone and hurry back over to her station. I give one quick look around and quickly grab the green bag and shove it into my purse. I don't want anyone else to wear my hair. The idea of another woman making a wig from my hair makes me really anxious. I am sure that it would be for a good cause, but I don't really care.

9
Emily

When I sit up in my bed the next morning, something immediately feels strange. I look around my room for a few minutes and contemplate what could be wrong. I check the walls, the carpet, and the paintings. I start to panic as I rack my brain. Then it hits me, and I burst out into laughter. It's my hair. Most of it is gone, and it feels like I lost about five pounds from the top of my head, but also it's 9 a.m. and I slept like a baby. I haven't gotten such a good night's sleep in years.

All evening I kept shaking my head back and forth, flipping it upside down to try and get used to the new weight, but it's going to take a while. I'm not complaining at all. I absolutely love it.

I get up to go into the bathroom and smile at myself in the mirror. Excitement runs through me as I see that this was all real. I didn't wash off my makeup last night and am surprised at how well it has stayed on my face. It's barely smeared at all. It must be some good makeup.

I crawl back into my bed and decide to treat myself today. I am going to order some muffins for breakfast, which are one of my favorite things to eat. When I was caring for my mother, she would sit in the kitchen with me, and we would talk or watch TV together while I baked muffins. Each week we would find a new recipe to try. Sometimes when she was at her worst during the chemo treatments, it was the only thing she would get out of bed for.

I grab my phone to call and order the muffins from a bakery in town when I see that I have two messages. One is from Harper: *So excited about the painting class tonight. What time is it at, and do we need to get tickets or just show up and pay at the door?*

I text her back, *Me too, so excited. I took care of everything. I signed us both up online. The flyer says bring your own alcohol, so I will get a bottle of wine for us to share tonight. If all of that is okay with you, then meet me out front of the art studio at 6:15.*

The other text is from Christina: *Call me as soon as you get up.*

Oh no, I have a sinking feeling in my stomach. Could this be bad news? Did the rental fall through?

I call her back right away, and she answers after the first ring. "Hey girl, are you sitting down?" Her voice is upbeat so she must be going to give me some good news. I don't sit down; I can't. "I talked with Brandi last night, and everything looks good to go on Plum Street. It will be most likely ready by the end of next week. They are eager to get all the units rented out as soon as possible. Would you be ready to take it by then?"

My voice gets caught in my throat. I try to speak but nothing comes out.

"Emily? Are you there?" I hear her say.

My voice bursts out in a croak, "Yes, I will be able to."

We end the call, and another text from Harper comes in: *That's perfect. I will see you there at 6:15.*

I sink into my bed, pull the covers up over my head, and scream into my blankets. I cannot wait to tell Harper tonight that it's official.

The Highball Painting class is at 6:30. I spend a ridiculous amount of time getting ready for it. Mostly because trying to implement the same exact techniques that Olivia used yesterday was a lot harder than I had anticipated. I am not going to lie, but there were quite a few text messages to Harper asking questions, but as usual, she was sweet and helpful and didn't seem to mind at all.

After I was finished, I put on a pair of tall brown leather boots and a short yellow frilly dress. I gave myself a look in the full-length mirror and felt beautiful. The yellow from the dress really complimented my new honey hair color. I have never in my life thought I could look so pretty and well put together. My mother would have loved to have seen me like this. She would have been so happy for me. Maybe she can. I would like to think she is watching over me from somewhere.

I stop and grab a bottle of pinot grigio from the organic market in Aurora on my way to the art studio. I don't know much about wine, but this bottle had a picture of a famous painting, which seemed fitting for tonight.

When I arrive at the studio at 6 o'clock, there are already a bunch of people gathered out in front of the building, all talking to each other. Most of them are women. That doesn't surprise me, though. The host of this event is very handsome, after all, and I am sure that there are quite a lot of females that come just to ogle him.

I stand among them, smiling and pretending to be a part of some of their conversations while I wait for Harper. I keep looking over at the building next door. I am dying to walk over to 322 and see if I can see anything inside again. The brown paper is still up in the windows, so I wouldn't be able to see inside anyway. There will be plenty of time for that later. It's coming sooner than I had expected.

At 6:20, Harper still isn't here, and everyone starts to make their way inside to grab their seats. I send her a quick text telling her that I will be inside and will be saving her a spot.

I walk in, and the studio is set up with about twenty-five easels in rows throughout the cramped room. Small groups of people have filled most of the stations, but I find a couple of seats near the door so Harper can find me easily. I settle in and start looking at all the items set up in front of me on the easel. There are various small cups of paint colors—yellow, orange, red, purple—covered with plastic, some paint brushes, sponges, and a cup of water. On the back of the chairs are aprons that have been splattered with paint from previous classes.

I start to feel a little anxious. Trying new things always makes me feel like this. I just wish that Harper was here. I don't know what I am supposed to be doing.

The room is filled with excited chatter, especially from the three women sitting next to me. They are animatedly talking to each other and laughing. I look over and each of them has their own bottle of wine already open and they are sipping out of plastic cups filled with the red liquid.

I take out the bottle of wine I brought from my purse and am thankful it's a twist-off cap. I don't want to go through the trouble of trying to find a wine opener and make myself look stupid trying to use it. I look around for the plastic cups they are using and see them on a table to the side of the room.

When I walk over and grab two of them, I hear from behind me, "Hi, I haven't seen you here before. Is this your first time here?"

It's a deep, husky man's voice speaking to me. I look up, and it's Hudson. He is holding out his hand for me to shake.

"I'm Hudson. I'm the instructor," he says.

"Emily," I say nervously and shake his hand gently and quickly. I hope he doesn't feel that my hand is shaking.

"So, is it?" he asks me.

I give him a puzzled look. "Is it what?"

An enigmatic smile spreads across his face. "Your first time here."

"Oh, um, yes it is. It's my first painting class ever," I say while looking back at the door, willing Harper to walk in.

"Well, I hope that I don't disappoint you," he says in a playful tone.

I smile shyly back at him and take the plastic cups back to my seat. I feel his eyes on me the entire way.

I begin to pour a small amount of wine into my cup when I hear one of the women next to me say, "Do you know Hudson?"

I look over and it's the lady sitting in the middle of the three speaking to me. I tell her no, I don't know him. This is the second time someone has asked me if I know Hudson. He must be a popular guy.

I notice that the woman closest to me has set her purse in the seat I was saving for Harper. "I'm really sorry, but I am saving that seat for my friend."

The woman in the middle speaks to me with a slight slur in her voice. "Candace, you can't put your purse in her imaginary friend's seat."

All three of them burst into laughter. Are they making fun of me? I don't know how to react to them, so I just turn my attention back to my canvas.

"She's kidding," the one named Candace says. "This is our one night away from our husbands and kids every month, so we might get a little crazy. Don't mind us."

Suddenly, the whole room starts to quiet down, and the three women start to squeal with delight. I look up to the front of the room, and there is Hudson standing there. Shoot, it's already starting. I look at my phone and it says 6:40 and there are no messages from Harper.

"Welcome, everyone," he says in that low deep voice. It booms through the entire room. He begins to instruct the class about what we will be painting today. A tequila sunrise, he explains. I try to focus on what he is saying, but I am starting to panic a little because Harper still isn't here yet.

I send her another text message: *Class has started.*

"Hudson doesn't like it when people are texting during class," the woman in the middle says to me. She must be the ringleader. I remember girls like her in high school, always in the middle of everything, always the center of attention. They love being bitchy to people to make themselves feel better. She is in her late thirties, a good fifty pounds overweight, wearing skinny jeans so tight that her muffin top is spilling over the waistband. I ignore them again.

I mimic what everyone else is doing in the class. I put on the apron that was draped over the back of my chair and unwrap the plastic from my paint cups. I dip my brushes into the colors and try to follow along with what Hudson and everyone else are doing.

I hear the ladies rambling on and on about how hot Hudson is. They make comments like, "If I weren't married, I would totally go for that." I laugh inwardly so I don't draw any more attention to myself. I'm not sure these ladies would be Hudson's type.

I glance over and half of their bottles of wine are already gone. They must be getting pretty tipsy by this point. Then I notice they are giggling and pointing in my direction. Probably making fun of my painting. I am not even caring about what I put on the canvas. It's hard to concentrate because I can't stop worrying about Harper.

I know that I should be irritated with these women, but I feel kind of sorry for them. Married with kids, husbands who are probably at home watching football right now, happy their wives are gone out of the house. They probably have cookie-cutter houses out in the suburbs, are stay-at-home moms, or work some meaningless part-time job and drive minivans. Their whole lives are based around that small bubble. That type of life does not sound appealing to me at all. When I am their age, I will take the life Christina has. Now that would be agreeable to me. These women are nothing like her.

I'm putting blobs of yellow and orange on my canvas when I hear Hudson's voice behind me.

"This is an interesting interpretation of a sunrise."

I try to think of what to say before I sense that he's right next to me, so close that I can smell his cologne. The same kind I smelled at the pub the other day.

I turn my head to look up at him. "Huh?"

"Your painting."

He points to my canvas. I look up and notice exactly what he means. My canvas looks nothing like anyone else's in the room. It looks like a toddler finger-painted something on it. The ladies next to me are roaring with laughter now.

"Hi, Hudson," they all say in unison.

He looks over at them hesitantly. "Ah, hello ladies. I see that you are out causing trouble again."

They all blush and giggle at him.

"We drove all the way downtown, from South Lebanon, just to see you," the ringleader says in an overly flirtatious tone.

I was right. They are from the suburbs, and South Lebanon has lots of families with the same cookie-cutter upper-middle-class houses. Exactly where I would expect them to be from. I go out that way quite often searching for furniture. There are a lot of nice thrift shops up there. People must be constantly redecorating their houses and donating things because I find tons of great items.

He turns his attention back to me. "I really like what you have done. The way you mixed the colors together works really well."

"You don't have to lie. I'm terrible at painting."

"I disagree. You aren't terrible at all. I love this painting. It's good to have you here, Emily." He glances at the empty chair next to me. "Are you here with someone?"

"She's here with her imaginary friend," the bitchy ring leader blurts out.

I am mortified. All I can do is mumble back, "My friend Harper was supposed to meet me here."

Before I can suffer any more embarrassment, my phone starts to ring. I look at the screen, and it's Harper, finally. I jump up, scooting my chair back, almost tipping it over, and sprint out of the front door. I answer as soon as I get outside the studio, "Harper, are you okay?"

"I'm on the way to the vet," she says frantically, and I can hear that she has been crying. "Monkey got hit by a car." She lets out a huge wail. "I had to wait for Ethan to get home, and we are driving him now." She sounds like she is hyperventilating on the other end of the line.

I hear Ethan in the background, "Sweetheart, please try and calm down. He's going to be okay. It's not that bad."

"I'm so sorry I am not there, I feel awful. I will call you later," she says, and the line goes dead.

Well, that sucks. I don't want Harper to be upset like that. My heart feels so sad for her knowing that she must be in so much pain right now.

I look back at the art studio. It will be so uncomfortable having to walk back in there, in front of all those people and those awful ladies, but I left my purse inside.

I look over at my new building. I stare at it for a long time. Then decide that I have been lingering out here long enough and walk back into the studio to grab my things.

Hudson is back up at the front of the class and watches me walk every step of the way to my seat. I go to grab my purse so that I can get the hell out of here when I notice that Candace has it in her lap, and the ringleader is rifling through it.

They see me walk up. "There you are." The ringleader is slurring her words badly now. "We were just about to go through your purse to see how we could contact you. We thought you had left."

I snatch it out of Candace's lap roughly, giving all three of them a dirty look, and walk out the door. I wanted to scream something at them, but there was no way I was going to embarrass myself any further.

I walk hastily to my car and freeze when I hear the yelling coming from back down the street the way I came. I turn and it's Hudson jogging after me. I turn back around and start walking away faster. I do not want to speak to him right now. I am so embarrassed and just want to get out of here.

"Please wait, Emily."

I resign my attempt to escape and slow down, allowing him to catch up.

"What happened? Is every okay? Why did you leave the class like that?"

I can feel my cheeks start to burn from humiliation. First the ladies in the class, then the incident with Harper, and now I just ran out and drew all that attention to myself. Everyone in there surely saw me. My breathing starts to get heavier, and my chest feels tight. I just need to get out of here as fast as I can.

I am not thinking when I blurt out, "My dog got hit by a car, and I have to leave right now."

I continue walking quickly away again. I hear him call after me, "I'm so sorry, let me know if I can do anything."

I get to my truck that's parked a few blocks away from the studio. I hop in and slump down in the seat. I try to calm myself down with my breathing techniques. Deep breath in and hold it tight, then let it out. After doing this a few times, I start to feel a little better. I probably shouldn't have said that about my dog, but what difference will it make? He would never know.

I hear my stomach growl. So much for heading out for dinner and drinks tonight. The only thing I ate all day was one of the muffins that I bought from the bakery this morning. I really don't feel like going into a grocery store to get something to make when I get home, so I google fast food restaurants near me. I don't even care what I eat. I am feeling really low right now and something fattening and delicious would cheer me up.

    I sit up in my seat and get ready to turn the keys in the ignition when I see the three suburban moms stumbling down the street toward me. They are cackling like witches hanging on to one another. I duck back down in the seat far enough, hoping they don't see me. I peek out the window just enough to see them.

    "Where are we going now, ladies?" the ringleader says.

    "I need to get home before the kids go to bed or Tom is going to be pissed at me," Candace says. "Last time he was so mad that we didn't get home 'til after midnight."

    Ringleader Mom reaches into her purse and grabs a set of keys. "Fine, Candace, be a loser, but we are stopping at the Waffle House on the way home. I'm starving." She clicks the button on her key fob, and I hear a beep nearby. I see the lights flash from a vehicle parked right in front of me. I duck down into my truck, close to the floor so they cannot see me at all.

    I laugh out loud. Of course, it's a fucking minivan. I knew it, and to top it off, it has a personalized license plate: *KOOLMOM*. I hear the doors slam, and the van starts up. I sit back up in my seat and watch them drive off.

    I hear my stomach grumble again. The Waffle House sounds so good. My stomach gets even louder thinking about a pile of steaming pancakes. *Ya know what?* I tell myself. *Screw it.* There is a Waffle House on my way home as well. I am going to stop and get some damn pancakes. But first I pull out my cell phone. I have to make an important phone call.

    "Nine-one-one. What's your emergency?" the woman on the other end of the line says.

In my most concerned tone of voice, I say, "Hello, ma'am, I am not sure if this is who I should call, but I am a business owner in downtown Cincinnati on Plum Street and I just saw three women, all very drunk, get into a silver minivan. When they pulled out of their parking spot, they hit a car parked in front of them, backed up and, hit another car behind them, then just continued to drive off. I don't think the lady driving was in her right mind to even know she had done that. Before they got into the minivan, I heard them talking about driving home to South Lebanon. That's an awfully long way to drive so drunk. I am worried they will cause another accident. I mean, they already hit two vehicles. What if they hurt someone? Thankfully I was able to get their license plate number."

The operator tells me I have done the right thing. I give her the *KOOLMOM* license plate number and hang up.

When I get to the Waffle House, I order a stack of pancakes with extra butter and syrup and savor every bite as I devour them.

10

Emily

I head straight to the drawer that contains my running clothes the next morning. I'm going to need to run for at least an hour today to burn off some of those carbs from yesterday. Between the muffin and the giant stack of pancakes and butter, I probably ingested two days' worth of my normal calories, and none of them were healthy.

I'm standing in my kitchen waiting for my espresso maker to drip a much-needed caffeinated drink when I hear someone knock at the door. It's not surprising to have someone coming by. For months people would come out to my workshop to pick up items they had purchased or to see items that I had listed online, but I took down all of my listings weeks ago when I started contemplating opening up a retail store. I decide to ignore it, drink my espresso, and wait for them to leave before I go outside to start my run.

I hear the knock again and this time it's much louder. I really don't have time to get into a conversation with anyone right now. I'm glad that all the windows in the front of the house have blinds and curtains so that no one can see through. Whoever it is, they are persistent. I'll just wait them out.

Once again, the knocking on the door comes, and this time it is so loud that I feel like the house is shaking. I slam my cup down on the counter, feeling irritated that people are here bothering me without even notifying me they were coming first.

I stomp over to the door, unlock the latch, and fling it open ready to scold whoever it is on the other side. I am ready for a fight when I am completely thrown off guard by who is standing on the other side.

It's Hudson Berman standing on my doorstep, wearing fitted jeans and a short-sleeve white V-neck T-shirt, and dirty white Converse sneakers. He has his arms raised up, hanging from the top of the doorframe. I can see his muscles bulging just under his T-shirt sleeve, and his T-shirt has ridden up enough to expose part of his stomach. He is filling up the entire frame of my doorway with his height looking very concerned and…well, very sexy.

I shake off any inappropriate thoughts I have of him as he walks past me into my living room, looking around my house as if I have hidden something in here from him.

"What are you doing here?" I say, enunciating each word slowly.

"I am so sorry to just show up like this, but I need to make sure you guys are okay. I texted and called you, but I didn't get an answer."

What in the hell is he talking about? Who are "you guys"?

"Oh no, it's not good, is it?" His eyes are sad as he looks down at me from his height of almost a foot taller than me.

Then it clicks. Oh my God, I forgot about the fucking dog. That's what he's talking about. That stupid story I told him about my dog getting hit by a car. I quickly avert my eyes from his so he doesn't see my reaction, and I walk past him quickly back into my kitchen.

I say as I'm walking away, "Everything's just fine. He just broke his leg. I mean, that doesn't mean it's fine, just that he didn't die anyway."

"Thank God. I can't tell you how relieved I am. I stayed up all last night thinking about it."

I watch him pacing back and forth in my living room, talking about animals, his love for them, and how upset this has made him. I find it strange that he would come all the way out here just to check on my dog. What if I lived with a jealous boyfriend or a husband, and—wait, how did he get my address?

"How did you know where I lived?" I interrupt his ranting.

He stops pacing and starts to look around my house again. "All of your information is on the receipt when you signed up online for the class. So where is your little guy?"

I am pretty sure that it's illegal to look up personal information online and show up at their house. I wonder if this guy is maybe a little crazy.

"He's not here. It was a dog that my ex and I shared. He drove down to get him late last night. We decided it was for the best, but thanks for stopping by."

I am not sure if any of this story seems realistic or not. I don't really care. I would say anything to get him to leave. I head toward the front door to open it so he can go.

He stops me and puts his arms on each of my shoulders. "I'm so sorry. That's a lot to go through. Are you okay?"

He is standing so close to me, and I see that his eyes are green. I thought maybe they would be blue, but no, they are a light shade of green with little specks of gold.

I shrug his hands off my shoulders. "I am completely okay. No need to worry."

He walks into my kitchen towards the sliding glass door and puts his fingers in between the blinds, opening them a bit so he can see through.

"This is one hell of a place. The orchard outback is amazing. What do you grow out there?"

"Not much anymore, just some apples and a few vegetables."

"Can I go outside and see it?" he asks excitedly.

"When, right now?"

He nods eagerly.

"No, I can't right now. I am really busy today."

"Come on, please? Pretty please?" he whines.

It dawns on me that this guy could be a psychopath, and maybe he wants to get me outside and murder me. Who just shows up out of the blue like this? No one even knows that he's here.

He's bouncing up and down on his heels like a little kid wanting to go outside to play, and I can't help but give in.

"Fine," I roll my eyes. "I will take you outside."

I unlock the doors, pull open the blinds, and slide them open. He steps outside and I go to follow him but turn around and grab a small knife from the knife block on the counter and put it in my waistband. Just in case.

Hudson is like a little kid in a candy store walking through the orchard.

"Wow, this is so crazy. I've never seen anything like this before. It's like we're in some spooky fairytale."

"Yeah, I kind of thought the same thing when I first saw it."

The orchard is so overgrown and unkept, and this time of year, the areas that I have managed to keep up with are starting to dye off for the winter. It looks like a setting for a creepy Halloween movie.

I lead him through the path in the orchard that I've cut clean so that I know where I can and can't walk without hurting myself. We get to the edge of the orchard, and he starts to walk quickly past me out into the open.

"I wouldn't do that if I were you!" I yell out to him.

That's when he sees it. "Holy shit." He walks closer and puts his hands on top of his head and stares in astonishment at the ravine in front of him.

"Yeah, holy shit is right. You could fall down there if you're not careful, and I don't think you would have just broken a leg."

"This is insane. I can't believe you have this on your property. Aren't you worried you might accidentally fall in?"

"No, I'm not worried. I know it's there, and I'm not an idiot. I would never just wander around and stumble into it; it's almost a mile long."

He walks as close to the edge as he dares to and looks down. I walk over and stand next to him. I am not entirely sure that he is not an idiot and will possibly fall over the edge.

The ravine is about thirty feet deep in this area and maybe the same distance across. I have walked up and down the entirety of it, and it gets narrower and shallower in some areas that aren't nearly as dangerous, but this spot happens to be the deepest and the widest across. Usually there is a small stream of water running through the bottom, depending on if we have a big rainstorm or, say, after a snow melt. We had a big snowstorm right at the beginning of spring earlier this year; it filled up halfway with water.

"Do you know how far across it is?" he asks.

"I'm not sure. I don't exactly have a measuring tape that long," I tell him sarcastically.

He grins at me wickedly. "Okay, then I'm gonna go ahead and get a running start and jump across it. Then I can determine how far across it is."

I'm not sure if he's kidding or not, so I jump forward and grab on to his arm.

"No, you will not do any such thing."

He laughs at me. "I'm kidding."

"Listen, I really have a lot to do today so I'm gonna need to end our tour."

"Oh, okay," he says, a little hurt. "That's cool. I have somewhere I have to be anyway. But hey, I was wondering…" He pauses and looks down at his feet. "Do you maybe want to go and grab coffee sometime or drinks, or maybe I could take you out to dinner?"

He is running his hand through his silky brown hair and kicking around rocks on the ground. Oh, geez, is he asking me out on a date? This went the completely opposite direction, from possibly getting murdered to eating dinner together.

"Um... No, sorry. I just can't," I tell him and start heading back through the orchard.

He follows closely behind me. "That's okay, I get it. You have got a lot going on right now with your dog and everything, but I texted you and called you a few times, so you have my number. Call me when you're ready."

I lead him around the side of my house, not wanting him to walk through my house again, and watch him walk to his car. He turns around and gives me a weak wave as he gets in his car and disappears down the driveway.

What a strange guy, I think. He's very attractive, but I have zero interest in going down that path again, so there will be no dates with him in our future.

I locate my phone in the bedroom on the dresser. I see that Harper has sent me two messages. I read the first and feel relieved when she tells me that her dog is perfectly fine. *All he had was a tiny scratch that needed two stitches and he'll be 100% okay.* The second one says, *Oh I also forgot to tell you a guy named Hudson from the painting class called me this morning and offered me and my husband two free tickets to the class since we weren't able to make it.* Why would he think Harper has a husband? *He also said that he tried to call you as well to offer you and your husband free tickets, but he couldn't get a hold of you. I told him you weren't married and that you were single. He sounds really cute, Emily.*

I shake my head in disbelief. Thanks, Harper. You could have potentially just told a serial killer that I am a helpless single woman all alone at home.

Then I see that I have five missed calls and three text messages from Hudson. Wow, this guy is very persistent.

It all makes sense now, why he just showed up here like that. He was only calling Harper, fishing, to see if I had a husband, and since he found out that I didn't, he came out here to hit on me.

Clever and very bold, Hudson, but no thank you.

11

Victoria

"Auntie Victoria!"

I embrace myself for impact as all four of Evelyn's kids are screeching loudly as they run towards me. I give them all big hugs and tiny little bags with gifts that I purchased for them before leaving Los Angeles. They all say at the same time:

"Tell us all about your trip!"

"We're so glad you're here!"

"Let's play hide and seek!"

"Settle down, kids. Victoria just walked in the door. We haven't seen her in a long time, so we need to give her a minute to acclimate herself. She's not used to being around so many little people," Evelyn says

They all run off screaming and laughing to various places in Evelyn's house.

"Get over here." She pulls me into a long hug, and I pat her on the back. "I have missed you so much," she tells me, teary-eyed.

"Me too. I am so glad to be back home. The house looks great. What have you done with it?"

"Matt and I upgraded the hardwood floors, and we changed the paint on the walls."

"It looks nice, and it smells so good in here. I have missed family brunch so much. I bought this for you." I hand her a small red box, and she opens it. Inside is a silver chain. Attached are two charms with our initials, V and E, on it.

She inhales a deep breath. "I love it," she says and quickly clasps it around her neck. I look at her wearing the silver necklace and instinctively reach for the charm bracelet around my wrist.

"Come sit down with me." She pours me a mimosa from a premade pitcher she has sitting in front of us. "We didn't talk long on the phone the other day. You never answered why Brent isn't here with you."

Now is the time I should tell her. She is looking at me as if she knows something is not as it should be. I take a huge gulp of my champagne and orange juice and steal myself for this conversation.

Just then, I hear Hudson's deep voice from the entrance to the kitchen. "Finally, two of my favorite ladies are back together again." He comes over in between us and pulls us into his arms. I almost fall out of my chair, he is so forceful. He kisses each of us on the head, messing up my hair. I smooth it down when he releases his grip.

"I can't believe it's been almost a year since you have been here, Vic. I can't wait to have you back for good." Hudson says.

"Well, I'm here now."

"How long are you staying?" Evelyn asks.

I try to start the dreaded conversation once again when Evelyn's husband, Matt, walks in the room, delaying it.

He is just like Evelyn and comes over, giving me an exceptionally long hug with the same "We missed you so much. Where's your other half?"

I try my hardest to put a smile on my face, but I don't know how to go about answering these questions.

"He's still in LA," is all I can manage to say.

"I'm surprised you are here without him. I don't think that Evelyn and I went more than a day apart from each other back when we were first married." He walks over and gives his wife a kiss on the cheek, and she beams radiantly.

"Well, not every married couple can be as damn cute as the two of you are. So, Matt, I hear that you have taken over at the brewery now."

"Yup, business is booming. We are doing some exciting new things. Your father has miraculously given me permission to do whatever I like. Evelyn is going to be coming on soon to help out." He wraps his arms around his wife.

"You are going to start working at the brewery?" I ask Evelyn. She has never taken an interest in our family's business. She has always hated the idea of being around people that are drinking and all that comes with the alcohol industry.

"Now that Addison has started first grade, all the kids are at school all day. I have plenty of time on my hands. After the first week they were all gone, I was already bored and lonely. Matt and Hudson have created a position for me there, creating content for the Facebook page. Trying to get more younger people interested in the brewery."

"You don't even know how to use social media," I scoff at her.

"I know how to use it. I just choose not to post everything I am doing for everyone to see, like you do. By the way, you shouldn't post so many photos of yourself with a drink in your hands."

"If you are so bored, why don't you just have another kid?" I ask her.

"Nope, no more kids. It's time that I get to have Evelyn all to myself," Matt demands, squeezing her tightly and kissing her head.

Evelyn and Matt are the definition of the perfect couple. They have four kids and make parenting look flawless. Their kids are all so well-behaved, but then again, Evelyn is the sweetest, nicest person you could ever meet, so I can't imagine any of her kids being anything but nice as well. They are the type of couple that after ten years of marriage still hug and kiss each other constantly, making everyone around them feel uncomfortable. I am surprised kids don't keep popping out of her every year.

"We will leave the procreating to you and Brent now," Matt says to me.

I quickly grab the mimosa pitcher and fill my glass back up to the top, then change the subject, not feeling brave enough to tell them yet.

"So, Mom and Dad are in Greece for three more weeks?"

"They were supposed to come back last week, but Mom extended their trip. She's out there living her best life," Evelyn says.

I am secretly glad they are not here and won't be back soon. I need that time to get my affairs in order so they don't think I am wasting my life away, and telling them is going to be harder than telling Hudson and Evelyn.

"Dad was a little upset because he wanted to come back last week. He was worried about the thing with Hudson and the brewery," Evelyn says.

I look curiously around at everyone. "What thing with Hudson and the brewery?"

"Oh, sorry, I didn't know you didn't tell her," Evelyn says to Hudson.

"It's fine, she should know," Hudson says. "I had to file a restraining order last week."

"What!" I say in alarm. "Against who?"

"I was dating this girl. Her name is Samantha Mercer. We dated for a few months, then I found out all this stuff about her.

She had been lying to me about a lot of things. You know how I feel about lying, so I broke it off. She got super psycho after that. She knew I worked at the brewery and started showing up there and would stay there for hours questioning everyone about me. She would call me at all hours of the night, so I blocked her number, then she started showing up at my house and just waiting out there, watching. That's when I had enough and had to call the police."

"Oh my god. That's scary," I say, worried.

"It's okay. She hasn't done anything violent, and I don't think she's much of a threat. I am sure she will just get tired of all these shenanigans and move on. I told Mom and Dad not to worry and that everything is fine."

"What was she lying to you about?" I ask.

"She made herself out to be this person that had a great job and a huge family. She would tell me all these stories about her brothers, sisters, and cousins. Once I started to get to know her better, I found out that she didn't have a job at all. She was sort of living out of her car. Then one night she broke down with me and told me that she didn't have any family. That she lied because she thought I would think that was abnormal. When I ended it, she accused me of judging her about her situation. Which was not the case. I wouldn't care about something like that. I ended it because of all the lies she had told."

"Well, that doesn't surprise me, Hudson. You have always managed to drive girls crazy. I'm sure this isn't your first stalker," I tease him. "Has she left you alone now?"

He sighs, "Not exactly."

"Wait—Hudson, you never told us she is still stalking you," Evelyn says. She and Matt look at him, concerned.

"I didn't want you guys to worry, but I have it under control," he assures them.

"Fine, but you let us know the moment something happens. I can't bear to think that something bad could happen to you," Evelyn says tearfully.

"Mommy, I'm starving," Evelyn's youngest, Addison, says, coming into the room.

"Okay, that's our cue to eat. Everyone, let's head into the dining room."

There is lots of food as usual. Evelyn makes some of the dishes herself but orders in some of the food from various organic markets around the suburb she lives in. She does so much for these family brunches. I don't know where she gets the time or energy.

She gets the kids all situated at the dining table while I pour another mimosa. I should sip this one. It's my third, but I can't help it. I gulp this one down too fast as well.

Everyone is sitting and eating when the inevitable questions start to come.

"How is the interior design business coming along?" Matt asks.

Evelyn looks at me curiously, waiting for my response. She knows something is going on. I can tell.

"Since the renovations are almost done, I can start helping you set up the showrooms," Hudson says.

"Already?" Evelyn asks. "Are you going to start setting up early? I thought you were waiting 'til the first of the year."

"Why wait? I'm right next door. We can get started over the holidays," Hudson says.

I can't take it anymore. My heart starts to beat fast while everyone else is having conversations about me and the stupid interior design business.

"I'm not starting the interior design business anymore," I blurt out way too loudly.

Everyone at the table goes silent and looks over at me. Even the children. I must have said that much louder than I thought I had.

I reach out and grab the mimosa pitcher and fill my glass again while everyone stares at me in silence.

"Brent and I are getting a divorce," I say and take a drink from my newly filled glass.

Wide eyes are staring at me from all around the table. I can see that my timing was definitely not right.

Evelyn finally breaks the awkwardness. "Let's finish brunch, and when the children go to play, we can all discuss this," she says in a poised tone.

We continue eating brunch. Evelyn gracefully changes the subject to how much fun the kids are all having in school and what they all want to wear for Halloween coming up next month. When everyone is finished, Matt ushers the kids outside to play, leaving Evelyn and Hudson inside to talk to me.

"Are you okay, sweetie? I figured there was something going on," Evelyn says to me, and I am so thankful she is treating me kindly, but Hudson is staring at me unbelievingly.

I tell them as much as they need to know about what happened with me and Brent. I explain that we jumped in too quickly when we got married and decided that we were not meant to be together. We are getting a quick dissolution since the marriage didn't even last a year, and we are going to remain friendly.

Hudson sits there in silence, staring at me. Evelyn, ever optimistic, asks me if we can work it out, see a counselor, or perhaps go away on a trip together.

"None of that is going to happen. We already signed the papers," I tell her, as her eyes fill with tears for me.

"Please don't do that, Evelyn. I promise everything is fine. I am not upset at all. I wasn't happy, and neither was he. It's completely mutual. As for the interior design business, I am putting a short hold on that. I am still going to open my own company, but I don't think it's the right place for me to be with the Alexander Group. It was way too much pressure for me. I am really glad that this all happened. It was too stressful."

Hudson finally breaks his silence. "Dad is going to flip out when he hears this, Victoria."

"I know, that's why I need the two of you to help me when they get back. Brent and I agreed that I would be the one to tell our family, then after I do, he will tell his. By the time they get back I will have my own apartment and will be on my way to finding another place to start the business. I already spent the last two days touring buildings."

"So, you're not moving into 322?" Hudson says sadly.

"I am sorry, Hudson. No, I'm not. And to be honest, I am glad. I don't want to be there."

That is the truth. I really don't want to be there ever again. That place doesn't hold many good memories for me.

12
Emily

Today is the day. I wake up with an excitement that I can barely contain. As Christina promised, 322 Plum Street is available to move into. She worked out all the details for me to rent the commercial unit downstairs. I meet with her and her friend Brandi this morning at 11. She's the one who does all the rentals for their Cincinnati properties and will have all the paperwork for me to sign and take me on a tour of the building.

Once again, I feel so incredibly lucky to have made a friend like Christina. She could never possibly realize how much this means to me.

The time doesn't go by fast enough this morning. I start to get ready at 8 a.m. Putting on my makeup and styling my hair is much easier now after a week of practice. I am done and ready by 9:30. I can't keep pacing around my house, so I decide to drive to the Alexander Group's office early and wait there.

I get there an hour early. The receptionist tells me to have a seat and that Brandi will be out shortly.

A few minutes before 11 o'clock, Christina walks in the front door. She looks around the waiting room and completely ignores me sitting there.

"Hey Shondra, I have an 11 o'clock with Brandi. I'm gonna head back to her office. We have another person meeting us here. When she arrives, can you please send her back?"

"She's already here, Christina," Shondra says, pointing to where I am sitting in the lobby.

Christina turns around and scans the waiting room. I have a huge smile on my face because I am going to shock the hell out of her in just a second. She hasn't seen me since I went to Harper's salon and got my makeover. Her gaze stops on me, and her mouth drops open in complete disbelief.

I start giggling and stand up slowly.

"Oh. My. God," Christina says, exaggerating the three words. "How…. When?"

"What do you think?"

I do a little twirl. This new look has given me so much confidence over the past week. I have never been one to turn heads, but all week people seem to look at me everywhere I go, and not just men, but women too.

"I think that you need to give me the number of whoever did this because that's where I am going from now on. You look amazing, Emily. No, not amazing—stunning. I barely even recognized you." She looks at me with admiration. "You need to tell me all about this later. Today is the day. Let's sign that lease and get you the keys to your future."

I squeal with delight, following her back to Brandi's office.

After we go through and sign all the paperwork about the rental, Brandi hands me a set of keys.

"Let's head over and get you set up."

The Alexander Group's office is about five blocks away, so we walk over to my new retail store. On the way, Brandi points out some of the other buildings that their company owns and describes some of their history and the history of their own company.

"It's been family-owned for over sixty years," she says. "George Alexander founded it in 1959, and when he retired, his sons Brent and Brandon took over. Now they have properties in Cincinnati, Chicago, and Los Angeles."

Just like Christina, she is quite knowledgeable and good at her job. As we pass Hudson's art studio, Brandi points out that they also own that building as well. I cautiously look inside. The studio has been transformed back into a retail store, with racks of art supplies and some easels set up toward the back. I don't see him inside and am glad that he isn't there. He has sent three text messages this week and I have ignored all of them. I know that it's very rude of me, especially since we are going to be neighbors now, but I made it perfectly clear at my house that I wasn't interested, and his text messages have all been a little flirty. I will have to deal with that all later. Instead, there is an older woman with a tie-dyed dress on, long gray hair, and wearing black-rimmed glasses. She seems like an interesting person. I hope that she is there most of the time instead of Hudson.

I use my set of keys to get into the front door of the building. The brown paper has been removed, and the room is gleaming from the light shining in through the large front windows. The two women smile sweetly at me as I walk around the space looking in every nook and cranny in awe that this is all mine.

Christina knows this means a lot to me, but she can't possibly know how much. How far I have come in life to get here. How much sacrifice I have made. When I look around at where I ended up, I know that it was all worth it. Everyone who ever doubted me was dead wrong.

Brandi leads me out a door from inside the rental into the hallway that I saw from the front-door window last week. She shows me the mail area with my parcel locker where I can receive packages. I follow her down the hallway to the back of the building, where there is a staircase leading down into the basement area.

She shows me which storage room is mine and I unlock the door and look inside. It's a spacious area with lots of room to store some extra pieces that I won't be able to fit upstairs, but right now half of it is filled with someone else's things.

"You and the six apartments share the basement. You have the largest storage room down here. The maintenance guys will be here later next week to finish getting all this stuff out of here. They were trying to salvage some of the things that weren't damaged in the fire when they did the renovations, but there is no need. Everything needs to be thrown out. The owner doesn't want any of it."

I look at the stack of items in the storage room to see if I can use any of it. There are some boxes, a bunch of pieces of furniture, some cue sticks for playing pool, and other things that look like junk.

The pool sticks are random. I wonder what happened to the table. It must not have been salvageable from the fire. I am excited that there are six or seven usable wooden furniture pieces, and they look like they are of decent quality. I can sand them down and clean them until the smoke smell is all gone.

"Is it okay if I keep this stuff?" I ask Brandi. "I could use some of it for my store. I will just throw out what I don't want myself."

She shrugs and tells me that's not a problem.

Christina invites me to join her and Brandi for lunch, and I accept. Brandi and Christina are fun to listen to as they talk with each other. You can tell that they have been friends for a long time. They talk about an upcoming trip they are taking to the Maldives. Christina is always traveling to places like that. I hope to be like her someday. She has an amazing life. They ask me dozens of questions about my new hair and makeup. I give them both Olivia's cards from my purse, telling them they have to go see her.

I head straight back to my home workshop after lunch. I have about five weeks to get everything ready for the store to open. I am going to open on Saturday, November 7th. It will be my twenty-third birthday.

13

Emily

I knew it was inevitable that I would run into Hudson. After all, he is right next door. He gave up on texting me last week. After no responses to the messages that he sent, he must have finally gotten the hint.

I worked harder than I ever have worked in my entire life this week since getting the keys to 322. I am having movers bring some of the items I have already finished into the store today, and a sign company is installing the custom-made sign out front that I created with my business name on it.

Teal Lotus is what I chose for the new name of my business. Modern Resale was okay before when it was an online store, but it was kind of boring, and this is a trendy part of town. I wanted something that would stand out and make a statement. So, I changed it on all my social media accounts as well.

The company that makes the signs was very helpful and gave me lots of designs to choose from. I designed my sign to have letters made from black iron in a typeface called Quiche Sands. The letters were made to stand half an inch out from a natural wood block as the background. It looks very modern yet old-fashioned all at the same time.

Today, while I am standing out front helping to position the sign, I see Hudson walking up the sidewalk toward our buildings.

He is dressed nicely like the other times I saw him, but today in a cream-colored button-up shirt, dark brown slacks, a brown belt, and some very expensive-looking shoes that are polished so shiny he could have just picked them up from the store. He also has the same gray backpack that he was carrying before. It's so out of place with his clothing. What does he always keep in there?

I debate whether I should run back into my store quickly so I can avoid him or pretend that I don't see him. I decide to stay outside. We are going to have to interact at some point. It might as well be now.

I focus my attention on the man hanging my sign and don't look in Hudson's direction. Maybe I can delay this a little while longer if he doesn't notice me. I dare not look in his direction as I listen for his footsteps. When I don't hear anyone pass me, I brace myself for this exchange. I look in his direction, and there he is. He stopped just a few feet away from me, staring at me in disbelief.

"Well, well, well, what do we have here? I think that we might know each other." A wide devilish grin starts to form on his face.

I sigh deeply. "Hello, Hudson, how are you?"

"Um, I'm good, but even more important, how are you?" He looks up and sees the sign being hung above us. "Teal Lotus?" he says, looking back at me skeptically.

I don't answer him. He walks over to the window of my store and looks in. He must see the furniture that has been moved in there.

"Are you the one who rented this place? I heard that they rented this unit out to someone with a vintage furniture store, but I would never have guessed in a million years that it would be you. But wait, there's no way this can be yours. I mean, wouldn't you have perhaps told me that? I was at your house after all. That might have been a good time," he says in a mocking tone.

"Well, it is my store, and you were at my house uninvited. I didn't owe you any explanation," I say back in a snooty tone.

"You told me at my painting class that you were terrible at painting, but from the looks of it, that's not the case." He looks back into the store. "You have some really nice things in there."

"Thanks. Now I need to get back to hanging my sign."

"I still have your tequila sunshine painting in my studio. I can bring it over to you later."

I shudder thinking about that awful evening. "No thank you, I really don't want that painting. Just throw it away."

"You know, Emily, you could have just texted or called me back. You didn't have to go as far as renting the place next door to get my attention," he teases.

"I didn't text you back because I told you that I am very busy and not interested in lunch, or coffee, or dinner."

He ignores my rejection. "Can I see inside?"

"No, you cannot. I am very busy," I raise my voice.

"Did you move all of that stuff in there by yourself?" he says, looking through the window again. "I can drop off my backpack and come help you."

"I have movers for that, and I don't need your help."

I know that I am being mean—the man hanging the sign must think I am being such a bitch to this poor guy—but this is the second time he has inserted himself into my personal space without being asked.

"Alrighty then. I will be just next door when you need my help."

"I won't need your help."

He smiles and starts to walk toward his front door.

"By the way, Teal Lotus is a great name. I love it."

14

Victoria

Hudson is avoiding me. It's been almost two weeks since we had family brunch and I haven't seen him once since then. Every time I call him, he doesn't answer and when I text all I get is a short message back with something along the lines of. *Sorry, I'm really busy right now. Let's get together soon,* but then that never happens.

I am going to go to the art studio today and force him to see me. Evelyn said that's where he spends most of his time after he gets off work from the brewery. So, I decide to ambush him there.

"So, this is what you do on Friday nights?" I say when I walk in.

Hudson is there sitting at one of his easels, painting something that looks like nonsense swirls of color to me. I have never really been one to understand art techniques, but Hudson is always painting something that he calls art.

"It's about time you came to see the place, Vic."

I look around the store. "It's quaint."

He narrows his eyes at me. "To what do I owe the pleasure of your presence?"

"I'm here to rescue you. You have been slaving away since I got back into town. We are going out tonight, plus I want to take you for a ride in my new car." I jingle the keys in front of him.

"You got a new car?"

"It's a brand-new Audi A4, all black inside and out. The guy at the dealership tried to get me to buy an A5 or A6, but I am being frugal."

"I hardly think a brand-new Audi is a frugal car, even if you got the cheaper model."

"You're going to love it. Come on, let's go."

"I can't. I already told you I'm really busy."

"Busy with what? I don't see any customers here. Just close the store, and let's go do something fun like we used to. I have been back now for weeks, and we haven't gone out at all. It feels like you're avoiding me. Is this because of Brent?"

"Vic, I hate to break this to you, but I don't really go out that much anymore. It's not fun for me to keep going out night after night, hanging out in bars and clubs getting drunk. It's more important for me to be here in the studio. And no, it's not because of Brent. I talked to him earlier this week and he seems indifferent about the divorce. Whatever happened between the two of you is your business. I am staying out of it."

"I had no idea that you two had spoken already. What did he say about me?" I ask nervously.

"Nothing, really. Just that you two agreed to go your separate ways. We didn't talk for very long. Evelyn told me that you talked to Mom and Dad."

"Oh, I see, you talk to Evelyn but not me," I pout.

"Stop it. You are more than welcome to come by here and talk to me whenever you want. We can go out for lunch or coffee, and when you need help moving into your new apartment or setting up your business, I will be happy to help, but the only thing you keep calling about is for me to go out to get drunk with you and Katie, and right now I need to focus on what's important."

I am so irritated with Hudson right now. As if I am not important enough to help me get through this hard time. Shouldn't I be top priority for him?

I push back my feelings. "Fine, for now, but I will get you to come around soon enough. When you get bored with all of this." I wave my hands around the room.

"I am not going to get bored. Things are going well here. Anyway, what did Mom and Dad say?"

"I FaceTimed the two of them a few days ago. I wanted to do it while they were still in Greece. That way they would be in too good of a mood to be angry with me. They both took the news well, especially Dad. I thought he was going to be mad, but he said that he wants me to be happy, and if I wasn't then getting divorced was the best decision. He was more concerned with what I am going to do for my job now that I'm not opening the interior design store with Brent."

"What are you going to do?"

"I am still going to open it up, just on my own. I still have plenty of money left in my trust fund that I could use to get it going. Dad said that I needed to meet with the family accountant to discuss what my options are."

"You've got this, Vic. When you get things going, I will be there to help you. When are you moving into your own apartment?"

"I signed a lease this week. You will love it. It's close to where you live. I don't have any furniture or a bed or dishes or, well, anything yet. So, I have been between there and Katie's place still."

"I know it's hard to leave Katie's penthouse luxury apartment, but you need to get out on your own. If you need furniture, you should check out the store that's opening next door. The girl over there sells vintage furniture. I saw her loading things in there today. It looks pretty cool."

"Vintage furniture," I say in disgust. "No thanks, I would rather just design it myself. Like I did when I decorated your place. Look what an amazing job I did there."

"You did a really good job, so get out there and put your talents to good use."

"So, someone is setting up over there, huh? I saw a sign up in front of the building. The Teal Lotus. That's a stupid name for a vintage furniture store."

"I like that name a lot. It will fit in perfectly on this block. Are you okay about it not being you?" he asks, concerned.

"Yes, of course. I am more than okay that it's not happening. It was going to be way too much for me to take all of that on. I need to start things slowly. I don't want to be a part of the Alexander Group. I want to have my own thing. Like what you're doing here. I know that I have made fun of you, but I am proud of you."

"Thanks, Vic. You've got this. I have complete faith in you."

"So, does that mean I can get you to come out with me tonight?" He chucks a paintbrush in my direction. "Okay, fine, I'm leaving, but I'd better see you again soon."

When I leave his studio, I walk past 322 and look into the windows. Hudson was right; there is a bunch of old furniture in there. This store probably won't be able to exist here for very long. The rent on this property isn't cheap. I can't see how selling used furniture would be able to pay the bills, but then again, I said that about the fancy soap shop that opened across the street two years ago and I see that's still there. Lather and Fizz. I have no idea where these people come up with these stupid names. I wonder if this girl that is renting this store knows Brent? Maybe he is giving her a deal to try and make me jealous. Well, not the case. My place would have been too classy to be down here anyway.

15
Emily

I could have never realized how much fun starting my own business would be. It was fun when I started selling my pieces out of my workshop at home, but being able to decorate my own store is another thing.

I spent the day taking photos of some fall scenes around the downtown area. The leaves have really started to turn now, and the colors look so vibrant. I took the images to a local print shop to have them made into large canvases to hang on the walls. I plan to do this every few months to capture the different seasons in Cincinnati.

Harper asked me to come out with her and Ethan and a bunch of their friends tonight, but I declined. I plan to spend the entire night here at my store working on this gorgeous reception desk that I got from a store closing sale. It's going to look awesome as the checkout counter here. Besides, I know what Harper is doing. She has been constantly trying to set me up with one of Ethan's male friends. Every time I get even a small hint that one of them will be around, I tell her I have to work on the store. I know that she understands, though. She has dropped by twice this week with what she calls "store-warming gifts." She is so incredibly thoughtful. She brought an adorable vintage

Open/Closed sign for me to hang in the front window. I can't wait to use it.

I've been so involved with this desk that I didn't realize it's already after 8 p.m. The last time I checked it was 5:30, and I was already starving then. Now I feel like I could eat a piece of wood, I am so hungry. I think about what I could order nearby. I am not ready to leave yet for the night. I just need some sustenance to keep me going for a few more hours. I hear a knock on the front door and look up to see Hudson standing outside, holding up two orange plastic bags in his hands. Doesn't this guy have anything better to do on a Saturday night? He must have other women that he could be bothering.

I walk over and unlock the door. Before I can say anything, he says, "I know, I know you are very busy, but I noticed that you have been in there working hard for several hours and that you haven't taken a break to eat. You must be hungry."

"Please tell me you are not watching my every move now," I snap at him. "Are you some kind of a stalker?"

"No, I am far from being a stalker."

"Don't try and deny it. Your actions scream differently. First you show up at my house, now my business."

"Okay, you're right. I was planning on kidnapping you and selling your organs on the black market."

I unintentionally laugh at that.

"Finally, I get you to laugh. I was beginning to wonder if you could."

I shake my head. "What's in the bags?"

"I brought you some food. Not food to share. Just food to leave here with you. I wanted you to have something good to eat. You must be hungry, and it looks like you have a long night ahead of you. I know how it is. When I first opened the studio, I was there around the clock nonstop. I barely left for food or drink."

I stare at the bags of food. I should just tell him no thank you, but I actually am hungry.

"Here." He hands out the bags to me. "I ran up and got you some bagels, cream cheese, some muffins, and a couple of organic juices. I wasn't sure what you liked so I just grabbed some things."

"What kind of muffins?" My mouth salivates.

"I think there is chocolate chip and blueberry."

A chocolate chip muffin sounds so good right now and I could really use some nourishment.

"I will take them," I say and reach out and grab the bags, my irritation waning just a little. "Only because I love muffins, but thank you."

He smiles. "You're welcome. I will see you around the block, Emily," he says and walks out the front door.

I'm surprised to see him leaving without a fight, but I don't care. I tear into the muffins and bagels. I guess I'm much hungrier than I thought I was. The muffins he brought are amazing. I look in the bag to see if there is a receipt as to where they came from. There isn't one in there and no writing on the orange bags. I finish eating the food and drink one of the mango blend juices that he brought, feeling satisfied. That should give me a couple more hours of energy for this desk.

I look out the windows to make sure that he isn't out there staring in at me, which is a ridiculous thought. I am sure that he isn't stalking me that badly. There are a lot of people walking around on the street. It's Saturday night. The bars and restaurants are all busy right now. For just a brief moment I think that I see the same blonde girl that I saw before on the sidewalk in front of Hudson's house, but that's ridiculous. Why would she be out in front of my store? I am sure it wasn't her. There are lots of women with blonde hair in this city, with me now being one of them, so I ignore it.

16

Emily

Time is nonexistent to me anymore. I spend every day either here at the store or in my workshop at home. I am working around the clock with very little sleep. When I do sleep, I dream about painting or sanding. It is getting to the point where when I wake up, I think I have already finished a project, but it turns out it was just in my dream.

I have been training one of the guys that helps me haul furniture to go out on his own and find pieces that I would like. He has been doing a fantastic job and is helpful at getting new items for me on his own. I have been able to send him to thrift shops, estate sales, all the places I would normally search, and he brings back things I would have bought myself. I pay him very well for what he brings me, and it saves me a ton of time. I have the storage area almost full in the basement with all my backup inventory. I will need to take all that other stuff that was left there to the dump soon.

For the last four days, there has been a different kind of muffin in an orange plastic bag that I find in my mail parcel locker. Today there is a muffin called lemon lavender. There is also a brown box with a candle in it from the Melted Hearts Candle Shop. I open the lid and it smells amazing. It's the perfect fall scent called pumpkin pancakes. Obviously, these are all from Hudson, even though I have not seen or heard from him all week. I guess this is him respecting what I asked him for in his own way. He just leaves these things in my parcel locker without bothering me. I have wondered several times how he manages to get them in there.

I don't say anything to him about the gifts. I know that it's not good manners to not thank someone for such generosity, but I don't want to lead him on. Maybe he will eventually get the hint that I am not interested.

I'm not going to kid myself, though: these muffins have been delicious. I have devoured them every day, and I admit, I did take the candle home and burn it in my house. It made the house smell just like pancakes in the fall.

My diet has fallen to the wayside lately. I have been eating a lot of crappy food, but I haven't gained back a single pound. I am sure it's because of the amount of work I have been doing. I have also managed to keep up with my running schedule. The weather here in Cincinnati has been beautiful for early morning runs. It's become chilly but not too cold yet. I still get to yoga, but only once a week now. I have already gotten two lectures from Shiva, but I tune her out. I just go there to see Harper. She is in full wedding planning mode now, with it coming up early next month. Today, she and I are going to a store in the Market district that she has been talking nonstop about. They make unique specialty wedding items. She is having them personalize a shadow box that will collect the corks from the bottles of wine they drink at their wedding reception. It never ceases to amaze me the number of creative shops there are here.

Harper walks into the store and immediately jumps up and down, squealing. The store is full of all sorts of wedding items. Decanters, wine glasses, serving trays, plaques, and signs, everything you can have personalized with your names. Harper almost loses it when she sees that you can have your wedding song printed on a canvas.

"I am definitely getting this made. Our song is "Something" by the Beatles, and that would look so freaking sweet on a canvas."

We are leaving the store and heading to have lunch when I hear that familiar husky voice call out my name from across the street. I look, and of course, it's Hudson.

He jaywalks across the street, almost getting hit by a car to get over to us.

"Fancy meeting you here," he says. "I thought that was you."

"Hudson, are you still stalking me?" I smile at him. I know that he isn't this time. I am just in an exceptionally good mood and want to mess with him.

"It isn't stalking if we run into each other in our own neighborhood." He looks back at the store we just came out of. "When's the wedding?" he teases me.

"Ha, ha, very funny."

Harper clears her throat loudly. I almost forgot that she was there for a minute.

"Emily, who might this be?" She looks at me with gaping eyes.

"Sorry, Harper, this is Hudson. He owns the art studio next to the Teal Lotus."

"Oh, right, you do the Highball painting."

"Harper, right, nice to meet you. I spoke with you on the phone. Now that you have some free tickets, you will have to come back sometime. It's usually the last Saturday of the month but this month falls on Halloween, so I am not going to have it."

"That's too bad, but I am so excited that Halloween is on a weekend night this year. Ethan and I go to this Halloween party every year at the Pink Ballroom."

"I have heard of that. I hear it's a really fun time," Hudson says.

Harper's eyes dart back and forth between us. "You two should come with us this year," she blurts out, and I cringe. Why is she inviting him to a Halloween party?

Before I can say anything, Hudson is telling Harper what a great idea that is. "Maybe you and I can have a couple's costume?" he says to me, raising his eyebrows up and down.

I know that he is messing with me the way I was with him, but I need to clarify that we are definitely not doing couples costumes.

"I'm not really into Halloween, but thanks for the offer, Harper."

"Did you enjoy the muffin today? I thought it might be a little out there, with the lemon and lavender, but I had one too and it was surprisingly good."

Harper's eyes are wide with curiosity now.

I don't respond to his question about the muffin. "Hudson, we have to go now. Harper is planning her wedding and we have lots to do."

"Always a pleasure. Ms. Lewis," he says coyly.

I grab Harper's hand and practically have to drag her down the street. We go to a Mexican restaurant for lunch, and we are sitting at our table looking at our menus when she says, "So, are we not going to address the elephant in the room?"

"What elephant?" I say, hoping she will drop the subject.

The server comes and brings us a bowl of chips and salsa. I order a jumbo margarita. I will need it for this conversation. I know I am not going to get out of explaining things to Harper.

"Since you are eating his muffins, you should let him eat yours."

I almost choke on the tortilla chip I had just put in my mouth when she says this.

"Harper, I'm shocked. You never say things like that. I don't think I have even heard you curse."

"Were you going to keep the extreme hottie that we just saw on the street—ya know, the one that brought you a muffin and wants to do couples Halloween costumes with you—a secret? I am going to need all the details right now." She is practically falling out of her seat with excitement.

I need to tell her something about Hudson, so I start from when I saw him at the painting class. I don't tell her the details of the mess that happened there or about me lying to him about the dog. After all, it was her dog that got hurt and she wouldn't like that too much.

"It feels like he is stalking me," I tell her.

"You think that an extremely hot guy who brings you food and gifts and asks to take you out is a stalker? Girl, you must be completely delusional because that is flirting, not stalking."

"Well, I have told him that I am not interested several times, and he keeps coming back."

"You're insane! Why wouldn't you want to go out with him? Do you need glasses? He is gorgeous."

"I know he is, believe me, I have eyes. I just don't want to date anyone. I have way too much going on."

"Have you googled him yet?"

"No, why would I do that?"

"To get information about him, what his past girlfriends look like. What kind of stuff he posts online. Maybe he has a criminal record."

"No, Harper, I have not googled him. I have no interest in what his past girlfriends look like or anything about him, for that matter. He's kind of annoying."

"What's his last name?" she demands.

"On the flyer for his painting class, it said it was Berman."

She pulls out her phone and quickly types in his name in Google.

"Emily!"

She yells my name so loudly that some of the other people in the restaurant turn to look at us. She turns her phone and shows me a picture of Hudson, staring at the camera with his green eyes twinkling out from the picture.

"Do you know who this is?"

I shrug.

"His family owns Berman Brewery. It's in Over the Rhine."

I shrug again.

"It's been around forever. It's a Cincinnati staple, like even before breweries were popular. Oh my god, we have to go there."

"Absolutely not. Nope, nope, nope. There is no need to lead this guy on anymore," I tell her emphatically.

"Okay, fine, I will just sit back and eat popcorn watching to see how this all plays out, and you'd better tell me every detail. No more holding out on me."

17

Emily

In front of my parcel locker today, there is a large brown rectangular box with my name written in a black Sharpie on it. I take it in my shop and set it down in front of my receptionist desk. There is a note taped onto it.

I open the paper and read it. *I'm sorry if I embarrassed you in front of your friend yesterday. I hope this makes up for it.* I look at the box and debate whether to take it back over to Hudson and tell him I don't want anything else from him. My curiosity gets the best of me, and I open the box to find a painting.

It's of a teal-colored lotus flower. It's so detailed and intricate. The colors are immensely vivid. So much so that I feel like it might be real. The shades of teal contrasted with the yellow core of the blooming flower are electrifying. It is the most beautiful painting I have ever seen in person. While the painting may be impressive, and I am sure that he painted this himself, I need to talk to him and finish this once and for all.

I go over to his store, and he's not there. Instead, the older lady I saw there before is working. I have noticed that she is the one that is always there during the day.

I bet he sleeps all day after partying all night like most other rich kids whose parents own breweries. I am sure that's why he doesn't come in until the afternoon.

"Hello there," the elderly lady says when I walk in the door. She is wearing a brown chunky knitted sweater over a long purple dress today. She always looks like she walked right out of the '60s. "I was wondering when I would have the pleasure of meeting you." She sees my confusion. "You're Emily, from next door, correct?"

"Yes, I am."

"I am so excited for you to open your store. Hudson says you have some really extraordinary talent."

I wonder how he knows that. He must have been looking in my store more than I realized.

"I was actually looking for him. Is he here?"

"No, sweetie, he will be here shortly after two o'clock."

Jeez it must be nice to sleep in 'til two. She walks closer to me, holding out a hand, each finger wrapped with turquoise and silver jewelry.

"I'm Frieda. I should have come over to introduce myself sooner, but you must be so busy, and I didn't want to interrupt you."

Well at least someone has some manners to not interrupt, I think.

"Nice to meet you." I shake her hand. "I love your rings; they're beautiful."

"Thank you."

"Have you worked here for a long time?" I ask.

"I have been here since Hudson opened this place, about six months ago now. I was one of his art teachers in grade school. I always knew that boy had talent. I was constantly pushing him to pursue his dreams of one day becoming an artist."

I am shocked to hear that Hudson hired his grade school art teacher.

"I hadn't realized that this place was so new. Only six months, you said?"

"Before it was an art studio, it was a small hardware store. I don't think there was much demand for that with the Home Depot and Lowes overtaking everything, so they closed. He was really excited to get to be on Plum Street. It has such an artist vibe, ya know. Your store is going to fit in perfectly here. We are so happy to have you on the block."

"Was this building affected by the fire that happened last year?"

"No, not really. The hardware shop had to shut down for a few weeks, but the fire was mostly over at your building. I saw the whole thing from my apartment. I live just down the street."

"Oh wow. That's convenient. Well, I can't wait for you to come by and see my store when it opens. Please tell Hudson I stopped by. And thank you; I am happy to be here."

Right at 2:15, Hudson is at my front door. I steel myself for the talk that I need to have with him. I need to let him know for the last time that he must stop with the food and gifts. Even though they are all very nice, I can't keep accepting them and leading him on.

I invite him in, and he spins around, looking at what I have done.

"This is amazing. You really are talented, Emily."

"Hudson, I have no idea what your intentions are, but the gifts and asking me out need to stop. I am not interested in dating anyone right now or anytime in the near future. Maybe never. I have the store to think about and that will keep me busy for a very long time. I need you to please stop."

It takes him a few moments to respond, and I hope that he isn't going to try and talk me out of my decision. I don't want to have to be mean to him.

"I get it, honestly, I do. I shouldn't be trying to date anyone either. I haven't had the best luck with relationships recently, and I told myself that I would take a break from dating while I got the studio up and going. So how about this: we become friends. We are going to be next door to each other for many, many years to come, so we might as well make the best of it. I promise I won't cross any more boundaries with you anymore."

"I accept that. Friends only." I grab the painting and go to hand it to him.

"No, please keep that. I made it just for this store. Don't think of it as a gift for you."

I look at the painting. It would look great on the wall next to the other pictures I took.

"Alright, I will do that. On one condition."

"Anything."

"Tell me how you got it into my parcel locker. You need a key or a code to get into the building."

"They never changed the mail code since doing the renovations. They changed all the residence pin codes but not the one the mail person uses to get inside."

"How do you know the mail code for this building?"

"My family is really close with the family that owns this building. They own mine as well."

"The Alexander Group?"

"Yeah, we have all been friends forever; our parents were friends before I was born. One of the sons, Brent, used to live on the second floor of this building. We used to hang out a lot and I would get his mail while he was traveling."

"That makes sense. For a minute I thought you were breaking in, but you're only doing something a little less illegal. Also, since you aren't going to be bringing the muffins anymore, I need to know where you get them."

"Findlay Market. It's in Over the Rhine. Haven't you ever been there?"

I shake my head.

"You've got to go, it's amazing. One of my favorite places in the city. I would ask you to go with me sometime, but I promised I wouldn't cross any more boundaries." He starts to head toward the door. "So I will tell you this… If you ever want a friend—*just* a friend—to go there with sometime, let me know. I go there a few times a week."

"Fair enough."

Just as Hudson is leaving my store, Harper walks in. She gives us both an all-knowing grin.

"Good afternoon, Hudson."

"Harper, so good to see you again. How is the wedding planning going?"

"Really good, thanks for asking." She looks him up and down. "Don't leave on my account."

"I need to get back to work. You ladies have a lovely afternoon."

"Is he always so charming?" Harper asks me after he leaves.

"Yes, unfortunately," I tell her.

"You are the only girl that would think a gorgeous guy like that being charming is unfortunate. I am beginning to wonder if you are medically insane." She shakes her head. "You know who he looks like…. Damon Salvatore."

I gasp. "You know what, you're right. I must have watched *The Vampire Diaries* like four times when I was a teenager."

"Four times?"

"Yeah, I watched a lot of television and movies back then. I had like zero social life. I didn't have any friends until I moved here."

"You didn't have any friends? Even when you were a teenager?"

"Nope. I had some friends when I was younger, when my mom and I lived in the city, but after she married my stepfather, we moved an hour away. My new school was hugely different from my school in the city. We moved out to this suburb area where there was lots of old money, and I just didn't fit in, not even with the dorky kids. They were even all too good for me. I stayed home and took care of my mother after she got sick, so she was kind of my only friend."

"When did you start dating your ex?" she asks solemnly.

"After high school."

"How did you meet?"

"I bought a lot of furniture from his mother's antique store. She had this huge store that had so much stuff in it from years of collecting. I don't think she knew what great things she had in there. She was in her late sixties and was getting senile a little bit. She wasn't all there."

"He turned out to be a jerk?"

"Such a jerk, the worst. I spent so much time wrapped up in movies and TV shows that made you think everything had a happy ending. I always thought that I would have this fictional happy family life and then later a fictional love story. When neither turned out that way, it was hard for me to deal with. That's a lot of the reason why I don't want to go there with Hudson. I don't want to go through another heartbreak."

"I can tell you firsthand that no one ever ends up with their first love. Those are strictly for heartbreak. Ethan wasn't my first love."

"He wasn't?"

"No, when I was in beauty college, I was dating this guy that I thought I was so in love with. He turned out to be a complete jerk and broke my heart, but then a few years later I met Ethan, and now I know that I have a true love story. I know that it does truly exist. Emily, you are so young and beautiful. You should give yourself another chance. It doesn't have to be with Damon Salvatore, even though you would be crazy not to, but at least with someone, someday."

"Maybe you're right," I say melancholically.

"Just when it happens, play hard to get and make him really work for it." She winks. "That drives them crazy."

I think about what she is saying. She might just be right. I am lucky to have her as a friend.

"Hey Harper, have you ever been to the Findlay Market?"

18
Emily

The art I had made into canvases came back from the printers today. I hung them up on the walls of my store. The way the fall scenes look against the whitewashed brick is gorgeous. I hang Hudson's painting up as well. He truly did beautiful work with the lotus flower.

I am admiring the walls when I see Hudson and Frieda walking arm and arm in front of the store. She stops abruptly when she sees me. The two of them seem to have some sort of disagreement with each other, and she drags him over to my door.

I walk over and unlock it. "HI, guys. How's it going?"

"Hello, Emily. Hudson and I were just heading over to have lunch at a deli a few blocks away. We were wondering if you wanted to join us?"

I look at Hudson, and he is looking shamefully at the ground. I can tell that he was not the one who wanted to stop and ask about lunch. Frieda has obviously made him.

Frieda nudges him in the side. "Yes, would you like to come have lunch with us?" Then he silently mouths, *Sorry*. I smile at them. This whole scenario is funny, and I like watching Hudson squirm.

"I would love to, Frieda, but I can't today. Thanks for the invite, though."

"Alright, dear. If you need anything while we are out, just text Hudson."

"Will do, Frieda. Enjoy your lunch."

I watch them walk arm in arm down the street. He is so sweet when he is with her, and Frieda is such a lovely person. Maybe I should have gone with them. I am kind of hungry and could really use a break from here. My brain is starting to turn into mush.

After an hour I see them walk back by, and they both wave as they pass. I smile and wave back. A few minutes later, I see Hudson at my front door holding a brown box.

"Frieda told me to bring you this," he says after I open the door. "It's the leftover half of my chicken salad sandwich. I know that's gross to offer you my leftovers, but she will have my head if I hadn't come to offer."

I laugh hardily aloud. I imagine Frieda scolding Hudson and him worrying who will be angrier—her for him not coming over, or me for him coming over.

I surprise myself when I say, "Ya know what? I am not in the mood for chicken salad, but what I would love is one of those lemon lavender muffins that you brought me before."

He stands there completely still and silent. He probably thinks this is a trick, and if he says the wrong thing, I am going to yell at him.

"Would you be interested in taking me over to the Findlay Market and showing me where you got them?" I ask.

Without hesitation he says, "Yes, of course. Let me just run over and tell Frieda, and I will be right back."

We hop on the bus that takes us the ten minutes to the market. When we get dropped off out front, I am amazed to see that this is not just some little farmers' market but a huge place bustling with people everywhere. There are musicians out front playing music, as well as food stands selling barbecue, empanadas, jerk chicken, and various other items. It smells so good in the air with all the food cooking, my stomach growls.

"Wow, this is pretty amazing," I tell him. "I thought you meant some little farmers' market. This place is huge. Is there some sort of festival going on here?"

"Nope, it's always like this on Saturdays. Wait 'til you see inside," he tells me with a wide grin on his face.

There are dozens of tables out front filled with people drinking out of red cups and eating from brown boxes that must have come from the food vendors or possibly from somewhere inside. I notice that the red cups are being served from a large outdoor bar area. The sign is written creatively with chalk. Someone took a lot of time to write in tiny chalk letters all the different beers, wines, and cocktails they have available.

"They have a bar here?" I say, astonished.

"They have a few throughout this place. Did you want to get something to drink?"

I look at the chalk menu and see that they have a cocktail called the Painkiller. The drawing next to it is expertly done with thin chalk of a glass filled with orange liquid, a tiny pink umbrella, and cherries on top.

"Yeah, I think I do. That Painkiller looks good. The chalk work is amazing."

"They change that every week or so to add in their new drinks and beers they put on tap. Someone puts a lot of effort into that."

We get two of the drinks and I follow his lead into the enormous building. There is a long walkway leading down the middle of the market to the back of the building, with thirty or maybe forty booths and mini-stores along each side. I am bewildered by how large it is inside here. It looked big from the outside, but it seemed to have grown twice as much when I walked in the door. What surprises me more is how many people are in here. There is barely any room to walk through the aisle due to the vast amount of people lined up in front of each counter calling out their orders. It is loud with the sound of laughter, chatter, and the vendors all talking at once.

Hudson lets me stand there taking it all in for a while. I look up at him, and he is staring down at me, waiting to hear my response.

"Wow," is all I can say, smiling.

We walk slowly through the crowd of people, sipping our drinks and looking at each vendor. There is a plethora of breads, meats, cheeses, spices, soups, pastas, pastries, and many other types of foods from different countries and cultures. No wonder he was able to get such a variety of muffins for me.

When we get to the middle of the market, I am surprised to see corridors leading right and left that also are filled with vendors.

"If you like that candle scent I got for you, this is where I got it from."

He leads me down the left corridor. This part of the market seems to be where the specialty shops are that sell soaps, handmade jewelry, and clothing, and I see the Melting Heart candle shop.

We walk outside the back of the market; there is a small stage with another band playing music to a crowd of people. Some are dancing and drinking. Kids and dogs are running around. There is another seating area and a smaller bar that serves the same cocktail.

"That drink was delicious. I am going to grab another," I tell Hudson.

"That sounds great. I will as well."

As we stand waiting at the bar, I notice him staring at me with an amused look on his face.

"Why are you looking at me like that?"

"No reason. It's just really nice to see you having some fun for a change."

We grab our drinks and have a seat to listen to the band. I take a few sips from my second drink and realize it's quite a bit stronger than the first one, but it's still delicious.

I sit there quietly for a while, thinking about his comment. I'm not offended by it. There is some truth to it. I don't go out and allow myself to have fun the way that other girls my age do. I spend all my time working on my business or myself. Since I've been here in Cincinnati, I've allowed a little bit of free time for the few friends that I have made, but not much. I never accept any of the offers to go out with Harper and her fiancé and their group of friends. I am always so afraid she is trying to set me up. That's ridiculous, though. I came to Cincinnati to start fresh and meet new people. To have new experiences. I am letting my past hold me back, and I need to let it go finally and let myself move completely on.

"I can be really fun, ya know. I am not always such a stick in the mud," I say to him solemnly.

"I'm sorry, I didn't mean it to come off like that. I just meant that—"

I interrupt him, "No, you're right. I really should get out there and have more fun. I am only twenty-two years old, and this is the first time I've ever sat and listened to a band play. I have never been to any parties or a dance club. None of the things normal girls should be doing."

"Really? You've never gone and watched a live band before?"

"Nope, never. I didn't have the chance to do things most teenagers and people in their early twenties do. I don't even have a driver's license."

"What?" Hudson almost falls off his seat. "Don't you drive a big truck?"

"Yes, but I just drive safely. I know I need to get one. It's just that no one took me when I turned sixteen. I was allowed to drive my mom's car whenever I wanted. There was just too much going on to care about getting a license, and then it just kept getting pushed back."

"Don't you get carded when you go out?"

"I don't go out very often, but when I do have a state-issued ID card that I use. That's all you need."

"That's true."

"I had a difficult life before I came here."

"I want to know all about you, Emily."

He looks at me, and I see that he is *really* looking at me. Not just at what I can be for him. I can see in his eyes that he is sincere, so I decide to share a little with him.

"My mother was diagnosed with cancer when I was in high school. She was extremely sick for years, and I was the one who took care of her. Going out with friends and having a normal life was out of the question. Which was fine with me. She was my best friend, and I wanted to be with her. She died when I was nineteen and then my stepfather died shortly after that."

"How did your stepfather die?"

"Also, cancer. It came out of the blue. Thankfully, he had a life insurance policy that helped me get here and get my life going."

"Man, that's rough. I can't believe that happened to you. What happened with the ex-boyfriend you mentioned? The one that took your dog."

"I started dating him shortly after my parents died. It was more of a long-distance thing. He was at college a few hours away and would come back sometimes on the weekends and during holiday breaks. That's the only time I ever saw him, and we never did much besides hang out at my house."

"Why did you guys break up?"

"He was just not a nice person and didn't treat me very well. He had other girlfriends at his college that I eventually found out about. He was the only boyfriend I had ever had, so I allowed it to go on for way too long before I ended things."

"You have only had one boyfriend? That's hard to believe. I can imagine you having guys lined up at the door to take you out."

"Nope, not the case. What about you? I am sure you have plenty of exes."

"Not really anyone serious. I am not going to lie, but when I was in high school and college, I was not interested in a serious girlfriend at all. I might have broken a few hearts because of that. Now that I am finding out what makes me happy, I have settled down a lot. I spent too much time with the wrong friends out partying night after night. Now I want what my parents have or my sister Evelyn has. She has been married to her husband for ten years, and they have four kids together. They still act like they are newlyweds."

I wonder if this is the sister that I saw at the Irish pub. The striking girl with the black hair.

"You have a sister?" I ask.

"I have two sisters, Victoria and Evelyn. Both are older. Do you have any siblings?"

"No, just me."

"I am really sorry to hear about your parents. That's a lot to have gone through already in life."

"Please don't feel sorry for me. I am okay, really, I am. I am still young, and ya know what? As of right now, I am going to get out there and start to enjoy my life more," I say, hopping out of my seat. "Let's get out of here and go do something crazy."

I finish my drink and start to feel bold and empowered. It's a little bit of the alcohol but also a sort of epiphany about my life. I take a deep breath of the crisp fall air and let it cleanse out any of the bad feelings that are left from the past. I make a pact with myself here and now to let my hair down more and enjoy what I have going for me now.

"Don't you want to get some muffins?" he asks.

"Nope, I want you to take me somewhere that's fun on a Saturday evening."

His eyes light up. "Okay, I know the perfect spot."

I follow Hudson out of the market, and we start walking up the street past the bus stop. We walk for a few blocks with him rambling on nervously.

"I know this might be a little awkward because I didn't mention this to you, but my family owns a brewery close to here. I want to take you there. If that's too weird for you, I understand. There are a lot of other places we can go around here, but if you want to go, I promise it won't be weird. It's not the type of thing that I usually do—ya know, bringing girls there—but I really want you to see it."

"Oh, I get it. You want to take me to the place you take all the other girls to," I joke with him.

He looks at me seriously. "No, I can absolutely assure you that I do not take all the girls there. My family is serious about us not using this as a party spot. They don't want any of us setting a bad tone."

We get to the front of the Berman Brewery. I had seen pictures online when Harper was googling Hudson, but I haven't seen the inside.

I am nervous as hell when we walk in the front door. The brewery is a huge warehouse filled with tables and a bar that leads down the entire length of the building

There are cornhole games set up indoors because of the high ceilings, along with giant Jenga and shuffleboard. Around these common game spaces are high-top tables that are already crowded even this early in the evening, with groups varying from young adults to older businessmen. This is definitely a place to be but doesn't strike me as overly party-focused, but just a fun, positive place to hang out.

Hudson introduces me to a few people working there, including a man who is his oldest sister's husband, Matt. We order a flight of different beers they have on tap and sit at the bar tasting them.

I am nervous about being here, but Hudson makes me feel so comfortable. He sits next to me the entire time and includes me in all his conversations with the people that work there and the regular customers who know him. He tells everyone about my furniture business and how talented I am. I blush so much throughout the evening that I feel like my face will be forever pink. I have never felt so secure in a social situation before.

Hudson is completely in his element. He is kind to all his employees, and everyone loves him. I am really surprised to learn that he also works here. Quite a bit surprised.

"I used to be here like sixty hours a week after I graduated college. My parents wanted me to take over this place after they retired, but I just couldn't do that. I want to be a part of the brewery, but I need to explore my other passions in life also, like the art studio. I would never be able to enjoy life not knowing what else I was capable of. I am fortunate that I can be flexible with both places. Now I am just here in the mornings during the week doing the distribution orders. Matt has taken over the role of managing everything else, from sales to head brewer. He's doing a really excellent job, way better than I could have done."

"Can I tell you something without you getting mad?" I ask him.

He looks at me suspiciously.

"I thought that you just slept all day."

His mouth falls open. "Did you seriously think that I'm just at home sleeping all day?"

"Yeah, I did. I figured that you didn't come in until after two because you went out at night and you needed to sleep during the day. Or maybe you were a drug dealer. You do always carry that backpack. Who knows what's inside." I slap him on the arm teasingly.

"I carry the backpack with me because I need to change after I get done working here into my clothes for the art store. It would be incredibly expensive to have to buy new shirts every time they got paint on them." We both have a good laugh at this.

I drink too much beer throughout the night and sample all the different foods they offer at the brewery. I laugh so hard throughout the evening that my jaw hurts. I start to feel way too drunk to be in here anymore and don't want to take it too far. I tell Hudson that I need to go home.

We head outside to say our goodbyes for the night.

"It's so gorgeous out here," I say, twirling around. I might be a little too intoxicated.

"How are you getting home?" he asks me. "Can I call you an Uber?"

I look over at him. It's dark outside now, and the way he looks in the moonlight is phenomenal. He is definitely the hottest guy I have ever seen, and he is here with me right now, making me feel like a princess all day.

"How are you getting home?" I ask him.

"It's a short bus ride, but I think I will walk. It's a nice night for that."

"Do you think that I could walk with you?"

He looks genuinely surprised. "To my house? Yeah, sure, of course. I would love the company."

The lights from downtown on the way to his house are so bright and beautiful. They give the city a magical look that makes me fall in love with it even more. The October air is crisp and a bit chilly, so he puts his jacket around me. I look over at him. He is not looking at the lights but at me in a way I haven't seen him look at me yet. My heart beats very fast, and for a minute, I feel like I can't breathe. I realize that I am very drunk, but I feel happier than I ever have.

We get to the front of his house, and I think back to the very first time I saw him peek his head around that maroon door.

"Would you like to come in for a cup of coffee? No pressure, just thought I would ask."

"Yes, a coffee would be amazing," I accept, wanting a steaming drink now after the chilly walk, but also, I want to see what the inside of this place looks like.

I am surprised when we get inside to see that everything is white or a different shade of white. The only thing that has any color is the hardwood floors.

"Wow, it's very, um…"

"I know, I know. My sister decorated this place. At that time, the trend was all white. Now I just think it's too sterile."

He brews us some coffee and we sit on opposite ends of his couch trying to warm up from the walk.

"I want you to know that I'm really happy that you came out with me today. I know that you don't want me to keep asking you, but I would really like to get to know you better. If you would ever allow me to take you out somewhere sometime, we could go anywhere you want. We could go see a live band or have dinner. Hell, I would even take you to a dance club. I'm not a good dancer, but I'll do it just for you."

I picture Hudson with his extremely tall body out on the dance floor, trying to throw down some dance moves, and I burst out laughing hysterically.

"It's a pretty horrific sight," he says.

"Okay, I will let you take me out. And Hudson, I have had a really good time today. Thank you for doing all of that for me."

"Well, that's good to hear because you deserve to always have someone doing nice things for you. There's something special about you. You are so smart and talented. What you do with the furniture is breathtaking. You have so much going for you. It takes a lot of courage to open a business at your age. Plus, you're absolutely fucking gorgeous. Since the very first day I saw you, I have not been able to get you off my mind."

God, he is being so sweet right now, and he's so damn handsome. I set my cup of coffee on the end table. I scoot across the couch and gently grab his hand. He grabs mine back and pulls me closer to him. I breathe him in deeply. Why does he smell so good?

We are just a few inches from each other's faces, looking into each other's eyes when I lose all sense of control and kiss him on the lips. Not a gentle kiss, but a hard kiss that makes him fall back into the couch. He wraps his arms around my waist and kisses me back but much gentler, still trying to be a gentleman.

I run my hands down the front of his T-shirt, feeling the bulge of the muscles on his chest and abs. I put my hands under his shirt and feel his bare skin against my fingertips. I start to lift his shirt up and off his body, but he pushes my hands away. I reach down and put my hands on his belt and take it out of the buckle. He puts his hands on each side of my cheeks and pushes me back from him.

"Are you sure?" he says, looking at me in my eyes, pleading for me to say yes, his chest heaving in and out.

I don't say anything. I pull the rest of his belt buckle loose and unbutton his jeans.

"Are you sure?" he whispers into my ear.

I bite his earlobe hard enough to let him know that I am serious. My body gets more and more stimulated from his touch. Heat is blazing from every pore on my body. Everything is throbbing.

He stands up, grabs me from the couch into his arms. He carries me somewhere in his house while I kiss his neck. I feel myself falling for a moment in the dark before I land on something soft and realize it's a bed. The heat dissipates because I no longer feel his body against mine. A light comes on in the corner of the room, and I see him walking back toward me. He stands at the end of the bed, looking down longingly at me. He is shirtless now. His belt and top button are undone on his jeans. The light shining from behind him shadows his muscles and elongates his frame, making him look taller than he is. My body shakes uncontrollably with lust towards him. I feel like I am going to explode if he doesn't touch me again.

"Are you sure?" he says again in a much more urgent tone.

"Yes," I tell him, barely able to get that one simple word out between my breaths.

19

Victoria

My phone starts ringing early in the morning. I look at the clock next to my bed, and it's 8 a.m. Who's calling this early on a Sunday? It's so early; I need a few more hours of sleep. I stayed out 'til two in the morning, and six hours of sleep is not going to do it. I sleepily grab my phone and see that it's Evelyn's number on the screen. I press the accept button.

"Evelyn, why are you calling so early on a Sunday morning? Don't you go out on Saturday nights anymore?"

"Nope, I am always in bed by nine. Victoria, you know that. Even when I did go out on a Saturday night I was always home early before anyone else. I am just not built like you. But fine, since you don't want to hear any gossip about your little brother, then I will let you go," she says.

"Fine, what?" I perk up, wanting to hear what she has to say.

"I was just having my morning coffee with Matt before all the little ones get up for the day, and he was telling me a very interesting story."

She pauses for too long and I have to nudge her. "What was the story?"

"Hudson was at the brewery last night while Matt was there, and you won't believe it, but he had a girl with him," she says with intrigue.

I sit up in my bed, now wide awake from this news.

"What? That's bullshit. I asked him yesterday to come over to see what I have done with my new apartment, and he said that he was going to be at the art studio late."

"Well, somehow, he ended up at the brewery around six last night," Evelyn says.

Since when does Hudson bring girls into our family's business? But more importantly, he told me that he was busy last night. Who would be with him there, and when did Hudson start lying to me?

"According to Matt, she was quite a stunning girl."

"A very pretty young lady," I hear Matt say in the background.

Evelyn continues speaking. "Apparently the two of them were extremely flirty with each other. They stayed for a few hours, and then they left together. I had no idea that he was seeing someone new. Just the other night at dinner he said he was taking it easy for a while, but I guess not."

"I am sure she was just one of his chicks that he runs around with. Wait, when was he over for dinner?" I ask angrily.

"On Wednesday. I texted you to see if you wanted to come too."

"Well, I didn't know that Hudson was going also. He never mentioned it. It seems like he is always avoiding me lately."

"Sorry, you guys should get together and talk it out, and no, I don't think she is just some chick. Matt said they were very close, and it seemed like it was more than someone Hudson just messes around with. When was the last time he brought a girl into the brewery like that?"

"What did she look like?"

I hear Matt in the background explaining her appearance. I must be on speakerphone.

"Typical Hudson type—thin, blonde, big blue eyes, boobs."

"Is this the girl he had to get a restraining order against?" I ask.

"Nope, definitely not. We were given a copy of her driver's license photo from the police officer who did the report. We still have it hanging in the breakroom next to all the other people that are banned from the brewery. Just in case she tries to come in and harass Hudson again," Matt says.

I know that Evelyn and Matt are calling me to give me this information, to be gossipy. The two of them have little lives outside their kids and the brewery and probably think this is funny, but I can't help but feel jealous. I have barely spoken to or seen Hudson since I got home. I ask him constantly to come out with me, and he always declines as if he's so busy, and yet here he is at our family's business with some girl. What the hell is going on? Is this girl the reason he is too busy for me?

"Well, we know how Hudson is, always the player. Just another Saturday night with another random girl," I say before getting off the phone with them.

I quickly press the call button for "Little Bro" in my phone. I know it's early, and he will probably try to resist, but I want to talk to him in person. I am going to get him out to coffee so I can figure out what his deal is, and I won't take no for an answer. However, the call goes to his voice mail after two rings, which means he declined my call. I call him back again right away.

"Hey Vic, I can't talk right now," he says when he answers the second call.

"Okay, no problem. Just meet me in an hour."

"Uhhh, sorry, I can't," he says in a distracted tone of voice. I hear the muffles of something and then it sounds like he is walking around. I keep him on the phone listening on my end for several minutes, waiting to hear someone's voice in the background. Most likely, the girl he was with last night is still at his house. I don't really care if I make her feel uncomfortable.

I can hear footsteps on his hardwood floors pacing around his house, walking up and down his stairs, doors opening and closing, and I wonder what is going on. He seems to do this several times. It sounds like he puts his hand over the receiver and calls out something. Was it someone's name? It's muffled, so I can't make it out.

"Listen, Vic, I got to go. I will give you a call back later," he tells me before the line goes dead.

Oh my god, he just hung up on me. What the hell is going on with him? It's already too much that he has been so distant. He is acting strange by bringing random girls around the brewery and now hanging up on me. Is he doing drugs or something? Maybe that's what it is, or maybe he is having some sort of a breakdown. That would explain a lot of things—like the art studio. I need to get him in person and find out why he is behaving this way.

20

Emily

I wasn't sure if I would be able to grab an Uber or a Lyft so late last night or, more like, so early this morning, but it was amazingly easy to get one from Hudson's house. I snuck out around 3:30 a.m. Hudson was sound asleep, snoring softly. I took Harper's advice to "play hard to get." I am not exactly sure if this is what she meant by that, but I am going to try it. I also don't want to wake up next to him and have things be awkward.

Thankfully, he was quite a heavy sleeper. I didn't want to leave anything behind and was trying to be as quiet as I could, but I was still a little tipsy from earlier in the evening and being in an unfamiliar place, I kept bumping into everything, looking for my things. I couldn't find my right shoe, so I had to abandon it.

I'm sure the driver who took me home was thinking what a slut I was. Makeup smeared all over my face, hair tousled, missing a shoe, and reeking of sex. But I didn't care one bit. I sat in the back seat, smiling out of the window the entire way home.

I got home and laid down in my bed and fell asleep right away. I slept hard and didn't wake up 'til almost noon. I can't even remember the last time I slept that late. It felt so good.

Hudson is the first thing I think of when I open my eyes. What will happen now with us? I need to just play it safe. He might not want anything more than what happened last night, and I don't know if I do either.

When I see him next door, I will simply act the same as before. Everything I say will be simple and short. We can be friendly with each other, but there is no need to hash out what transpired last night. We will just chalk it up to two consenting adults having a fun time together.

I pull the covers over my head. I close my eyes and begin drifting back off to sleep when I hear my phone's text alert beep on the nightstand. I briefly wonder if it's Hudson. *No, I can't wonder if it's him,* I scold myself. *You don't need to look at the phone. Just go back to sleep.* I can't stop myself. I grab my phone and see six messages from Hudson that came throughout the morning.

Did you leave?

I searched the whole house and you're definitely not here. Except your one shoe.

I'm not gonna lie, I'm a little sad you're gone.

Okay, more than a little sad.

Text me when you wake up, just want to make sure you got home safe.

Please Emily, I am so close to coming out to your house.

I feel bad that he is worried it is almost the afternoon. So, I text him back, *Just woke up, got home no problem, all good.*

Immediately another message from him. *When will I see you again, maybe we can get dinner tonight.*

I can't, I have to get back to work. Short and simple. Play hard to get.

I see the bubbles pop up on the screen indicating him typing back. They disappear and I watch and wait for his message to come through. After a few minutes I see the bubbles pop up again and toggle back and forth for several seconds, then a pause, and then they disappear again. I click out of messages to make sure my phone isn't glitching. It beeps. It's a message from him.

I hope you have a wonderful day. I won't bother you, but text me if you need anything.

I wonder if this is the message he originally meant to send. It looked like he changed his mind several times.

I head downstairs and make a coffee to take out onto my front porch. The October air is crisp and chilly but it's exactly what I need today. I wrap a thick warm blanket around me, sit in my rocking chair, and think about last night. My stomach starts to tickle with the feeling of butterflies floating around. I can feel my face blushing thinking about me and Hudson last night. I am going to have to be very careful with this situation. I can't allow things to get out of control like before.

A little red Honda Civic pulls up the driveway so slowly that it takes several minutes for me to see the person inside. It stops in front of my house, and out of the car comes a thin brunette girl.

She walks hesitantly around the front of her car and stops.

"Can I help you?" I ask her.

"Yes, I saw your Facebook Marketplace page Teal Lotus and saw that you sold vintage furniture. I wanted to take a look."

"I don't have anything listed for sale there anymore. I will be opening a store downtown in a few weeks. It's on Plum Street. You can come by there after it opens."

"Oh, that's too bad. There was this chaise lounge that you have photos of that looks exactly like one my grandmother had in her house before she died. I was really hoping to see it," she says as she walks closer to my porch.

I wonder how she was able to get my address, but I am sure there are plenty of previous posts on the Marketplace that have it listed in the comments. I make a mental note to go through all the posts and take down anything that has my personal address or phone number.

"I haven't had any chairs like that listed for a while now, but like I said, you are more than welcome to come check out the store."

She stands there, not replying, and starts looking around the front yard. I realize now that she is closer, she is familiar to me somehow. She turns back to face me, and that's it. I have seen her before. I am pretty sure that this is the blonde girl I saw out in front of Hudson's house the first day I saw him, only now she has brown hair.

"What did you say your name was?" I ask her.

"Chloe," she tells me.

Yeah, right. I would bet a hundred bucks her name is not Chloe, and I know she is not here to look at a chair. This is definitely the girl from Hudson's house. I can see it in her eyes now.

"Well, Chloe, if you give me your number, I can call you and give you the details of what I will have at the store."

Her thin frame stiffens when I ask her for her phone number. She stares at me wild-eyed. Her blue eyes are bright and blazing.

"That's okay, I will just stop in."

She looks at my house, then around the yard one more time before heading back to her car. She drives back down the driveway much faster than she did coming up.

There is no way that was a coincidence, her stumbling across my Facebook page. I don't even have anything listed on the Marketplace right now. She would have had to look back over my past photos to see any lounge chair. She could have gotten my address from there, but how would she have known to look for me online in the first place? She must have seen me with Hudson and somehow figured it out.

My intuition tells me this will not be the last time I see this so-called Chloe.

21
Emily

Hudson doesn't come into the art studio after he gets done at the brewery on Monday, and then again, he is absent on Tuesday. Frieda leaves around 4 p.m., and then the store has just been closed each day. I haven't been next door to see him for very long, so I don't know if it's unusual to not have his store open in the evenings. I know he mentioned on Saturday that he has quite a bit of freedom having the studio and can come and go when he pleases.

I could just text him and ask him where he is, but I don't want him to think that I am checking up on him—and I'm not, of course. I am just curious if everything is okay. He did say to text him if I needed anything, though. After thinking more about it, I ditch the idea. I have no idea what I would say, and Harper did tell me to play hard to get. I don't want to seem needy. But the fact is, I cannot stop thinking about him. Every time I try to focus on what I am doing, my mind floats back to Hudson standing over me without his shirt on, then Hudson kissing me and how strong his arms were wrapped around me.

Stop it, Emily. This is ridiculous. I am sure he has other things to do. Maybe he got wrapped up with work at the brewery.

By Thursday afternoon, he is still not there. I haven't been able to sleep all week, not knowing what happened to him. I finally get the courage to go over and ask Frieda how Hudson has been.

"Hi Frieda, I was wondering where Hudson has been. I hadn't seen him in here all week. Is everything okay?"

"Darling Emily, you look beautiful as always. He took a few days off and went to his parents' house. They have a cabin up north. You should give him a call."

"Oh no, I don't want to bother him."

"I don't think you would be bothering him, considering he has called me every day this week to ask how you were doing. But you didn't hear that from me." She puts her index finger over her mouth in secrecy.

I blush with excitement. My heart beats so hard in my chest. I don't want to be this thrilled to hear this, but I can't help it. I thank her and head back to my store.

I go to check my mailbox and pick up my packages. I feel a twinge of sadness because I miss getting the gifts that Hudson used to leave in here. I never thought I would hear myself saying that a week ago.

I take everything inside and start opening my packages. There is a box that is handwritten addressed to me from Knox, Ohio. I don't remember ordering anything from there. I open the package and find some aged rum, Cream of Coconut, grated nutmeg, some cocktail cherries, and pineapple and orange juice in a freezer bag with ice packets. I read the card inside and see a recipe written in some beautiful cursive handwriting.

I am confused about what all this is for. Then I read the name of the recipe and remember that it's the recipe for the cocktail Hudson and I had at Findlay Market. The Painkiller. This is obviously from him, but it doesn't look like his handwriting. Not at all like the writing that was on the note when he left the painting. Who writes in beautiful cursive like this anymore?

I can't stand it any longer. I pick up my phone, take a photo of the contents of the package, and send it to him.

Is this from you? I text.

My phone starts ringing quickly after the text. It's Hudson.

"Nice handwriting," I say, answering the phone.

"It's my mom's handwriting. She still writes everything in cursive. It's way nicer than mine. I wanted the recipe to look nice, something you would want to keep."

The idea that he had his mother write out a recipe for me is so endearing. I'm sure he didn't tell her who it was for, though.

"The juice is going to spoil if we don't drink it soon. When will you be back?" I ask him, gritting my teeth. Hoping he doesn't shoot me down.

"I will be back tomorrow evening. You could just put it in your fridge, and I will be at your place by 8 p.m."

"Sounds good. I am salivating for another one of these cocktails," I say and hang up the call.

I clap my hands together and draw my breath in sharply. What am I going to wear?

❊

Hudson's car comes racing up my driveway at exactly 8 p.m. on Friday evening. I can't help but smile at how prompt he is. I have the door open before he can knock.

I chose to wear a white sleeveless cotton dress that is tight and very short. I cover it with a thin flannel. That way I can let it drape off my shoulder when I see fit, exposing my shoulders and my black bra underneath. Hudson sees me and his eyes travel from my face down to my feet then back up again.

"Wow, you look amazing."

"Just what I always wear around the house," I say coyly.

He narrows his eyes at me, smiling. He is wearing black jeans and a black T-shirt, and I have to contain myself to not look him up and down because he looks so sexy. There is something about him and his tight jeans that make me insane. But no matter what he put on, he would be hot.

I step aside to let him pass. As he walks in, he runs his hand along my bare upper thigh, and my whole body tingles. I take a deep breath to reacclimate myself.

"How was your trip? You were visiting your parents?"

"It was good. My parents have been out of the country for the last six weeks and just got back on Monday. No one knew exactly when they were coming back. My mom just called me out of the blue Monday morning and said they were home. They sort of just come and go as they please now that they are retired. I always get concerned about them when we go too long without seeing each other. They are usually back here in Cincinnati every few weeks, or one of us goes up there, but since they were gone so long, I needed to go up there and make sure they were settled back in."

"That is really sweet, and your mother has beautiful handwriting."

"She does, and she was thrilled that I was having her put it to good use."

"Does she know who it was for?"

"Maybe." He smiles at me, and my heart skips a beat. "I really love this place. Your style is exactly the aesthetic I would want." He points to my TV stand. "Did you make this yourself?"

"Yes, it was a vintage buffet."

He walks around my living room, checking out everything in here.

"And the art?"

"Yes, even the art on the walls. Most are pictures that I took and had blown up into canvas prints, some were left here in the house from the orchard back in the day. It's the same in my store too."

"Photography, too! I love how artistic you are. Living out here on this land must be a dream. It's so beautiful out there," he says, looking out my back door. The sun is almost down on the horizon, and the orchard does look pretty this time of night. "Do you plan on growing more fruit in the orchard again?"

"It would be a lot of work, but maybe that will be my next endeavor after getting the store up and running and hiring some employees."

"I would love to come out and help you."

"Really? I wouldn't have pegged you as having an interest in agriculture."

"No way, I love being outdoors. My parents' cabin is on twenty acres of land. I am always out there exploring their property. I find new things every time I venture out. I can't wait to get out to explore that ravine. I am embarrassed to say I have spent too much time thinking about it."

"Why do you live in the city, then?"

"I bought that house right after I graduated college. It was close to all my friends, the brewery, and my sister. I was into going out a lot and partying. At the time, it just seemed like I needed to be in the city, in the center of it all. Now I would much rather have something like this."

I am surprised. My place is the complete opposite of what he has. I think about how blindingly white everything was in his home and how cold it felt.

"Alright, let's get to making these cocktails." He claps his hands together and heads to my kitchen.

I have everything laid out as nicely as I can. I don't ever have anyone over to serve drinks to, so I don't have many tools for drink mixing.

"How did you know what is in them?" I ask him.

"On my way out of town earlier this week, I stopped by the market and asked."

Hudson takes the lead by mixing and pouring everything into the glasses I laid out. We sit at my kitchen island and take the first sip of our drinks.

"Yum, even better than the ones at the Market," I tell him, and I mean it. These taste amazing.

We talk about how things have gone for me this week with the opening coming up soon.

"Now that I am back in town, I would love to come by and help you. I do have a little bit of skill in the painting department, so I can be of some assistance."

"I just might take you up on that offer."

Our stools are very close to each other, and I feel Hudson brush his fingers along my bare leg. I want to touch him so badly. I want to press my mouth to his and feel his lips on mine.

I let my flannel fall off my shoulder and stand up, pushing my stool out from the island. I step over and wedge myself in between his legs. He puts his hand on my face and pulls me in and kisses me. Softer and more tender than I kissed him the other night. It's more intentional, not the hard fury of passion we couldn't contain before.

He grabs me by the waist and hoists me up on the counter without any effort at all. I wrap my legs around him tightly. He is so tall that sitting on the counter, I am face-to-face with him. I let my flannel fall off both my shoulders and shimmy out of it, then I pull my dress up over my head and throw it on the kitchen floor, revealing my lacy black bra and matching panties. I reach behind my back to undo my bra when he grabs my arms and pulls them around his chest. He grabs me tightly and lifts me up off the counter. I wrap my legs and arms around him tightly and put my face into his neck and kiss him just like we did the other night. The way he picks me up and carries me is so tantalizing.

"Where is your bedroom?"

I point down the hallway to a door at the end.

We spend most of the night exploring each other's bodies. The night seems to go on forever and that's okay with me because I don't ever want this to end. This time no one sneaks out and we eventually both fall asleep from exhaustion, soundly wrapped in each other's arms.

We don't get out of bed at all the next day. We order food and wine to be delivered in and nourish ourselves in between various sexual activities all day, most of which I have only seen in videos. We order greasy cheeseburgers that are the best I have ever eaten, wolfing them down ravenously with nothing but underwear on. We order things like ice cream, cool whip, and cherries and lick them off each other's bodies.

By Sunday morning, I am exhausted. Exhausted in the way that makes you feel weak but satisfied. I think I may have gotten five or maybe six hours of sleep in the last two nights. Hudson lies there with his eyes closed, still sleeping. The blanket is covered up to his stomach, one of his legs is draped out of the side, and his bare chest is exposed. His arms are raised up above his head, his muscles bulging. His hair is a mess, but he looks adorable.

I watch his chest expand and release air and listen to his shallow breaths until he opens his eyes and looks at me. He stretches out his long body on my bed, making his length even longer, and lets out a long, satisfying grunt. He reaches out, grabs me around my waist, and pulls me closer to him. He kisses me deep and hard. I want him again so badly. I am already naked, so I swing my leg over his waist and straddle him.

He grabs my hips and gently eases me off him. "No more for you right now. We have to get ready to go. Do you mind if I shower here?" he asks as he hops out of my bed and heads into my bathroom.

I am completely at a loss for words, not understanding what just happened.

"Where are we going?"

"To my sister Evelyn's house," he says from inside the bathroom. I hear the shower turn on, and he peeks his head around the doorframe. "It's family brunch day and I won't take no for an answer," he says as he closes the door to the bathroom. I hear him singing some song that sounds vaguely familiar from inside the shower.

His sister's house for brunch? I want to say no because that would be an incredibly uncomfortable situation for me, but I also want to say yes. I would love to go and meet his family.

I make a choice to step out of my comfort zone. I get out of bed and head over to my closet. What do I wear to a family brunch?

22

Victoria

Hudson is late. I got to Evelyn's early, hoping to talk with him before brunch started, but he is not here yet, and I am very disappointed. After he hung up on me last weekend, I tried to get him to talk to me, but he left and went up to our parents' cabin for the week and still barely talked to me while he was there.

"You confirmed with him that he is coming, right?" I ask Evelyn.

"Yes, I spoke with him on his way back from Mom and Dad's on Friday. He said he was coming."

"I sent him a few text messages over the weekend, telling him I need to talk today, but I only got one back, and it was a vague 'sounds good.' What do you think is going on, Evelyn? I am at my wits end trying to understand why he is avoiding me."

"Hello?" I hear a woman's voice coming in the front door. It's Katie.

She is looking radiant in a black dress that ties in the front, her auburn hair swept up in a twist with perfectly quaffed tendrils around her face. She recently started dating a new guy that she met on one of her hideous dating apps. I knew that would happen sooner than later. Katie is the type of person who can't bear to be single for any amount of time. She's so needy.

I pull out my phone and get ready to call Hudson when I hear him call out from the front room.

"Hello, I'm here! Sorry we were late. We stopped by the store to grab some champagne," he says, walking through the front room toward the kitchen.

"You know we always have plenty of that here already. You didn't need…" My voice trails off when I notice that he is not alone.

Walking just a step behind him, holding his hand tightly, is a girl with light blonde hair and dark blue eyes that are darting all over the room nervously. She's wearing a pink dress with a pair of gray ballerina flats. She looks young, much younger than Hudson. Why is she here right now?

Evelyn turns from what she is making on the stove to greet Hudson, and when she sees them walk in together, her face lights up. Was she informed he was bringing someone today? I can feel my face burning. I am indignant, trying to figure out who this is and why she is here.

Katie looks wide-eyed at the girl, then over to me. She knows me well and can tell I am not too happy about this situation. I have talked with her several times about what is going on with me and Hudson, and she knows how important today was to me.

"Everyone, this is Emily," he says.

We all stand there staring for a moment. Evelyn is the first to break the silence.

"Hello, Emily. It's so nice to meet you."

She grabs a dish towel and wipes her hand off as she crosses the room to shake the girl's hand.

I, however, do not make a move at all. I just stare at her incredulously.

Just then, Matt walks into the room carrying some plates. He notices the girl holding Hudson's hand.

"Emily," he says warmly to her, "it's so good to see you again." He walks over and shakes her hand.

"You know each other?" I ask Matt.

"I met her at the brewery last weekend."

"Welcome to our home. Come sit down," Evelyn says to her in her always-cheerful tone. "Can I pour you a mimosa?"

So, this is the gorgeous blonde that Matt and Evelyn called me about last weekend. She's the one who came to the brewery. You have got to be kidding me. First he takes her there, and now here to our family brunch. If our parents were here, they would not be too happy about this. I look her up and down. She is pretty, but by no means is she gorgeous the way they described her.

Evelyn pours her a glass from the pitcher of mimosas with fresh strawberries and oranges we had made earlier.

"I picked these from my orchard," she says shyly, handing a tray of sliced apples over to Evelyn.

"Emily has this incredible orchard on her property out in Aurora. You guys have got to see it," Hudson says.

Evelyn begins asking her questions about this orchard. I use the moment while the girl is occupied to whisper, "What is going on, Hudson? Why did you bring some girl here?"

"I am just bringing a good friend to family brunch, and she isn't just some girl. Anyway, you have a friend here." He nods over to Katie and goes back to the conversation, smiling. Is he really that dense?

I smile weakly at this girl when she turns her attention back to Hudson. I watch them intently. Questions are racing through my mind. Why would he bring a date to family brunch? Why didn't he tell anyone beforehand? And why are they holding hands like they have been together for years?

I feel a tug on my wrist and turn to see it is Katie. "Victoria, don't freak out right now," she whispers. She knew from my three phone calls this weekend that I really needed a chance to talk to

Hudson, and now that this girl is here, I probably won't have that opportunity.

We hang around for a while making small talk, sitting at Evelyn's kitchen island. She is acting like she is making a new best friend, putting this Emily at the center of attention. I want to completely ignore anything she has to say, but my skin is tingling and the hairs on my arm are rising. I feel like I need to be on high alert and learn whatever I can about her.

"I think that we can all head to the dining room now. The food is just about ready," Matt calls out to everyone.

I sit down at the dining table, fuming. Why didn't Hudson tell me ahead of time he was bringing someone? Is he trying to punish me for something? He has ignored me for weeks. He knew that I wanted to talk with him. He knows that I am upset we haven't spent any time together. Family brunch is supposed to be for the family. This is just so fucking rude. And why is Evelyn being so nice to her? Doesn't she also get how rude this is? I am almost ready to explode, I am so angry.

"How were Mom and Dad?" Evelyn says. "They have been calling me every day since they have been back. You would think that Mom would just want to relax now that they are back from Greece, but she is making plans for everyone to come up next weekend."

"We had a really nice time. Mom was in good spirits, and Dad was just happy to be back in the States so he could watch American football." Hudson laughs. "She mentioned talking to you about Halloween. She is dying to take the kids trick-or-treating, and of course she is excited for your birthday coming up."

"I know, I can't wait. The kids will be so excited to go trick-or-treating with their grandmother," Evelyn says.

"You're coming up too next weekend, right Victoria?" Evelyn asks me.

"Of course I am. Why wouldn't I? That's ridiculous."

"She's just making sure, Vic. It will be nice for all of us to be together again. No reason to be snippy," Hudson says to me.

"It's been almost a year. Can you believe it? I am just so excited for everyone to be back up at the cabin," Evelyn exclaims.

"How did you two meet?" I ask Hudson.

He starts rambling on and on about seeing her at his stupid painting class, their first date, their drinks, their time at our family's brewery. They went to Findlay Market of all places. He can't possibly like this girl that much if he took her to that old farmers' market for a date.

"She has been working downtown for almost a month now and hasn't been there yet," he says.

"Where are you working, Emily?" Evelyn asks her.

"She is renting 322 Plum Street," Hudson says. "She is the one I was telling you guys about with the really cool vintage furniture store."

"You're the one renting 322," I nearly jump out of my seat with this realization. Hudson has some nerve bringing her here. Doesn't he realize how upset this would make me?

He goes on about how amazing she is and how great all her stupid used furniture is. I was supposed to have a classy interior design company there, and he is thrilled about used furniture. Why isn't anyone concerned about that?

I look over at Emily, and Evelyn's daughter Addison is talking to her, distracting her. I need to talk to Hudson.

"What the hell is going on?" I lean over and say to him.

He looks confused when he says, "What?"

"Why would you bring the girl that is renting my store here today?" I hiss. "Can you even imagine how upsetting this must be for me?" I try to keep my voice low. I don't want to upset the children, but we need to have a serious conversation.

"Vic, you said that you were relieved that you weren't going to be on Plum Street. You said you dodged a bullet. I thought you would be happy to meet her."

"I do not understand how you can be so dense."

Hudson looks at me with surprise. "Fine, if this is such a big deal to you, then we will leave."

"No, *I* am going to leave," I tell him.

I stand up and announce that I am not feeling well. I need to go right away before I can allow anyone to stop me. I storm toward the front door.

Evelyn and Hudson follow me. They act like they are so concerned but they can't possibly be with the way they are acting with this girl who seems to be stealing my life.

"I don't want to speak to either of you right now. I just want to go home and lie down."

They both start spouting out words that I do not want to hear. I walk out the front door and slam it behind me.

23

Emily

Hudson leads me into Evelyn's massive house, holding my hand tightly, and I am so thankful that he is. I have no idea what to expect from today. I am so nervous and anxious, but he has assured me how great his family is and that I will love them.

We walk into the kitchen, and it's beautiful. It has all modern appliances; the walls are a creamy white with navy-blue accents and lots of wood cabinets. Brightly colored rugs cover the natural wooden hardwood floors, and dark blue and gold velvet chairs line the gigantic island. Hudson introduces all of us. His sisters are both beautiful, but the one named Victoria is absolutely striking. She is the one I saw at the Irish pub that day with Hudson.

Evelyn looks very much like her brother, just not nearly as tall as him. She is more my height, but she has the same bright green eyes and the color of hair as him only, with more curls. She seems to be much older than him, also. Hudson told me she has four kids. So, I would think she has to be in her thirties, but you would never be able to tell that with how put-together she is.

We sit at her enormous island, big enough to seat eight people, and she pours me a mimosa. I give her the apples I picked this morning from my orchard and sliced for us to eat.

After some small talk, we head into the dining room to be seated. Hudson has been holding my hand tightly. He must sense how nervous I am. The table is set with a huge amount of food, pastries, breads and jams, bagels, and a variety of cream cheeses. Matt and Evelyn bring in plates of hot food—quiches, meats, scrambled eggs, and avocado toast.

The table looks like it would be out of a home magazine. The whole house does, but not sterile the way Hudson's place is. This house is decorated with a homey feeling. More for a family.

I sit in between Hudson and Victoria's friend Katie, who seems completely uncomfortable. I get the sense that she is confused about why I am here with Hudson. Maybe they used to have a thing. She doesn't ever look in my direction and hasn't said more than hello to me. His sister Victoria practically runs to the table to sit next to Hudson.

Just then, four kids chasing after each other come running into the dining room. They are all young and close together in age. Three boys and one girl. They all look like mini versions of their mother.

His sister Evelyn tells them to stop running and take their seats at the table in a calm Mary Poppins voice. I am surprised to see that all four of them obey immediately and sit down, but not with any fear, just happy to listen to what their mom tells them to do. The youngest of the four, a little girl with light brown curly hair wearing a light pink dress sitting right across from me, stares at me intently. So much so that I wonder if I have something weird on my face.

Evelyn introduces them all to me. They all give a little nod or wave and sit patiently while she dishes out various foods for them. There is conversation going on all around me. It's hard for me to concentrate on what everyone is talking about. I can't shake my nerves. Being here with all these new people is so out of the box for me. I have never had a boyfriend take me to meet his family, or anyone for that matter.

Evelyn walks around filling mimosa glasses. Alcoholic ones for the adults and nonalcoholic sparkling grape juice for the kids. It's adorable that she does that for her kids. You can tell she is a good mom.

I notice that the little girl is still staring at me. I am not sure if I should be creeped out by this or think this is normal. I don't have any experience with children, so I am not sure why she is looking at me like that.

Everyone has gotten their food and begins to eat. Hudson is having a conversation about the cocktail we made the other night. I am filled with joy when he explains that we had it on our first date together. I want to interject and tell them it wasn't really a first date, but it is so sweet the way he is talking so passionately about it. I can't bear to burst his bubble. I guess that since the casual outing to get muffins turned into meeting his coworkers turned into the best sex of my life, it kind of could be construed as a date.

"Where was your first date?" Evelyn asks.

"Findlay Market," Hudson says proudly.

"I just love that place!" Evelyn responds. "Remember when we used to go there almost every Sunday before all the kids?" she says longingly to her husband.

"Ah, yes, back in the good ol' days."

They look at each other lovingly. Hudson was right; they are sweet together.

There is more conversation going around the table. I am trying hard to keep up, but I am so nervous and worried that I will look or sound stupid by trying to speak, and this little girl will not stop staring at me, so it's adding a bit more nerves. I take a bite from the food on my plate; she takes a bite from her plate. I drink out of my water glass; so does she. I scratch the top of my head, and so does she. Is she mocking me? Trying to be silly? I have no idea.

"Renting 322 Plum Street," I hear Hudson say out of context.

I bring myself back to the conversation around the table.

I notice that Victoria's face is flushed bright red and she doesn't seem happy about this information at all.

"You're the one selling used furniture at 322?" she spouts angrily at me.

Is she mad at me? I have no idea why she should be. I want to correct her about it just being used furniture, but Hudson does that for me, which I am very appreciative of. I can't manage to get any words out. The air in this room feels thick, and I am trying to catch my breath. It feels like there is a dark cloud hovering over us.

He goes on to tell them all about my furniture business, gloating about what an amazing artist I am and how they should all come in to see the store when it opens. I am a little taken aback that he is describing me this way to his family, but it brings a huge smile to my face, and my nerves calm down a little bit.

I look over at Katie, sitting next to me, and she is shoveling food into her mouth as if she hasn't eaten in days. She still refuses to make any sort of eye contact with me. There is definitely something strange going on here.

Victoria seems really upset, but Evelyn, Matt, and Hudson are speaking with one another in such a cheery tone that I think I may be misunderstanding the situation. It's my fault, though. I am always so awkward around other people, and this is a lot of new people all at once, so I am sure that it's just me.

"That's wonderful. That is a great location to have a place like that. You have to check out all the other shops in that area. My favorite is Serendipity. It's this adorable little shop that sells matching mom and child outfits," Evelyn gushes.

"Oh, that sounds really cute. I haven't seen that one yet," I reply to her.

"These apples you brought are delicious. I should bring the kids there to do some apple picking," Evelyn says.

"Maybe next year." I explain to her and Matt about the ravine and how dangerous it can be for kids to run around there. "At some point I will get a safety fence put up along my property line, but since it's just me there right now, I don't need to."

I feel a tug on my arm. I turn and see the little girl Addison standing next to me. The one who has been staring at me the entire time. I brace myself for what she might do next.

"I really like your dress," she tells me. I then realize that I had chosen a pink dress that was almost the same color as hers, only mine has a different pattern and shape to it. "And your shoes are pretty too. When I grow up, I want to have shoes just like that."

"It looks like we must have coordinated our outfits together this morning." She must be around four years old and probably has no idea what coordinate means. I have no clue how to talk to children.

"You are really pretty," she says.

I soften quickly when she says this. I wasn't sure what the staring meant, but now she is being so kind. She seems to be a lot like her mother, Evelyn, who is smiling and seems genuinely happy to have everyone here at her table, even though there is something strange going on with Victoria and Katie.

I look over, and Victoria and Hudson seem to be having a heated conversation. Hudson's face is bright red, and he looks upset. Victoria seems to be scolding him for something.

"Thank you so much. You are even prettier," I tell Addison, and she heads back to her seat.

I can no longer eat any more food. It is all so delicious but there is just something in the air that is making me uncomfortable. The food and the mimosas seem to be churning in my stomach. I reach over to grab Hudson's attention. I need to tell him somehow that I am not feeling well and that I need to leave. God, this will be so embarrassing. I wait patiently for his and Victoria's conversation to be done.

Evelyn and Matt are fussing with their kids. They seem to be completely unaware of any disturbances. Katie is pouring another mimosa, still not looking in my direction. I feel like I'm not able to breathe, and I really don't want to embarrass myself. I try taking in a breath and letting it out slowly so no one notices.

Before I get the chance to explain that I need to leave, Victoria has stood up and is telling everyone that she isn't feeling well and that she needs to go home and lie down.

Evelyn is trying to find out if she is okay, offering any sort of remedies. "Do you need Tylenol? Pepto-Bismol? Or maybe you can lay down in the guest room for a while?" she says.

I sit in silence as Victoria leaves the table, and Evelyn and Hudson follow her to the front room. She doesn't even say goodbye to her friend Katie, Matt, or the children.

I look at everyone left around the table. Addison is back in her seat, and she and her siblings are happily eating their food as if nothing is happening. Matt is staring at his plate of food longingly. He seems disappointed that he has to wait to finish eating. Katie is slumped back in her seat, taking large gulps of her mimosa.

Hudson and Evelyn come back to the table. I half-expected Victoria to be with them, but she isn't. Damn, I definitely can't leave now. I have no idea what to do.

"That is really cool that you are so young and starting up your own business." I look over and am shocked to see that it's Katie who is talking to me. "When I was your age, I was doing absolutely nothing with my life. Cheers," she says, holding out her glass of mimosa to me. I pick mine up and cheers her back, very confused about this exchange. "I am downtown also at the Spencer agency. It's Just a few blocks away from Plum Street."

I smile gratefully at her.

There is no explanation of what has happened from anyone around the table. But what I do know is that the entire mood of the room has changed. Hudson, Matt, and Evelyn are not pining over what just happened with Victoria; they are talking about next weekend and going to see their parents. They all seem happy, as if nothing has happened.

"We should bring them something special," I hear Evelyn say.

I no longer feel so sick to my stomach. There was an atmosphere in the room while Victoria was here. Now that she is gone, everything is much lighter.

"I am really impressed with you, girl." Katie slurs her words and holds her glass up to cheers me again. "Owning your own home and your own business. How old are you anyway?"

"Twenty-two," I tell her.

"Wow, that's awesome, and to look as hot as you do at twenty-two, you could rule the world," she gushes over me, and I am beginning to realize that maybe Katie has had too much to drink.

Katie stays for another twenty minutes, talking to everyone for the first time since I got here. It turns out she is a nice person. There doesn't seem to be anything weird anymore between her and Hudson. Before she leaves, she even asks me if we can grab drinks after work sometime. I tell her yes, but I get the sense that we will never get those drinks, but I am thankful for her kindness.

Evelyn and Matt send the kids outside to play. I peek in the backyard and see that it is a dream oasis for children. Their backyard is like its own park. They have a huge jungle gym playset with a gigantic slide, a trampoline with a safety net, an obstacle course, and a whole variety of sports equipment strewn out all over the yard. So much play equipment. I would have been in heaven to have something like this when I was a kid.

"Do you mind if I go to Matt's office to talk about work stuff?" Hudson asks me hesitantly. "We are launching a new beer, and I am going to look at the graphics."

"Oh, of course, go right ahead. I am going to help Evelyn clean up."

He kisses me on the mouth longer than a kiss in front of other people should be.

I help Evelyn clean up the table, boxing up food she wants to send home with me and Hudson. The little girl, Addison, runs back in from outside several times to make sure I haven't left yet.

"She really seems to like you, which is strange—no offense—because she doesn't normally talk to people like that. Do you want to have kids someday?"

"Um…" I struggle with how to respond. "I haven't really thought of that."

"I am so happy that Hudson has finally brought a girl around."

"I am relieved to hear that. I got the feeling earlier that your sister wasn't so happy about me being here," I tell her.

"Don't worry about her. She has always been overprotective of Hudson. She is just going through a hard time right now. I am sure that Hudson told you about the divorce."

I shake my head. "No, I don't think so."

"Well, I am sure that you will hear all about it. It seems to be all we are talking about lately," Evelyn sighs. I am surprised to hear Evelyn say that about her sister going through such a tragedy. "Sorry, that came off as rude. It's just that Victoria hasn't made the best choices. I know that she is going through a hard time right now, but she always seems to be going through a hard time. I had just really hoped that getting married would have made things better for her, but now they are getting divorced, and she's lost the interior design business. I am just worried about what she will do now."

Something niggles in my brain about what she has just told me.

"Victoria does interior design?" I ask.

Evelyn shakes her head sadly. "She was supposed to open in the same building you have your furniture business. I'm afraid that is the reason why she was acting so strangely today."

Just then, Hudson walks in and overhears our conversation. He puts his arm around me and kisses my head.

"I am sorry, Emily. I didn't realize that Victoria would behave like that. I didn't know that she was that bothered about the building. Did you know she was?" he asks Evelyn.

"No, she has only told me how glad she is that she didn't end up getting involved with that. We have talked about it several times, and not once has she mentioned being upset about it. And you know Victoria; if she's upset about something, she will let you know."

"I have only had a few conversations with her about it and she said the same thing. To be honest, we haven't really talked that much. I have been so busy with the brewery and the studio that I haven't gone out with her. Now I feel bad. She has asked several times for us to go out, but I keep avoiding her. I just don't want to get back into the way things were before."

"And you shouldn't, Hudson. Don't encourage that from her. From the looks of her social media, she is out partying and drinking a lot. I am worried that she will end up in trouble like before."

It all clicks now. This is the person Christina told me about the day she took me to see the building. Victoria is the wife of the owner who had an affair. I don't say anything to Hudson or Evelyn about what I have heard, but I do make a mental note to call Christina later and find out all the details.

We say our goodbyes to everyone before heading out. Little Addison brings me a plastic bag filled with all sorts of foliage from their backyard—pinecones, leaves, and some dirt. It's the cutest thing anyone has ever given me, and I have gotten some adorable gifts in the last few weeks.

    I leave their house really hoping I will get to see them all again, but I don't want to get my hopes up too high.

24

Victoria

"Three-twenty-two Plum Street. She is going to be renting my store!"

I slam my purse down on my table as soon as I walk in my front door, knocking the contents out onto the kitchen floor.

Of course, they don't understand why I'm so upset. I thought that coming home would make everything better. Everyone knows that I am getting divorced, but no one is coming around to help me. Least of all Hudson. He's always so busy with work and that pathetic art studio. Way too busy for me, and now he has a girlfriend. Is that what she is, a girlfriend?

Evelyn has the kids and Matt, so I get why she is so busy all the time, but Hudson was supposed to be my rock. We were supposed to be together like old times.

I get home and realize that I left Katie at Evelyn's brunch, but this will work to my advantage. She will gather all the dirt on this girl, and hopefully she makes her so uncomfortable she never wants to come back again.

I open my computer to google Emily.

I go to Hudson's Facebook page and scroll down his friend list, looking for her name, but I don't find any friends named Emily. I look for her business page, the Teal Lotus, and find that name on his friends list.

I scroll through her account expecting to find more information about her, but she only has posts about her furniture. There is nothing about her personal life except her first and last name and the address of her new store, 322 Plum Street. A surge of anger runs through me again. That is not her address! That was supposed to be mine. What's even stranger is that all her social media accounts were created just eight months ago.

There are a bunch of websites that will give you more information about anyone if you have the person's full name and a city they have lived in. If you have other personal information like their age, relatives' names, or previous cities, that is also helpful. For a small fee you can get the entire history of that person. Criminal records, past addresses, emails, phone numbers, relatives, all sorts of juicy information.

I try her name, Emily Lewis, and the city of Cincinnati in the search box of the People Finder website. After several minutes waiting, the website pops up with dozens of Emily Lewises in or around Cincinnati, most of whom couldn't be her because they are nowhere around her age. I don't know her exact age. I would put her in her early twenties. She must be at least twenty-one or Hudson wouldn't have brought her into the brewery. The ones that could be here don't have addresses anywhere around this area.

I open a bottle of wine and spend several hours sifting through her photos on her social media accounts. I also find it strange that the only photos she has of herself are of her painting pieces of wood, or using a saw or a sander. They are all photos of her working, usually with safety glasses on, covering her face. What young girl doesn't have a million selfies online? What's even more out of place is that all her personal photos of herself were put up within the last month. There is none of her before that.

By the time I get to my second bottle of wine, I am desperately trying to figure out ways to get more information about her.

Maybe I could call Brandi. She deals with all the Cincinnati properties at the Alexander Group. She would have more information about her. I could make up a story about needing to get in contact with Emily Lewis, renting from them somehow. I don't know how she would react to me calling her, though. Brent has assured me no one knows about the affair, so she shouldn't treat me badly if I call, even though I know she doesn't like me very much.

I keep searching her photos and am getting very tired of looking at all her ugly old furniture and all the "It's so beautiful!" comments when I come across a comment that has her address confirming a pickup.

I quickly search the address on the internet and find the owner is an LLC.

"Damn it!" I yell into my empty apartment. Why would someone like her use an LLC to buy a house? I try to google the name of the LLC, and nothing comes up.

I decide to go ahead and call Brandi. I'm desperate now. I call her number and it goes to the Alexander Group's office voice mail. It's Sunday and there is no answer, so I leave a message.

My phone starts ringing back right away.

"Brandi?" I answer.

"What? No, it's Katie."

"Thank God, Katie. I need you to get over here pronto."

"I can't today. I am heading over to meet Lucas."

Gross. Lucas is a douchebag that she met on one of those dating apps. I can't believe she is sinking so low to use them. That is so trashy.

"Fine, then tell me everything that happened after I left today. How horrible is she? I need all the dirt you have."

"There is no dirt, Vic. She seems like a nice person. I really think that if you would have stayed, you might have actually liked her."

I am so inebriated now I can't help myself from screaming into the phone, "Oh, that's great! First she steals my business, then she steals my brother, and now my best friend!"

I know I am being irrational, but if I can be that way around anyone, it's Katie. She understands what I am going through.

"Stop it. You know that's not true," she says.

"Katie this is bad. I googled her, and I can't find her on the People Finder website. All her social media accounts are recent, with no photos, and the home she owns was bought under an LLC. There is something fishy about her. We need to get to the bottom of it." I can hear my voice slurring. I look at my table and see that I have almost finished my second bottle of wine. "Isn't that super fucked up?"

"No, not really. My condo is also under an LLC. That's the way my father made me purchase it. He says it's way smarter financially. Listen, Vic, I am going to call you first thing tomorrow morning. Do not do anything else today. Put your phone away and go straight to bed."

I hang up the phone before she says anything else. I sit there numb. No one seems to want to help me.

❀

I must have passed out at some point because I woke up on my couch with a massive hangover, and from the looks of it, I drank two bottles of wine all by myself. I find my phone on the floor and it's almost dead.

There are two text messages and a missed call with a voice message. One text is from Katie to call her as soon as I wake up, and one from Evelyn letting me know she's here if I need to talk.

I click on the voice mail. It's a message from Brandi.

"Victoria, I got your message from yesterday. I have to say I was very surprised to see that you called me. I was under the impression that you were no longer a part of the Alexander Group.

There should be no inquiries about any of the units on Plum Street, and there needn't be any further communication between us."

I quickly erase the message. The embarrassment crashes over me like a tidal wave. I cannot believe I called there yesterday. What an idiot I am. All I need is for Brent to hear I drunk-called them.

I completely freaked out at brunch. Hudson probably hates me. I need to do some serious damage control. I send him a series of text messages telling him how sorry I am and how badly I overreacted. I told him I was just having a really hard time with the divorce and need to figure out what I'm gonna do with my life, and I took it out on them. I tell him if this is going to be a serious thing with Emily, then I would like to meet her again and apologize. I lie and say how happy I am for them.

He messages me back and tells me we can meet tomorrow afternoon. He wants to meet at that dingy little Irish pub. Gross, I don't want to go back to that place, but I have to play nice. I need to compose myself and figure out a game plan if I am going to find out what is up with this girl.

25

Emily

Hudson apologized profusely for his sister Victoria's behavior. He explains more about her divorce and her interior design business. I get the impression that he doesn't know the whole story about what really happened with her and Brent. Christina made it sound like something way worse was happening than just getting a divorce.

"She hasn't had an easy life, so this whole ordeal must be hard on her. I haven't been there for her the way I should have since she's moved back. I really need to make an effort now. I guess I was just disappointed that they were splitting up. We were all so happy when Brent and Victoria started dating. She had been on a bad path before that, drinking and acting wild. My parents were really worried about her. Then she got a DUI and they completely flipped out. I had never seen my dad so angry."

"What happened to her?" I ask.

"Victoria isn't my biological sister. My parents adopted her when she was thirteen. Her parents were in a car accident and they both died. Our mothers were sorority sisters in college and were best friends, so after the accident, my parents brought her home to live with us. I was nine at the time, but I remember it being extremely hard on Victoria."

"Oh, that's awful. I guess I can really relate to that. No girl that age should have to lose her parents," I tell him.

"The two of you have a lot in common. I think that you would be good friends," he tells me.

I hear what he is saying and start to understand why she was so upset. If she lost her parents, her marriage, and now her dreams of opening her own business, then she must be devastated. I soften thinking about this.

"She is so lucky to have your family there for her," I say.

"Yeah, she really is. She started acting out in high school, sneaking out with boys, and she got caught drinking a few times. She went away to college, and we didn't see her much. She had a boyfriend that she lived with and seemed happy. I was just graduating high school when she came back and was getting ready to start college myself. That's when she and I started to get really close to each other. We went out all the time together. She partied harder than any friends I had. Everyone loved 'Party Victoria.'

"My parents were getting increasingly mad because she hadn't gotten a job and was living off her trust fund. Then she got the DUI, and my parents took her money away and told her she had to go to a rehabilitation center and get a job before they would give it back. That all really scared her because she pulled her life together quickly. She and Brent started dating right after all that happened, and within a few weeks they announced that they were getting married."

"Wow, that's a whirlwind romance," I say.

"It was. It was only three months from the time we learned they were dating, got married, and off, on a plane to Los Angeles."

"Did she ever go to a rehabilitation center?"

"Nope, she didn't. At that point, my parents were just happy she was marrying Brent. They didn't care about that anymore."

I think about Victoria's story and realize that she and I are a lot alike, and I start to feel bad for her.

"Why did they get divorced?"

"She said that they married too soon, and they weren't happy. So, there you have it. My sister in a nutshell. I am not excusing her behavior, but I do need to try and help her get back on track."

"I get it, I really do, and I'm not upset at all about brunch. It was an amazing day for me."

"Would you be willing to meet up with her? She wants to apologize. The three of us could go to this Irish pub that I really like. Please? I want you and Victoria to be friends. It would mean a lot to me. Plus, I know you two would really like each other. You both have such similar pasts."

"Of course. I would love to get to know her better. And really, no apologies are necessary."

"You're the best. Now we need to talk about more important things."

I get scared for a moment. What could be more important?

"What things?"

"This weekend, Halloween at my parents' house. We need to decide what we are going to wear. I was thinking, Morticia and Gomez Adams."

I am shocked. He wants me to come to his parents' cabin? When they were all talking about it at brunch, I never assumed that I would also be going. I don't think I am breathing, and I can't get any words out.

"Are you okay?" he asks. "Look, I know that this is moving a little fast, so if you don't want to come this weekend, I get it. I could try and come back on Saturday to hang with you on Halloween. We could go to that party with your friend."

I rush over to him, jump into his arms, and kiss him hard.

"Yes, yes, I will come with you to meet your parents."

"Good 'cause you will be a really hot Morticia."

26
Emily

We plan to meet Victoria at Killarney's today. I find it ironic that we end up meeting her at the same place where I saw the two of them for the first time, but of course they don't remember seeing me there.

I call Christina on the way to meet them to ask what she knows about the Alexander Group and the wife that was supposed to be setting up an interior design business at 322. She is curious why I am asking, but I don't want to go into any details about it. I hadn't even told her I was dating anyone yet, and I don't want to talk about it with anyone until I know that it's for sure. I haven't even told Harper yet. She seems suspicious but still tells me what happened.

"Remember when you got the keys from Brandi, and she was telling you about the two brothers that owned the company, Brent and Brandon?"

"Yes, I do remember that."

"Well, Brent's wife began having an affair with his brother, Brandon. They were caught red-handed one night naked in Brent's own bed. He had come home early from a business trip and walked in on them in the act."

My jaw drops to the floor. "You're kidding me!"

"Nope. Brandon told Brent everything that had been going on out of guilt. Apparently, they had been sleeping together for three months, and Brent hadn't even been married to her for a year, and she was already having an affair."

"How does Brandi know all of this?" I ask, wondering why she would know and Victoria's own family doesn't know.

"She is really close with Brent. She has worked for him since he took over the business when his father retired. I am sure she had to help with the damage control."

This gives me a whole new perspective on Victoria. I was feeling bad for her, but why should I feel sorry for someone that would do something like that? She was given the chance of a lifetime to marry a great guy, who owned a company and was willing to give her a part of it to start her own business, and then she had an affair with his own brother. This is all so salacious.

I really hate cheaters. There are a lot of things I can overlook, but cheating is a big deal to me. When my mother got sick, my stepfather started completely checking out of our lives. He would be gone on so-called business trips constantly. We barely saw him. Thankfully, my mother had me to take care of her because he was never around. I started following him and learned that he wasn't going on business trips, he was going to other women's houses. Not just one, but several. I would follow him and watch him taking them out to dinner, shopping at the mall. He even bought one of them a brand-new car. He never bought anything like that for me or my mother. He gave her a car, but it was already ten years old when she got it. I was furious with him. My mother was at home on the verge of dying, and he was out screwing other women.

I meet Hudson at the pub after he gets done at the brewery. He is already seated, and as soon as he sees me, he stands up and gives me a long kiss as he always does. The way he looks at me when we break our embrace is always the same, like I'm the most beautiful person in the world. It melts my heart every time.

"You look so cute today," he says to me.

"You already saw me this morning. I look the same."

"I am still standing by my statement. So freaking cute," he bites his lower lip.

God, it's so sexy when he does that.

Victoria walks in dressed incredibly inappropriately for happy hour on a Tuesday. Not to mention it's forty degrees outside today. She is wearing a very short tight black cotton dress. It's a little see-through because of the sheer cotton material and I can see that she has a red bra underneath. At least she has long sleeves covering her arms, but her legs must be freezing.

"Hot date later?" Hudson says, standing up to give her a quick kiss on the cheek.

"Maybe," she says with a wink.

"I love this place, Hudson. I am so glad you brought me here again."

She sits across from us and looks right at me.

"Emily, I am so incredibly sorry for the way I acted the other day. I am sure that you have heard that I have some dreadful things going on in my life right now." She glances at Hudson with a sad pouty face.

"I explained everything to her," he says.

Victoria hangs her head down. "Yes, it's just been so hard on me. I thought Brent was the love of my life, but I guess life throws you some curveballs."

I stop myself from laughing out loud in her face. Maybe if she didn't screw her husband's brother then she would still have the love of her life. I just nod, trying to keep my face neutral.

The server comes to our table, interrupting Victoria's pity party. We all order our drinks. Wine for me and Hudson and double vodka and soda for Victoria.

"Anyway, enough about that. I'm still young and have plenty of opportunities to find love. I mean, I am only twenty-eight. How old are you, Emily? I want to get to know you," she says to me, and her whole demeanor changes from a sad, pathetic divorcée to being my best friend in five seconds.

"Twenty-two," I say.

"Did I hear that you just moved here? How long have you been here?"

"Since February."

"Where did you move here from?"

I feel like she is asking a lot of direct questions. Like she is cataloging information about me. The server arrives with our drinks.

Hudson raises his glass. "Cheers to Victoria being back in the city and to Emily's opening day coming up in eleven days." We clink glasses.

"Did you get everything moved into your apartment?" Hudson asks Victoria.

"Yes, I had this amazing decorator come and help me. You need to come by and see it soon. It's gorgeous."

"Why would you hire a decorator? You could have just done that yourself. That is what you went to school for, and you're really talented."

"I have just been so busy with other things. I have started to look for a place to start my business. Tell me about your store that you are opening, Emily."

I begin to tell her about it, but I get the feeling she isn't even listening to me. She is nodding her head, but she keeps texting on her phone in the middle of our conversation.

Hudson's phone starts to ring. He looks at it.

"It's a call from Matt about the brewery," he apologizes, and leaves the table.

As soon as he leaves, the air gets thick, and Victoria's demeanor changes again.

"So, what exactly are your intentions with my brother?"

"I'm sorry, I am not sure what you mean?"

"You know he's a Berman, right? Our family has quite a bit of money."

"I am not interested in money."

Is she seriously talking to me like this right now?

"How will you pay that kind of rent selling used furniture? Prices are not cheap downtown. Did Hudson get you some sort of deal from Brent, or did you already know him?"

She seems to be fishing for information. I am not going to bite, though.

"I don't know who Brent is," I lie, "but to answer your other question, I will have no problem paying the rent. I don't just sell used furniture. I have quite a huge following for what I do, and I'm really good at it. I don't need Hudson's money. I have my own family money just like you do."

"I saw your social media accounts. Funny, though, I didn't see any personal accounts. Everything was just created recently. Seems very strange to me."

"So what? I don't post everything to get attention like you do."

I am not going to back down from her. I have known girls like this before. This is exactly what the rich girls in my high school did when I started going there. They backed off after they realized I wasn't going to take it.

"What do you have to say about your house being bought under an LLC? I did some research and found out that people do that to hide something."

"No, Victoria, people do that to save money on taxes. Also, for legal purposes. You know a little about legal issues I have heard."

I am ready for a fight with her when I look up and see Hudson walking back. She changes the subject the moment he gets back to the table.

My stepfather didn't teach me much, but he worked for a security company, and I learned from him the importance of keeping your identity safe. People get their identity and their lives stolen from them just by posting personal stuff on the internet. Buying my house and store under an LLC is just a smarter way to keep personal information safe.

"Remember the twins, Ava and Emma?" she asks him. "They used to have the biggest crush on you."

"I do remember them."

"I ran into them the other day, and they asked about you. You should come out with us sometime."

"Definitely not, no way. I have no interest in hanging out with them."

He squeezes my hand tightly under the table. He must sense how uncomfortable Victoria is making me.

The server comes by, and she orders a second vodka and soda. Me and Hudson have barely touched our wine yet.

I notice that she has been fidgeting with a silver charm bracelet on her right wrist. She caresses each of the charms one by one in a meticulous way.

"Emily is coming to meet Mom and Dad this weekend," Hudson tells her.

It looks like the blood rushes out of Victoria's already-pale white skin.

"That's not a good idea, Hudson. Mom would be very upset."

"It's okay, Vic, I already talked to them, and they are thrilled to have Emily come up. Mom already knew a little bit about her already."

I look at him curiously. "What do you mean?"

"Well, when I had her write the card for our cocktail ingredients, I told her about you."

I must be blushing because I can feel my cheeks getting warm. I look over at Victoria, and she does not look pleased at all. She is looking at me like I'm a bug that she needs to crush. This is obviously not going very well. I know that Hudson can't see what's going on, but I certainly can. I don't think that there will be much of a friendship between Victoria and me.

I excuse myself to go to the bathroom. I am going to take control of this situation right here and now. While I'm in here, I pull out my phone and send a text to Hudson.

I can't stop thinking about this morning. The way you licked me all over my body, even my toes, was so hot. I want to go home and do that to you. Right when I saw you walk into the pub, I felt like I was going to explode. I can't wait to get out of here.

When I am walking back to the table, I see that Hudson's face is a little flushed. I sit down next to him and put my hand on his thigh with my pinky finger grazing the zipper on his jeans.

"Okay, well, we have got to leave now," he says to me. "Frieda texted while you were in the bathroom; she needs to leave early today."

"Oh no," I say, feigning disappointment that we have to leave. The look on Victoria's face is priceless.

"You never told me where you were from?" she says as we are paying our tab.

We stand up quickly to leave. Hudson barely gives her a moment to beg us to stay.

"Sorry, Vic, we have really got to run now, but we will see you this weekend."

Before I know it, he has my hand in his and is leading me out of the pub.

I look back at her and say, "I'm from Missouri."

So many questions about me. I know exactly what she plans to do with all my answers. She wants to search about me on the internet. That's fine, Victoria. You won't find anything.

On the street outside, Hudson pulls me in close to him. "I cannot wait to get you home."

"Your home or mine?"
"Your place is definitely home for me."

27

Victoria

I was hoping that Hudson and I would have some time to talk alone at the Irish pub before Emily got there, but I was running late. So, when I walked in, they were already sitting next to each other. He stands up to greet me and it's as if I am a stranger to him.

I give my apologies to her right after I sit down to get that out of the way. I need to get to the important reasons why I came here and get information about her. I need to figure out why she has everything hidden about herself, why she keeps her identity such a secret.

She and my brother are sitting so close together. They both order the same wine, and he talks about her so gently, as if she is breakable. I hate watching this. This girl is not someone that Hudson should be dating. There is something clearly off about her. I just can't understand why I am the only one who sees it. Even Evelyn is fooled.

I try my hardest to put on a fake face and have a conversation with her. I keep telling myself I need to be nice in order to learn more about her. Hudson gets a phone call and leaves the table. Finally, I can talk to her woman to woman.

"How can you afford that place? Did Brent give you a deal?"

I need to find out first if she is involved with the Alexander Group in any way. She tells me about her own family money just like me. I guess Hudson has told her a lot more about my past than I had expected.

I ask her about her social media accounts, and she seems to evade all my questions. Then she lies to me about the reason she bought her house under an LLC, instead making a jab about my legal issues. There is no way Hudson would tell her about my past troubles with the law. She must have googled me and found that out.

When Hudson comes back to the table, she closes herself off completely, which is what I assumed she would do. Classic sign that someone is hiding something.

When Hudson says that she will be coming to our parents' house, I almost lose my temper again. I take a deep breath in and tell myself that this is actually a good thing. Mom and Dad will see right through this girl. They can do my dirty work for me.

She excuses herself to go to the restroom, and I can finally get a moment to talk to Hudson.

"Victoria, maybe you should slow down," he says, pointing at my drink.

"What, it's only my second drink. I'm fine."

"Okay. You just seem a little off today."

I fight back my irritation. "Tell me, what is going on with the two of you?"

A smile overtakes his entire face. "I think that she might be the one, Vic," he says to me proudly, and I almost throw up the vodka. A sinking feeling in the pit of my stomach begins rising up.

"What? There's no way. You have only known her for a week!"

"It's been almost five weeks. I know that's not a huge amount of time, but I have never felt this way before."

"You need to give it more time. I mean, you never know if these types of girls are after your money or not."

I realize by the look on his face that I need to dial it back so that I don't upset him again.

His phone beeps, and he picks it up and reads the text message. His face immediately goes red.

"Is everything okay?" I ask, concerned.

"Umm, yeah, just fine, but I am going to have to leave here shortly. Frieda needs to leave the studio early today. There's an emergency. So, I need to head over there."

"Just tell her to lock it up for the day."

"No, I can't do that. I really need to get there."

I fight back my anger. We are supposed to spend the evening together. I haven't learned as much as I needed to about Emily.

Just then, she comes back to the table. He tells her they need to leave, and you can tell that she's thrilled about this and can't wait to get away from me. She obviously knows that I am on to her.

I have learned what? Just her name and her age. There are so many more questions that I was going to ask. As she is leaving, she tells me where she moved here from. Missouri, but not the city. That's okay, at least I have that to go by.

They leave the pub quickly and I am left sitting there all alone, thinking about everything Emily said. I finish drinking my vodka, and after a while, I decide to walk over to the art studio. I don't know why I feel the need to go there. There's just something that feels off about them leaving so abruptly.

I walk down Plum Street until I can see their buildings, but not close enough for them to see me. All the lights are off in both stores. Maybe he hasn't gotten back here yet, but it's been almost a half an hour.

I pop into the soap shop across the street and smell all the soaps once, then twice, trying to kill time while peeking out the windows waiting for Hudson to arrive. The person working in the shop asks me if she can help me twice while I am in there. I don't respond to her, I just give her a nasty look. Can't someone just shop in peace anymore?

I leave the soap store after forty-five minutes. I can't keep wasting time there. I walk across the street and peer into the windows. There is absolutely no one in the art studio. I see that the sign on the door says closed with the hours written on it. *Due to the holidays, we have limited hours. Monday through Friday 8am till 3pm. Evening hours are limited. Please call for a private appointment.*

It's not even supposed to be open at this time of the day. So, what was he talking about Frieda having to leave? He was lying to me, again. He also lied to me the night he went to the brewery with Emily.

I look next door and I don't see her in there either. I am fuming with anger that Hudson is behaving this way.

Then it clicks. This was her doing. I remember him checking his phone. She must have sent him a message from the bathroom. Whatever she said got him to lie to me and made him leave the pub quickly.

This bitch is messing with the wrong girl.

I get back to my house, and I go right to my computer and type in all the new information that I have about her. Lots of Emily Lewises come up in Missouri. I can't find anyone that's twenty-two years old, but some of the results don't have specific ages. I try narrowing my search by adding a few of the big cities in Missouri. I still get nothing. I wonder if she has lied about that as well. Maybe that's not where she is from at all. I could put her name in other cities and states but that would take so long, and I still don't even know if I have the correct information.

Is Emily Lewis even her real name? Maybe Hudson has been lied to this whole time also. Maybe he is being duped. That's the only explanation. I put my own name, city, and age in the search, and my information pops right up. Victoria Alexander, also known as Victoria Berman, also known as Victoria Sellers. The last name on the record makes my heart drop. I don't even remember a time when I was Victoria Sellers, nor do I want to. The pain of thinking about my parents is too much. I grab my charm bracelet and push those thoughts out of my mind. I don't want to go there.

 I shriek into my apartment. This is so frustrating! I try to search for the LLC again in Missouri and nothing comes up. It's clearly some fake name that she created. I type her address into google again and begin to scroll.

 I freeze when I see the articles that come up. There are hundreds of news reports related to this address.

 The first article headline reads, "Two Dead in an Apparent Murder/Suicide."

 I skim the article as fast as I can, then move on to the others. There are so many stories about the couple that used to live in Emily's house and their horrific deaths. They were well known in the city of Aurora for owning a country store for over fifty years, and the man just went mad one day. I can't believe that she lives in the house where all of this took place. A man drowned his wife and then shot himself in the head. The articles mentioned he may have been suffering from mental illness and dementia.

 There is no way that Hudson knows about this. How could he possibly go there if he knew, and they invited Evelyn to go see it sometime? She would freak out and would never accept an invitation to a place where people were murdered.

 I make a bold decision and decide to drive out to this house. I want to see this place for myself and find out if anything else strange is happening out there.

 The house is so far out of town. Who would want to live out here? I have never even heard of Aurora. I pass a town center that doesn't have very many options to choose from. I am surprised to see there is an organic grocery store. I wouldn't think people out here would shop at a place like that.

When I get to Emily's address, I slowly drive past the long driveway that leads up to the house. It's so long and windy that I can't see what cars are parked there. I can't even see the house itself. There are too many trees lining the driveway. I don't know if they are here or at Hudson's house. I doubt they are staying out here, though, when they have Hudson's house right in the city. He would never like being this far out of town and in such a secluded area.

I turn back around and pull into the driveway and stop my car. I don't want to take the chance that I would go all the way up and have them be here. Hudson knows what kind of car I have now, so I can't risk it. I will come back later when I know for sure they aren't here.

I back out and head back the way I came. I drive through the little shopping area and pull into the organic grocery store. I need a minute to think before heading back to the city. I could call Hudson and see where he is, and if they aren't there, I could go back to the house and check it out. I call his number and it goes to voice mail.

I decide to go into the market and walk around. I will give it a little while before I try calling back again. I could get some wine for later.

This must be a good place to shop. The parking lot is full and there are a ton of people coming in and out of the store. I pull into a parking spot and head inside. I wander around in a daze, wondering what I should do. I try calling Hudson again and he doesn't answer. I buy a few bottles of wine and decide just to head back home.

As I am walking closer to my car, I see a piece of paper flapping in the wind from underneath the windshield wiper. I pull it out, annoyed that people still try to advertise this way, and almost throw it on the ground. I see that there is something handwritten on it, so I decide to take a look.

You park like a fucking moron. You deserve every inch of that mark along the side of your ugly black car. You're lucky that I didn't put that mark on your body, gutting you from your mouth down to your ass.

I quickly look at my car and see the long silver streak along the side of it. It's very noticeable against the brand-new black paint.

Someone has keyed my fucking car! Obviously, the same person that wrote this note. I frantically look around the parking lot, trying to see who might have done this. After all, I wasn't in the store for very long. All I see are dozens of people walking to and from their vehicles. It could be anyone. I unlock my car and quickly get in, locking the doors immediately. I uncrumple the paper and read it again.

My mind automatically goes to Emily and if she could have possibly done this. I know that Hudson and she are together right now. The lie he told me about going to the studio was obviously a cover because they were heading off somewhere together. Hudson would never ever do anything like this. I mean, we have played some silly sibling pranks on each other in the past but nothing even remotely like this. This is morbid and sick. Still, though, I wonder if this was her. If she somehow knew I was here and followed me.

I speed away from the store and that horrible place back to the city. I don't ever want to go out there again.

28

Emily

Hudson and I get back to my place and spend the next few hours in bed—my bed—in the place that he just called home. He falls asleep quickly, poor guy. We have barely slept at all for days. I am used to not getting very much sleep, but he must be exhausted, so I decide to let him nap while I run to the market to get some things to make for dinner.

I get in my truck and start heading down my driveway when I see a black car backing out of my driveway. Someone must have been lost and in a hurry, because they speed off out of the driveway, kicking up rocks everywhere.

I pull out onto the road that goes to the town center just a mile up, following the black car. We pull into the same market, and it's very busy. The parking lot is full of cars driving up and down the isles trying to find a spot, but that's usually what it's like here. I see that two cars are pulling out right next to each other. Nice, we can both park. The black car in front of me waits until they both pull out and then pulls into the spot. I drive up next to the car to get the spot next to it and see that the person has parked in the middle of both spots crossing way over the line, making it impossible for even a small compact vehicle to park there. Let alone my truck.

What a jerk. I almost roll down my window and yell at the person, but I see another spot in the next aisle open up and drive over there quickly to grab it. I am parked facing the black car when the door opens and the woman that steps out is unmistakable with her dark hair and fair skin.

It's Victoria. Why is she here? She lives in the city. Why was she pulling around in my driveway? There is no reason for her to be out here in Aurora. There is only one explanation. She is out here to spy on me. She already tried to collect a bunch of information earlier today, and when that didn't work out for her, she decided to drive out here.

This means war, Victoria. Why are you bothering me? I have done nothing to you. Are you just a jealous sister, or do you just not like me for some reason? My anger turns into a lump in my throat. I get ready to open my truck door and run after her to confront her, but I force myself to take deep breaths. I breathe in and out until my anger wanes a little.

I have a better idea. Rather than going after her, I will just simply leave her a message. I dig into my glove box and find a pad of paper and pen and write her a note. I take it and my keys and head over to her shiny black car.

After I leave the note on her car, I move my truck and find an inconspicuous spot in the parking lot so that I can still see Victoria's car.

I don't have to wait long. I watch her walk to her car in anticipation. All my anger quickly dissipates when I see her reaction. She frantically begins to look around the parking lot before jumping in her car and speeding away. I burst out laughing. That will teach you a lesson.

So, I wonder what else little miss Victoria has been up to. I am sure she has been trying to find out what she can about me online. She won't find anything. The funny thing is that I know some things about her, though. Like the real reason she is getting divorced, the real reason she isn't at Plum Street. I will keep that in my pocket for a while until I figure out how to use it.

29

Victoria

After the incident in Aurora, I put everything aside with Emily until we get to Mom and Dad's cabin. I have faith that my parents will see right through her, and if not, I will figure out what to do next when I get back. Besides, I really need a break from worrying about everything. Mom and Dad already know about the divorce, so I don't have to have a talk with them about that. I can just get up to the cabin and have some much-needed family time. I really wish that Emily wasn't coming, but there is nothing I can do about that.

I get there early on Friday. I am the first to arrive, so me and Mom spend some time talking.

"Sweetheart," she says, "I know that things are really rough on you right now. This whole divorce mess and starting your life over must really be taking a toll on you."

"It is, so much so," I tell her.

"Evelyn has told me that you are feeling pretty badly about things, and I want you to know that I am always here for you. From the moment you came into our lives, I was always going to be here for you no matter what."

"Thanks, Mom. I am having such a hard time right now. I need my family close. It's especially hard on me because I feel like

Hudson and Evelyn are so busy now, and they don't have any time for me."

"They will come around, but now is the time you need to get started with your new life. You have an apartment, now you just need to figure out a business plan, but if you still need to take some more time to heal, then you do that. Now that Dad and I are back in town, I will make sure that we all spend more time together, the whole family. That should help."

"It will help, Mom."

I am so thankful that she is saying all of this to me right now. She pulls me into her arms and hugs me for a long time. I breathe her in deeply. This is exactly what I needed.

She pulls away from me and ruins the moment with one sentence: "So, tell me about this new girl that Hudson is in love with."

I almost choke on her words. "He is not in love with her, Mom. They just started dating a few weeks ago. She is just one of those girls that Hudson has hanging around."

"I don't know, sweetheart. From the way he was behaving the last week he was here, he sure seems to be lovestruck."

"You make your own judgment when you meet her, but the impression I get is that they are not really that great of a match. Hudson will get bored and move on."

"He's got to settle down sometime with someone. He isn't going to be a bachelor forever."

"He's only twenty-four, Mom. I can't imagine him settling down until well into his thirties."

I am right; this is just a girl that he has been seeing for a few weeks. He will get tired of her the way he does every other girl he dates. Maybe that's the bad feeling I get from her. They will break up, all in good time. I will just wait it out and let Hudson come to his senses, and if he doesn't, I will make him.

30

Emily

After Hudson took me to meet his family, things have been heating up like crazy. We spent every moment together this week either at our stores or at one of our houses, besides when he is at the brewery. He even took me to finally get my driver's license.

I was so nervous walking into the DMV, but he held my hand the entire time until they called me up to take the computer test, then outside and take the driving portion. I thought for sure I would fail, not because I am a bad driver, but because I was shaking so badly behind the wheel and couldn't remember any of the rules of the road. It didn't seem real that I had passed until I heard them call out my name in the waiting room.

"Lewis," the lady behind the counter called out to me.

She took my photo and then handed me a temporary piece of paper until my real card comes in the mail. I looked over to Hudson and he was smiling so proudly at me.

At yoga on Thursday, I tell Harper that I am not going to make it to the party for Halloween. She goes crazy with excitement when I tell her everything that has happened with me and Hudson over the past two weeks and that I am going to meet his parents over the weekend.

"You go and meet your future in-laws," she says to me with her usual enthusiasm. "Besides, we might not be out that late anyway since we are leaving Monday morning for Joshua Tree. As soon as I get back, we will celebrate your store, your new relationship, and the fact that I will be Mrs. Ethan Myers."

"Oh, we are definitely celebrating when you get back, but first, do you have time to stop by my store before you head home? I have a gift for you."

She excitedly agrees and we head there when class is over. I had the sign company that made the sign for my store create a beautiful wooden plaque that has her wedding song carved into it. She had said she loved the one that was on canvas, but this is so much more in tune with a wedding that is taking place in a national park.

When we get to the store, there is a note tucked into the crack of my front door. I grab it and put it in my pocket to read later. Harper is so excited when she sees the wooden plaque. She loves it, I knew she would, but I didn't know how hard she would cry over it. I hug her tightly, holding back laughter because she is just so cute and sweet. She is never going to make it through her wedding ceremony without ruining all her makeup.

After she leaves, I open the folded piece of paper and read it. *Leave Hudson alone or else,* is all that is written on the paper. Oh, Victoria, you couldn't have been a little more original? Or else what? You're going to come to my house and pull into my driveway again? You are so boring. Do you know that I am the one who wrote you a note first? I doubt it. I am sure that you would have said something to Hudson right away. You are so bad about keeping your emotions in check.

I throw the note in the trash where it belongs.

❦

On Friday, after Hudson gets off work, we pack up and head north. It's a three-hour drive to the Bermans' cabin. I am so excited to have all that time in a car alone with him. It's our first road trip together. Hudson is a chatterbox for the first hour. He is excited for me to see their cabin.

"I can't wait to show you all my secret spots!"

He explains his parents always dreamed of living in a cabin up north in Knox. A couple of years ago his dad, Bob, had some health problems, and their mom, Betty, made him retire from the brewery, letting Hudson and Matt take over. He didn't like this at first, but he accepted that if he didn't step back, Betty would have been upset. "What Betty wants, Betty gets," Hudson explains. Bob comes down every few weeks to check on things, and they make him feel like he's the one still in charge.

I finally get the courage to bring up our situation to Hudson. I thought about it all day, trying to come up with the perfect words to tell him what has been on my mind. I don't want to sound overbearing, but I want to let him know I am ready for a relationship whenever he is. I have completely torn down my walls with him and can accept that we could possibly have a great future together.

I have been quiet for too long, trying to get the words out before Hudson finally speaks.

"Something else I wanted to talk about," he says, breaking the silence.

I look over at him and he is gripping the steering wheel so tightly that his knuckles are white.

"Yes?" I say nervously.

"I told my parents that you are my…" He pauses, "That you are my girlfriend. I hope that's okay. If you need some more time to decide if that's what you want, then I totally understand."

I scoot over closer to him and kiss him on the cheek, feeling excitement surge through my body. If he wasn't driving, then I would ravage him right here and now.

"Yes, Hudson. It's one hundred percent okay. I would love to be your girlfriend."

"Alright, now this is going to be a great weekend."

We pull up to the cabin and I gasp when I see that this is not just some cabin in the woods but a huge, beautiful place that looks more like a ski lodge, surrounded by forest that seems to go on forever. There are warm glowing lights emanating from every corner of the building, welcoming us.

Betty and Bob are extremely welcoming. They greet me kindly when I arrive. Betty pours me a glass of wine and takes me on a personal tour around the entire cabin showing me everything she put into the architectural design when they built it. The rooms are endless. There is a place for everyone to sleep, including a few rooms that have four bunk beds in each. She shows me to the room where Hudson and I will be staying, and it looks like a mountain retreat hotel room. I was surprised that she was allowing us to sleep in the same room, but he did tell her I was his girlfriend, and we are adults.

"My parents used to take me to vacation in the Smoky Mountains in Tennessee growing up with all my cousins and siblings. I always wanted to have a place of my own where everyone could visit. I didn't want to move away as far as Tennessee, so we decided to build here in Knox. I want this place to be filled with love and lots of grandkids, and hopefully I will be around for great-grandkids. I want you to feel at home here, Emily."

"I'm speechless. I have never seen anything like this. You truly have an extraordinary imagination to design such a gorgeous place," I tell her, and I mean it. I have never been anywhere even remotely as gorgeous as this.

We head back down to the giant den where everyone is hanging out. Evelyn's kids are all sitting around their grandpa, listening to his stories about Greece. He is obviously embellishing the story he is telling about how magical it is there, but it is adorable all the same.

I look over at Hudson. He is just as enthralled with the story that Bob is telling as the children are. Victoria is tapping away on her phone, not paying any attention, like usual.

For a moment I wonder how so many kind people can be related to her, but then I remember that she was adopted.

After Bob is finished, Betty announces that we need to leave in a few minutes to make our dinner reservations at Antonio's.

We all decide for who is riding with who, and once again, me and Hudson get to be alone together. Betty orchestrated it that way.

"This is our parents' favorite restaurant. We come here all the time," Hudson tells me when we get in the car. "It's an Italian place that serves the best fettuccine alfredo you will ever have, and if you want something a little healthier, there's a specialty salad they make. They bring all the ingredients to the table and make it fresh right there in front of you, including the dressing."

"That sounds amazing."

"My mom doesn't cook very often for us anymore. She tells us every time we come to visit that her days of slaving in the kitchen for us kids are long over. She wants to use her time to be with the family."

"That's fine with me, I love going out to eat. We should definitely get the fettuccine to share."

The restaurant is amazing, and so is the evening. All eleven of us sit around a large table, eating, drinking wine, and enjoying the conversations. I feel like I am in a Hallmark movie. I am glad to see that this kind of thing does actually exist in real life. Even Victoria seems happy. She is laughing with her mom and Evelyn. I see her playing with her silver charm bracelet again.

"Your bracelet is beautiful," I tell her. "Are the charms all different?"

She looks down at her bracelet and goes silent. "Thank you," she finally says, and the adults at the table go silent. "My mother gave this bracelet to me when I was five years old. Every year on my birthday, she would add on a new charm. For my seventh birthday it was a ballet slipper for my first ballet recital. Then on my tenth it was a silver Eiffel Tower for my first trip to Paris. When my wrist started to grow, she took it into the jeweler and had the silver band extended. It's incredibly special to me."

There is a sadness in her eyes, and I want to like her, I really do, but she is making it impossible. Maybe this weekend will get her to change the way she behaves toward me.

Betty stands up and raises her glass in the air. "Let's make a toast to Victoria coming home and starting a new chapter in her life." Everyone raises their glasses.

"Cheers!" everyone says.

"And to Hudson for bringing this wonderful new person, Emily, into our lives. We are really glad to have you here."

Again, everyone cheers. Even Victoria.

31

Emily

On Halloween day, we carve pumpkins with the kids and play all sorts of Halloween games. When it starts to get dark, we head up to our rooms to put on our Halloween costumes for trick-or-treating. I begin to worry that mine is a little too revealing for a family affair, but Hudson assures me it is not. I purposely didn't buy the Morticia Adams dress they had at the Spirit store because it was incredibly low cut and had a slit up the side that revealed…well, it revealed everything. Instead, I bought a long black ribbed dress from the mall that went down past my knees with a modest collar made from a thick sweater material. It was still very tight, and Hudson could barely keep his hands off me after I put it on. We put on our wigs and head downstairs.

Betty is gushing over how wonderful we look.

"Oh, I just love the Adams family! It was my favorite show when I was a little girl."

Bob is wearing a bacon suit and she is in a matching costume dressed as an egg. I laugh so hard at seeing the two of them as breakfast.

Bob tells me, "What Betty wants, Betty gets."

Evelyn, Matt, and their kids are all wearing different Disney character costumes. They really put a lot of effort into

Minnie, Micky, Cinderella, Buzz Lightyear, and Woody. Addison is Elsa from *Frozen* and looks so cute.

Victoria walks out dressed in a very tight black leather dress with black gloves coming up to her upper arms.

"What are you supposed to be?" Hudson asks her.

"Duh, Posh Spice," she says condescendingly.

He laughs heartily at her. "Aren't you supposed to dress like that with the other three Spice Girls?"

She walks over and hits him hard on the shoulder. "Don't be an ass. Who are you supposed to be, the Crypt Keeper?"

Trick or treating is a blast. I can't help but feel a little bit sad that I have never gotten to do this before. Growing up in the area I lived in was not great for trick-or-treating, so I never went, and by the time we moved in with Brooks, I was too old for it. I laugh and smile more than I ever have in my life. Hudson is like a little kid running up to all the doors asking for candy with his nieces and nephews. Addison is attached to my hip holding my hand the entire time, singing every song from the *Frozen* soundtrack.

When we get back from trick-or-treating, Victoria suggests that the adults all go to this local bar. At first Evelyn refuses. She doesn't want to leave the kids, but Betty insists that she and Matt have a nice time out while she and Bob stay home with her kids and doesn't take no for an answer.

"Fine, but I am taking this costume off. I am not going out dressed as Minnie."

Me and Hudson go upstairs to change out of our costumes also.

"Nope, don't even think about it," he says to me when I start to take off my dress. "You look so hot in that dress tonight. You are definitely wearing it out." He comes over and gropes my butt and starts pushing me toward the bed.

"Hudson, stop," I say teasingly. "I am not going to fornicate in your mother's house."

He looks me up and down. "Fine, but when we get back to the city, I need you to wear this dress again."

I leave the dress on but take off my wig and tone down my overly-done black makeup into something I would normally wear.

We spend the next few hours at a local pub. It's small and serves wine and beer and small specialty plates for sharing. Victoria seems in her element. She is content being out with her siblings, laughing, joking, and drinking. She is even being nice to me.

At ten o'clock, Evelyn and Matt announce that they are now turning into pumpkins and need to go home.

"This is the latest I have been out in a long time," Evelyn says.

"Stop being an old hen, Evelyn. Our family owns a brewery, for Christ's sake, but you act like it's a tea shop. It's Halloween night. You have to stay out with me," Victoria whines.

Evelyn gives her a dirty look. "Not all of us can be rockstars like you. I'm not telling you to come back with us too. You three stay out."

"Actually, I need to get back also. I am golfing with Dad and Matt tomorrow morning at 7 a.m."

"Seven in the morning? That's ridiculous!" Victoria blurts out.

"Bob is an early riser, you know that."

Victoria looks so sad, and I feel a tiny bit bad for her.

"But listen, it's early. Why don't you and Emily stay out later? You can Uber home when you're done."

Hudson looks at me, pleading for me to say yes.

I wish he wouldn't have suggested that. I would much rather go home with him, but I look at Victoria, and her face has lit up, then back at Hudson's face, and he does the same. I give in.

This will be a good opportunity for me and Victoria to get to know each other better. Maybe try and work out some of the kinks.

"That sounds like a great idea. I could go out for another hour or so," I say apprehensively.

After everyone leaves, Victoria suggests that we head to a different bar.

"This bar is boring and closes early. I know a much better place we can go to. Me and Hudson used to go there all the time before I moved. He would have loved to go there tonight if he would have stayed out with us."

I look at my watch and it's nearing 10:30 now. We can stay for an hour or so and then I can be home in bed with Hudson before midnight.

"So how serious are you and Hudson?" Victoria asks me while we are in the Uber, heading to the other bar.

"He asked me to be his girlfriend, so I am not sure if that means we are super serious or just casual. I am not used to the whole dating thing," I tell her.

"Really? You don't peg me as the type that doesn't date."

"Hudson is only the second boyfriend I have ever had. I was dating someone before I moved here, but it didn't last long, and I broke it off right before I came here."

"Do you still have feelings for him? Do you two still talk?"

I find it strange she would ask me that, considering me and Hudson are dating now.

"No, absolutely not. He was mentally abusive and treated me very badly. I would never speak to him again," I assure her.

We pull up to a place called the Barnyard, and when we park, I can see that she is right. It's a popular spot. The parking lot is filled with cars and the patio is full of people holding various drinks and smoking cigarettes. Inside, the place is packed with people, a few wearing costumes, but most are not. People stare at us as we walk toward the bar. You can tell this is a local place where most people probably know each other. They can tell that we aren't from here.

Victoria orders us two bottles of beer and two shots of tequila.

"No thanks, I am not taking shots. I can't. I will get way too drunk if I drink them," I say as she is pushing one of the shots into my hand.

First, I am not the kind of person who drinks shots. I am a lightweight, and I don't want to feel out of control here with Victoria. And second, I don't want to give Hudson's parents the impression that I am a wild partier if I come home drunk later tonight.

"Come on, you have to. We are here to have fun. Just take one for me, please?" she begs.

"Okay, fine. Just one."

We both put the shot glasses to our mouths and then slam them down on the bar counter. While we are sucking on the limes that came with them, I tip my glass over and let the tequila that I never actually swallowed spill out all over the counter. Victoria doesn't notice. The bar is so packed with people and is already filthy from the hundreds of other drinks that have passed over it, spilling various other liquids along the way.

I sip my beer and look around the crowded room. The first thing that stands out to me is how many males there are in here. I would say the bar is about 75 percent male, and it doesn't take long before Victoria has some of them in her sights. She grabs my arm and drags me over to a table. There are four men sitting there, all much older than me, maybe in their thirties, but I realize this is what Victoria would be looking for. She is almost thirty herself. These guys don't look like the type that she would go for, though. They are all dressed in baggy jeans, T-shirts with band names on them, and dirty sneakers. Three of the four have ball caps on. She seems more like the type to go for the well-dressed businessman.

"Hello, I'm Victoria," she says and holds out her hand to shake each of theirs.

The men all introduce themselves, staring at us as if they have just won the lottery. I don't pay attention to what any of their names are. I am not here to make new friends, and I really don't want to spend my time talking with these guys. I stand two steps away from the table and nod. I am not shaking hands with any of them the way Victoria is.

They maneuver their seats to make room for us to sit down. I don't want to sit down with these guys, but before I know it, Victoria gets into a deep conversation with one of them, talking awfully close to his face. I look at my phone. One hour and that's it. I don't like the vibe of this place at all.

The guy she was talking to leaves the table and comes back with six shots of a dark liquid for everyone.

Victoria claps and cheers, "Yah, more shots!"

The guy pushes one into my hand, spilling half of it on the table in the process. While everyone is taking their shots, I make sure to quickly put my glass upside down on the table, spilling the rest out. There is no way I am taking a shot, especially from a random stranger. Victoria is so stupid to drink that. I watch her gulp it down. She has no idea if they put anything in there.

"You girls are definitely not from here," one of the guys slurs. "You are way too fucking hot to be from here."

I just smile at him. I don't think he really wants a response.

Victoria is having conversations with all of them, and they are eating it up. I am sure that each one of them is hoping to have a chance with her tonight.

I pull out my phone and see that Hudson has texted me.

Hope you two have a great time tonight. I can't wait till your warm body crawls in bed next to me later. Wake me when you get home.

I feel a pang of sadness. I would so much rather be there with him in that big warm bed, cuddled up next to his snugly body, but instead I am here with Victoria, who somehow managed to have yet another shot of a dark liquid in her hand. Everyone is staring at me now, and I notice there is one sitting in front of me.

"I have to use the lady's room."

I walk away from the table quickly.

I try to spend as much time in the bathroom as I can before it gets awkward. When I get back, Victoria is in full flirting mode now. She has both of her arms around two of the men and is telling them a story about when she was in college.

"You're back," she says cheerfully. "Take your shot, you're falling behind."

All the men start chanting for me to take the shot.

"No more shots, Victoria. We should really be getting ready to leave soon."

"No way, you girls just got here," one of the guys says. "Sit down and enjoy this beautiful evening."

I notice that I left my bottle of beer sitting on the table while I went to the bathroom. I am definitely not going to drink that now, and it's a good excuse to get away from this table again.

"I'm going to head up to the bar to get another beer," I say to Victoria.

"Get me one too," she replies.

How can this girl drink so much all the time? I'm sure that she is tipsy right now, but she seems to be fine. I would be on the floor if I had that much to drink.

One of the guys follows me to the bar. Great, just what I need. I was trying to get away from them. He slides in next to me close, way too close. He reeks of cigarette smoke.

"So, you're from Cincinnati, just here visiting for the weekend, I hear," the creep says to me, inches from my face. "What are you looking to get into tonight?"

I am disgusted by this guy's behavior. I don't even know how to reply to his statement. I know that I told Victoria that I would stay here with her, but I need to get her to leave. I don't answer him before walking back to the table.

I hand Victoria her beer. "After this, we have to go, okay?"

She doesn't respond to me. She is too busy talking to the guy without the ball cap. Their faces are so close together that I wonder if they are going to start kissing.

The creep that followed me to the bar comes back with more shots for the table. Instead of arguing about taking it again, I just pour it behind my head, hoping there is no one behind me.

My phone says that it's midnight now, and Victoria was right, this place does get wild. The bar is even more packed than it was an hour ago. The voices start to get louder, with everyone trying to talk over the blaring music, and I start to feel hot and can't breathe. I take deep breaths because I don't want to get too overwhelmed. All the guys that were at the table before have gone off somewhere, leaving Victoria with one of them. He must think she is a sure thing tonight. Sorry, bud, that is not happening.

I want to leave so badly, but no matter how many times I ask her, she keeps brushing me off. Fine, I will wait this out, but I will never, ever go out with her again. I sit there watching her and this guy. She is so sloppy right now, slurring all her words and laughing so loud at this guy's dumb jokes. She takes a drink of her beer and misses the table when she goes to set it down. It crashes down on the ground. I amuse myself by coining her Sloppy Victoria.

She gets up to leave, walking toward the bar.

"Where are you going?" I ask.

"I'm getting us some real drinks," she says.

"No, Victoria, we need to drink some water. I am not having any more drinks tonight. I'm going to order our Uber here in a few minutes."

"No, let's stay just a little bit longer. That guy is totally into you, and he's cute. You should go and talk to him some more."

I stand there disbelieving what she just said while I watch her walk up to the bar. Talk to that guy? What the fuck? She knows that I am dating her brother. Is this why she brought me here, to get me to flirt with other guys? Just when I thought we could make some progress. I am so pissed off right now; I just want to leave. I pull out my phone to order the Uber. I will drag her out of here by her hair if I must, but we are leaving.

The app keeps toggling over and over, trying to find a driver in my area. It finally comes up with no drivers available. Dammit, I completely forgot that it's Halloween and we might have a tough time getting home. I can just call Hudson. I really don't want to wake him up, but I'm sure he will understand, especially when I tell him that his sister is really drunk and she needs rescuing from these creepy guys.

Victoria gets back to the table and hands me a red solo cup with clear liquid. I am grateful that she has come to her senses and got some water for us to drink. It's so hot in here with all these people crammed in, so I take a large gulp and immediately spit it back into the cup.

Coughing, I say, "What is that?"

"Vodka." She smiles wickedly.

"I said *water,* Victoria."

I'm fuming now. It's obvious that the entire night she has tried to get me drunk and flirt with other guys. What if she tells Hudson that I was? I know that I haven't been, but what if that was her plan all along? It's not like she hasn't done other things like this. I wonder how Hudson is going to take it when she tells him we came to this bar and hung out with four guys the whole night. Will he understand that I was just there to appease his sister?

The Uber app finally connects me to a driver who is thirty-four minutes away. Fine, at least we have a ride. I can hold out for that long.

"The Uber is going to be here in a half an hour! I am going to go pay our tab and then we are going outside to wait!" I yell over the crowd at her.

She sits up straight and rolls her eyes at me, seemingly able to sober up quickly.

"Fine, whatever!"

"Hey, no, we are going to my house for the after party," the guy she has been hanging on all night says.

"I wouldn't come back to your house even if you paid me a million dollars," she tells him, and the guy looks taken aback by this comment.

I head to the bar to pay our tab. On my way up there the creep from before is next to me again.

"Hey, babe. Are you ready to leave soon?"

"What do you mean?" I ask him.

"Your friend over there told me that you needed a place to stay tonight."

"What else did she tell you?" I say, holding back my anger.

"She said you are looking for a hookup tonight. That you and your boyfriend just broke up and you wanted to get really wasted to find a guy to go home with. She even slipped me a fifty to keep the shots coming."

My body convulses with rage, and all I can see is red. I barely hear what the guy is saying to me anymore. She tried to set me up. She had this planned the entire time. She would have been perfectly fine tricking me into getting drunk and going home with this disgusting random guy.

He grabs my arm and shakes me momentarily out of my rage.

"She said you thought I was really hot."

I rip his hand off my arm. "Does it seem like I think you're hot?" I yell at him.

I order two more beers and pay the tab. I can use the buzz from the alcohol right now, so I don't lose my temper with Victoria. I chug half of it down before getting back to the table. I hand one to her.

"One last drink before we go. The Uber will be here in fifteen minutes."

We clink bottles, and she drinks hers fast like I do.

The guy is still trying to get her to come back to his place. I am watching my app, waiting to see when the driver pulls up in the parking lot.

Victoria starts slurring her words very badly. She leans her head down on the guy's shoulder and closes her eyes. He starts rubbing her leg and she doesn't stop him.

I shake my head at her and think, *Sloppy Victoria.* I pull up my camera and snap a few pictures of her like this. If she tries to say anything to Hudson about me, I will show her family exactly why I had to stay here with these men. To protect her.

The app tells me that the Uber has finally pulled up out front.

"Victoria, are you coming? The Uber is here."

She mumbles back, "Everything's fine, no leave yet."

"She will be fine here with me. I promise that I will take good care of her," the guy says.

That's it, then. I am done with this stupid game. I walk right out the door and get in the Uber alone.

32

Emily

When I get to the Bermans' cabin, it's completely still—as it should be since it's almost 1:30 in the morning. They left plenty of lights on for us to come home to. I tread as quietly as I can into the kitchen and pour a glass of water from the refrigerator. I stand there sipping it, breathing in and out over and over, slowly calming myself down after what has happened this evening.

I wait for fifteen minutes, then thirty. By the time an hour has passed, I see on the clock that it is 2:30 in the morning and the Barnyard has been closed for half an hour now, and Victoria never made it home.

I go upstairs and wake Hudson up.

"Hey babe," he says groggily. "How did it go?"

"Can you try and wake up, please? Something has happened and I'm really worried."

He sits up more alert, rubbing the sleep out of his eyes.

"What's wrong?"

"Victoria got really, really drunk tonight. She met some guy, and he kept bringing her shot after shot. I was trying to get her to slow down but she wouldn't listen to me." I pull out my phone and show him the photos I took of her. "She was all over this guy."

Hudson scans the photos and sighs deeply. "Victoria, Jesus Christ."

"I stayed there with her all night, hoping she would come to her senses. I only had one beer the entire time because I wanted to make sure she was okay. I just wanted to watch over her. I told her I was getting an Uber. She said she wasn't going to come with me. I begged her and begged her, and she wasn't being rational. She went outside with this guy to go smoke a cigarette, and I followed her out there, but there were so many people and I lost her. I think she may have left the bar with him. They were closing and kicking everyone out, so I had to leave."

Hudson is wide awake now. "Oh my god, I can't believe she did that to you."

"I told the Uber driver to speed home so I could wake you and tell you."

He pulls out his phone and calls her number. No answer.

"God dammit, Victoria! This is so typical of you. Always doing this kind of thing," he says angrily at her voice mail.

"What should we do?" I ask.

"You stay here. I am going to go and see if I can find her. Mom and Dad will be so upset if she doesn't come home tonight."

"No, I am coming with you."

He nods in agreement, and he gets up and puts his clothes on.

"Where were you guys at?"

"Some place called the Barnyard."

"Oh god. That is the last place you should have been at. That place is well known for all sorts of trouble."

Funny, Victoria said Hudson loved it there. I should have known she was lying.

We head back to the Barnyard. The parking lot is mostly empty by this time, with only a few people loitering around. Hudson tries the doors, but they are locked. He knocks as hard as he can. A large man, who I think was the bouncer, opens them.

"We are closed, man," he says.

Hudson asks him if there are any girls left inside the bar. He starts to describe her, and the man interrupts him.

"There's no one left here, dude," he replies, and closes the door.

We go back to the cabin. Hudson calls and texts Victoria several times. He finally throws his phone down on the bed, exhausted.

"Well, that's that. I at least tried."

"Do you think she's okay?" I ask.

"She's fine. I told you before, she does this kind of thing all the time. That's what led to all her problems last year. Getting drunk, making bad choices. That's just her MO."

"I'm so sorry, Hudson. I should have tried harder to make her come with me."

"No, stop; this is not your fault. I could tell that Victoria has been back to her old ways ever since she has been back. I know that her and Katie have gone out drinking around town almost every night. That's why I was keeping my distance from her. I didn't want to get caught up in all that. I didn't realize she would do this crap while we are here up at the cabin with Mom and Dad, though."

We talk for a while longer and doze off around 4 a.m. We get a few hours of sleep until the alarm goes off at 7 a.m. when Hudson is supposed to go golfing with his dad.

We get up and search the bedrooms, couch, and bathroom to see if Victoria came home while we were sleeping. She is nowhere to be found. Betty and Bob come downstairs chipper and alert, ready for the day even though it's early in the morning.

"Good morning, kids. I will get the coffee started. You're up awfully early, Emily. That's sweet you are up to see Hudson off."

I don't say anything. I let Hudson take the lead with this.

"We need to talk," he tells them.

She starts the coffee pot. It's a large silver and black contraption that looks like it could brew enough coffee for twenty people.

Hudson tells them the whole story from when he left me and Victoria at the bar last night, until now. Betty's face stays solid as she listens. This woman is clearly a strong person, and she doesn't seem to be surprised about Victoria's behavior. She doesn't even flinch. Bob, on the other hand, is pounding his hand on the table and cursing about Victoria.

Matt comes walking down the stairs looking well-rested from being home and in bed so early. He sees that we are all sitting at the table looking serious and hears Bob's outburst, and turns around to walk back up the stairs. *Smart guy,* I think.

"We should have put that girl in rehab when we had the chance!" he yells.

"Sweetheart," Betty says to me kindly, "are you okay?"

I am surprised that she is being so kind. I thought she would be angry with me.

I nod slowly.

"I knew that it was a bad idea for Hudson and Evelyn to leave you out with Vicky. That poor girl has no problem getting herself into trouble. I am just so thankful that you made it home safe." She puts her hand on mine and gives it a squeeze. "Now, may I please see these photos?"

I hesitantly pass over my phone and Betty looks at the photos.

"Okay, did she say anything else to you that might be helpful for us?"

I take a deep breath in. "She told me that she was having a really tough time with the divorce. She is sad that she hurt her husband so badly. It seems to be weighing heavily on her. That's probably why she was drinking so much last night."

"What do you mean, hurt her husband badly?" Hudson asks.

"Ya know, the reason they got divorced."

"What reason, dear?" Betty asks.

"The affair she had," I tell them.

Their faces all look aghast, even Betty's this time.

"I'm sorry, do you all not know? I thought that everyone knew why she was getting divorced. She talked to me about it quite a bit last night."

"It's okay, sweetheart, go on and tell us everything. It's important that we know so that we can try and help Vicky."

"She said that she hates herself for having an affair, and now Brent will never speak to her again, after he walked in and caught them. She didn't mean for it to go on for so long, but she was just so confused because they got married so quickly."

Hudson's face has now turned white.

"Who did she have an affair with?"

"I think she said his name was Brandon."

Shock roars all around the table. Bob slams his hand down again, making the entire table move about an inch. Hudson stands up and begins pacing back and forth in the kitchen.

"His own brother!" Hudson yells.

"Hudson, I am so sorry. I didn't know that you were not aware. I should not have said anything."

He comes back over to me and kneels to grab both of my hands.

"You have done nothing wrong. I am the one who needs to apologize. I should have never put you in that position last night."

Just then, Victoria walks through the front door, looking disheveled. Her hair is a mess, and her makeup is smeared down one side of her face. She walks slowly to the table as if waiting for her death sentence.

"What's wrong?" she says when she sees Hudson and her parents so upset.

"First of all, Brandon, Victoria? His own goddamn brother! And second, going home with some guy last night. How could you? We have been so worried about you. And what you did to Emily... She has been up all night, scared to death. We went looking for you and called you several times," Hudson says.

She just stands there completely stiff.

"My phone died," is all she says.

"I just want to know if you are okay," Betty says.

"Yes, I am fine," she answers.

Betty nods and then gets up and walks upstairs away from us, clearly disappointed with her daughter.

I don't make eye contact with Victoria. I am sure that what is happening is humiliating enough for her.

"I have no idea what the actual hell is going on with you, Victoria, but you need help—serious help," Hudson says.

"Well, I guess golf isn't happening today. We are going to have to have a family intervention to figure this out," Bob says, following Betty up the stairs.

"Can I please talk to Emily alone?" she asks Hudson.

He looks at me, and I nod in agreement. He leaves to go upstairs to give us some privacy. I brace myself for this conversation.

"What happened last night?" she asks.

I tell her the exact story that I told her family.

"After you started crying to me about your divorce and what happened, you went to go smoke a cigarette with that guy you were talking to all night, and that was the last I saw of you."

"That's great. I was smoking cigarettes too on top of everything else?" She sounds exhausted. "Well, I guess the cat's out of the bag. Now everyone knows what happened with Brent."

"I'm sorry, I had no idea that they didn't know. I was just trying to smooth things over about why you didn't come home. You told me last night that Brent had already told your family."

"Did I say anything else to you? If I did, please run it by me first before you say anything else to my family. I was completely out of my mind last night."

"If I think of anything, I will tell you first. Are you okay?"

"I'm fine, just really fucking hungover. I cannot believe I went home with that loser last night. Thank God he was nice enough to just put me to bed. I woke up with all my clothes on, so at least I have that going for me."

"I'm glad you're home safe. I was so worried about you," I tell her and walk upstairs to find Hudson packing up our things.

He rushes over and gives me a huge, long hug.

"Promise me that you are okay. This is not how I wanted this weekend to go at all."

"Hey, it's okay. I'm fine, I promise. Let's sit down." I lead him to the bed. "When I was growing up, my mother had a lot of issues with this very same thing. She didn't drink a lot, but she did have many different boyfriends. She let men treat her like dirt. It wasn't unusual for her to not come home at night. So, this doesn't bother me at all. I can handle it."

"You haven't shared much of your past with me. Thank you for telling me that. I want to know everything about you."

I kiss him long and hard after he tells me that. I wonder if I did share some things with him about my past, would he accept it? I don't want to ruin anything by telling him now. Maybe I will…at some point.

33

Victoria

Hudson and Emily left quickly after everything went down. Before I am allowed to leave the cabin, I agree to have a family intervention later this week when my parents come down to Cincinnati for Evelyn's birthday celebration. She was filled in harshly by our dad after she woke up. My parents and Evelyn don't want to hash it out now with the children being here. My mom wants to enjoy the last day with them.

"We need to come up with a strict plan to get things back on track, Victoria," my father said sternly. "There will be severe consequences for your actions last night."

On the three-hour-long drive home, I have plenty of time to think about what happened last night. How did everything go so wrong? It was Emily that was supposed to get drunk and go home with some guy, not me. That was stupid of me to try and do that in the first place. But for her to take those pictures of me? That was really low.

I am lucky that the guy I ended up with didn't take advantage of me being as drunk as I must have been. I don't even know what his name was. Waking up next to him this morning was the most humiliating thing ever. His bedroom was disgusting. Dirty clothing and dishes everywhere, pictures of half-naked women and cars on his walls, as if he was a dirtbag teenager. I still had all my clothing on, and he told me nothing happened. That I was out cold and "doing chicks that are passed out wasn't his thing." I still feel so dirty, nevertheless.

Leaving the room and walking through his house was even worse. Two of the other guys from the table at the Barnyard were there, sitting on the couch playing video games at seven in the morning as if they hadn't yet gone to bed from the night before. The looks and whistles they gave me as I hurried out of the house were mortifying.

The thing is, though, I don't remember being that drunk. I try to remember the events of the night and how many shots I had to drink. Maybe three shots and one full beer. I wasn't even drinking half of the shots the guys brought to the table, and I spilled most of the beer I was drinking on purpose. I was only having them bring them so that Emily could get drunk. Then suddenly, I was so out of it. Then I remember nothing. I don't remember telling Emily about Brent at all, and I certainly don't remember going outside to smoke cigarettes or leaving with that guy. What time of night was that at? Maybe just after midnight, closer to 1 a.m.? Hudson said the bar was closed when he went back to look for me. During that time must have been when all of that happened. I just can't figure out why I don't remember any of it. I would never in my right mind confide something like that to Emily or not come home to my parents' house. The only person I have ever told is Katie, and I can trust her with anything. I don't trust Emily at all. So why would I tell her one of my deepest secrets?

The realization that I could have possibly been drugged hits me hard. It makes perfect sense. I have blacked out plenty of times before while drinking, but never from a few shots. The guys were bringing drinks to the table. They could have slipped something into my drink very easily, but Emily wasn't drugged. She was perfectly fine to stay up and help Hudson search for me.

I would text her and ask her, but it's not like she would be honest with me.

After I get back to Cincinnati, I decide to stop at a store and get a drug test. The package says that it can test for fourteen different drugs, from marijuana to opiates.

When I get to my apartment, I fill the little cup with my urine, dip the stick in, and wait for the results. Bile fills my throat when I see that the test comes back positive for benzodiazepines. I don't even know what that is. I quickly search the internet for benzodiazepines and spiking drinks. Tons of articles come up about this particular drug being popular for what they call roofies and the date-rape drug. It's a tranquilizer that lowers inhibitions, causes blackouts, memory loss, unconsciousness, and the list goes on and on to the point where it could easily cause death if taken too much.

I knew that I wasn't just drunk. One of the assholes from the bar obviously put it in my drink. I feel so sick that I run into the bathroom and vomit. I stick my finger down my throat and try to vomit as much as I can to get it all out of my system. Which I know is futile, considering it's already in there from the test results.

I also google how long it will stay in your system. Mom and Dad are coming into town this week to go over a plan of action for my sobriety. They drug-tested me when I got the DUI. I can't tell them that I was drugged; they would never believe me. They would just assume I took this drug on purpose. They would most definitely ship me off to rehab. I just hope that this is all out of my system before they get here.

I can't believe that that guy drugged me. I should go back up to his house and bring the police or do something. I can't let him get away with it. What if it wasn't him, though? Wouldn't he have had his way with me while I was passed out? He didn't. I can tell from the way I feel that nothing sexual happened, and my clothes were still on. What if the person that did this is much closer to home? Could it have been Emily? Is she capable of drugging someone? I shudder uncontrollably. If this is true, what else is she capable of doing?

34

Victoria

"Of course I am still coming to your birthday celebrations this week, Evelyn. We have the spa tomorrow and dinner on Wednesday, right?" I ask Evelyn when she calls me to talk about what happened Saturday night.

"Yes, but I just don't want to do it if you are not feeling up to it. I know that everything that happened must be hard on you. I am not gonna lie, I am really disappointed at what you did, but I need to make sure that you are okay."

"I know you are, and I am going to get this all figured out, but I wouldn't miss your birthday for the world. I am okay. Mom and Dad want to put everything aside until after your birthday. Besides, a day at the spa with you and Mom for your birthday sounds amazing. I could really use that."

"And Emily," Evelyn says.

My stomach roils. "What? No, don't invite her. I want to just spend time with you and Mom. I just need my family right now."

"I know that you have something against Emily, but she is a nice girl, and Hudson is completely in love with her, so it's likely she will become a part of our family soon, Vic. I want to include her. Besides, Mom told me to invite her so I already did, and she is excited to come."

Of course, no one seems to be mad at poor helpless Emily after Saturday's incident. She is just the victim that got caught in the crossfire of my problems. That's what my dad said to me on Sunday. And my mom, well, she is just smitten with her. She couldn't stop talking about her. I thought for sure they would be able to see what I see. It's so frustrating that I can't get rid of this girl.

"Hudson is not in love with her. They haven't even been dating that long, and he is not the type to fall into something like that so easily. She will probably be out of the picture by the end of the year. It's probably one of those cuffing things."

"What is cuffing?"

"It's when you get together with someone over the winter, so you have someone to spend the holidays with. Then it's over like it never happened."

"I don't know, I disagree. But can you just play nice for now?"

"No problem, Evelyn," I say with my fakest voice. "I will be there tomorrow, and I promise to play nice."

I will show up with a happy face. There is no way I am going to let Emily know that this has upset me whatsoever. This will also give me a chance to get the information I was trying to gather before. Maybe a clue to her past. Maybe I can find out if she is the one who somehow drugged me.

35

Emily

"Thank you so much for inviting me," I tell Evelyn as I give her the gift that Hudson and I picked out for her birthday. "I have to admit that I have never been to a day spa before."

"Then I am thrilled to be the first to bring you to one. We do this every year for my birthday. You are going to love it. Manicures, pedicures, facials, and massages. A whole day of drinking wine and being pampered. My favorite thing ever. Mom and Victoria should be getting here in a little bit, but I am glad you are here early. I really wanted to talk to you alone."

"Is everything okay?" I ask.

"Yes, I just wanted to apologize for Saturday night. I hate that you got caught up in that."

"No, I am the one who should apologize," I say. "I feel awful. I haven't been able to shake it off since it happened. I was really surprised when you invited me here today. I thought for sure everyone was mad at me."

"You did nothing wrong at all, Emily. We were all so glad that you were there. Lord knows what might have happened if you hadn't been. I am just happy that you are in our lives. I really hope that someday I can call you my sister."

I beam with happiness when she says this to me. I have never had any siblings, and having a sister would be so amazing.

Victoria and Betty walk into the spa, and we all greet each other nicely, even Victoria. She seems perfectly fine, as if nothing had happened, but I can tell it's all a big show she is putting on for everyone.

"Sorry we are late, sweetheart," Betty says to Evelyn. "We had to stop by our auto shop to have them look at Victoria's car and they took a little too long."

"What's wrong with your car?" Evelyn asks Victoria.

"Someone keyed it," she says, looking directly at me.

I know that she has probably considered the possibility of it being me, but she would never be able to prove it.

"Oh my god, that's awful. Where were you at?" Evelyn says.

"The grocery store by my new apartment," Victoria lies.

"Okay, noted. I will not be shopping there,"

Victoria is a horrible liar, or at least I can tell she is. Her mom and sister seem to believe her, but I know the truth.

The day is so wonderful. We get all the different treatments the spa has to offer. I can't believe I have never done anything like this before. I will most definitely be coming back more often. I feel more relaxed than I ever have in my life. We are all sipping white wine and chatting during our last spa service, our pedicures, when I notice that Victoria has a huge scar on her forearm. I never noticed it before, but now that I think about it, she is always wearing long sleeves.

"My goodness, what happened to your arm?" I ask.

"It's just a little road rash from a biking accident last year," she replies.

"Did you ever get that cream I told you about for scars?" Betty asks her.

"Yes, I did, and I tried it and many other creams. Nothing works for it. I saw a doctor who said there is a procedure they can do that will make it less noticeable. I am considering having it done."

I stare at the scar and realize that she is lying again. That is not road rash from falling off a bike; that is a burn from a fire. I can tell by the way it has bubbled the skin. I know very well because my mother had an awful burn like that on her leg. We had a small fire in our apartment when I was little. I wonder why she has made up a different story. She said last year, so it must have been something that happened when she was having all her troubles.

"Emily, you said that you were from Missouri, right? Whereabout?" Victoria asks.

"St. Louis. I lived downtown with Mom until I was fourteen. Then she got married and we moved out into the suburbs."

"What made you come to Cincinnati?" Victoria asks.

"After my parents died, I didn't have anything left to stay there for. I just really needed a change of scenery."

"I am so sorry to hear about your mother and your stepfather, Emily. It must have been hard to lose them so close together—and losing both of them to cancer is just so tragic," Betty says. "Hudson told me all about it. I hope that was okay."

"Thank you. It was rough, but I know that my mother is still watching over me."

"What about your stepfather? Isn't he watching over you?" Victoria asks in a bitchy tone.

"Victoria!" Evelyn barks at her. "What is your problem?"

"It's okay," I say to Evelyn. If Victoria wants to come at me yet again, I have plenty of ammunition to fight back with. "No, not my stepfather. We weren't really on speaking terms when he got sick. When my mother was battling breast cancer, he began having affairs with many different women. I was the only one that took care of her while she was sick. Maybe if he wasn't cheating, she might have had more strength to make it through, but that wasn't the case. Infidelity ruins so many people's lives."

"Didn't you have any friends that you wanted to stay there for? You mentioned a boyfriend to me before. What happened to him?"

I can tell that Victoria is obviously fishing for more information like before.

"I had a boyfriend, but we broke things off, and that was the end of that. There was nothing left in St. Louis for me anymore."

"You said that you had family money. Where did that come from?" Victoria asks.

Evelyn and Betty are looking at each other wide-eyed, not knowing what exactly is going on here, why Victoria is speaking to me like this.

"When my stepfather died, there was a life insurance policy through his work."

"Lucky for you," Victoria scoffs.

"That's about enough of that, Victoria." Betty scolds her. "I am not going to sit here and listen to you interrogate Emily."

I look up at her and see a fire in her eyes directed right at Victoria. I didn't even see that from her on Sunday when she came home from that guy's house.

She sits back in her chair quietly, heeding her mother's warning. When I look up a few moments later, she is smirking at me.

※

Later that night, the celebration for Evelyn's birthday continues back at her house. This time everyone is there—their whole family, along with some of their friends and children. They have dinner catered in and a hired bartender to make drinks.

Evelyn gets dressed up in a gorgeous ankle-length emerald-green dress. She looks beautiful and seems to glow with happiness.

Hudson has his arm around me all night and keeps kissing me on the cheek. Every time I look over at Betty, I see that she is staring at me and smiling, and she keeps winking at me. I find this funny and wonder if she has had too much to drink.

"I am just so impressed with what a driven young woman you are. Already at such a young age, you own your own home and your own business. Soon I am hoping that you will receive more good news," she says to me.

"What news?" I ask.

"I am hoping that maybe soon you and Hudson might be the next to get married."

She winks at me again, and now I know the wine has gone to her head. Hudson and I are nowhere near talking about marriage. I don't even want to get married. I don't believe that is something everyone should do to commit to each other. You can have a perfectly happy, long relationship without the piece of paper.

"It's just such a shame about Victoria and Brent, but I guess I always knew they wouldn't make it. Just a feeling I had. After Vicky went through all that last year, with drinking and the DUI, then the fire, I thought that maybe she latched on to Brent, thinking he would save her."

"The fire?" I ask.

"Yes, that fire that was in your building last year. Brent used to live there on the second floor, back when the second floor was all one big apartment. Victoria was house-sitting for him while he was out at his office in California. He went for a few weeks getting everything ready for them to move there. She wasn't there on the night the fire happened. Thank the Lord for that, but I know that it scared her badly. Who knows if she had been in that apartment what could have happened. I say a prayer thanking God every night that she went on that biking trip."

"I wasn't aware that anyone was around when the fire happened. Did anyone get hurt?" I ask.

"The business downstairs was closed. It was the middle of the night, and the firemen were able to rescue all the people on the third floor. There was a little boy that lived up there who had some burns but nothing major. The fire hadn't spread much beyond the second floor before they were able to put it out. But that second floor was not in good condition; they had to renovate the whole thing. That might be why she is so hard on you. I don't think she has healed from all her trauma. But don't you worry, our family is going to make sure she is well taken care of this time."

"I am sure that you will, Betty. You're an amazing mother."

"Is that how she got that scar on her arm? From the biking trip?"

"Yes, that's the one. She had gone away for a few days with some of her friends down to Hocking Hills to do a two-day bike ride and had fallen off her bike."

I would bet a million dollars that Victoria was actually there the night of the fire and not in Hocking Hills. She lies about everything, and there is that horrible burn on her arm that she is lying about. She said that she got it during that biking trip, which just so happens to have taken place at the same time as the fire. But why would she lie? That's the big question.

We all head into the dining room to sit and have some after-dinner drinks with the adults while the kids are all playing a game in the family room.

"Has anyone seen the weather reports for next week? Looks like we are going to be getting quite a bit of snow," Betty says.

"I saw that too," Matt says, "and already so early in the year. It's only the beginning of November."

"Well, I am perfectly fine with that. I absolutely love a good snowy winter," Hudson says excitedly.

"Me too, I love the snow. I loved going out and playing in the snow every winter when I was a kid," I say.

"I didn't realize they had a lot of snow in St. Louis," Victoria says suspiciously.

I change the subject quickly. She is trying to bait me into a fight again.

"Did Brent used to have a pool table?" I ask out loud as if I am just making casual conversation.

"Yes, why?" Victoria asks worriedly.

"Just wondering because the pool sticks are still there at my building. Betty was just telling me that Brent lived in that apartment. I have always wondered where the pool sticks came from."

"What do you mean the pool sticks are still there?"

Victoria seems very worried now. I decide to push things a little further.

"There was a bunch of stuff still there. Boxes, furniture, and some other stuff they salvaged from the fire. It was all still in my storage unit when I got the keys."

"How much stuff?" She really seems worried now.

"A whole storage unit is full." That's an exaggeration, but I want to see how she reacts. "That is such a blessing that you weren't there that night. All that stuff reeked of smoke. You could have gotten smoke inhalation or, worse, burned. The funny thing about fire is that it will burn some things and not others. Apparently, there was asbestos in the building, so it didn't all burn to the ground. There were lots of things that remained that hadn't even been touched by it, while others had only been charred. I assumed since the pool table wasn't there that it had been burnt all up."

She just stares at me, blinking her eyes. I can tell that her mind is going in circles trying to figure out what to say.

"I should come by and go through all that stuff. It's the least I can do for Brent. I know that there might be some things he would have wanted."

"Oh, they came and took it all away to the dump weeks ago."

"All of it?" she asks suspiciously.

"Every last bit," I say, smiling.

36

Victoria

I need to get into that storage room. There was something in Emily's eyes that told me she was lying about the things going to the dump. Was she smiling at me strangely? Does she know anything? There's no way she could. But I need to be sure. I need to see if there is anything left in the storage unit.

I excuse myself from the party. I tell everyone that I need to get an early night's sleep because first thing in the morning I am getting started searching for a rental for my business.

"That's wonderful, sweetheart. You are going to find something great, I just know it. Are you coming to the jeweler's with me and Evelyn tomorrow? I brought everything down with me that I needed polished, and I can take your bracelet as well."

"No, Mom, I don't think I will make it tomorrow. I have a busy day," I tell her, trying to get out of Evelyn's before Hudson and Emily leave.

"Just leave your bracelet with me. I will take it in for you."

I take off my bracelet without thinking too much about it and give it to my mom quickly.

I ask Hudson if he is staying for a while longer. I tell him I don't want to leave if everyone else is too, for Evelyn's sake. He assures me that he and Emily are having so much fun and they intend to be there a little while longer.

Because of Her

I race over to Plum Street and walk up to the building. I quickly type in Brent's code, hoping that it will still work. It doesn't. Dammit. I push the buttons for all the apartments, and I only get one answer. I try to convince the lady on the other end to buzz me in. I tell her that I forgot my key. She rudely tells me no and doesn't answer again when I buzz her back. That's fine; I wouldn't have been able to get into any of the storage units anyway. I guess I hadn't thought this out well enough.

I try to think of how I can get in there. I remember that I still have a key to Hudson's house. I don't think that he would have changed the locks, but it's worth a try to see if there is a set of keys for the building in his house.

I head over to his house and thankfully, my key still works. I go inside thinking maybe Emily's keys will be there or perhaps Hudson will have a set. It's a long shot, but I need to try. I look around anywhere for a purse or a set of keys.

I am really bummed when I don't find any, but I do notice that a lot of her things are here. Half his closet is her clothing, her toiletries are in the bathroom, and a hot pink yoga mat. Yuck, they must really be getting closer. It disgusts me that the house I decorated is now riddled with her things.

There is a computer sitting on his kitchen table. I don't recognize it, and it can't be Hudson's because it has flower stickers that are stuck on there. This must be Emily's computer. I open the lid, and when the computer boots up, I expect there to be a screen for you to enter a passcode. There isn't; it automatically goes to what she was looking at the last time she used it, which is her Facebook account.

I almost pinch myself thinking that I just hit the jackpot. I start scrolling through all her messages. There must be something in here. I don't know how much time I have, and I don't know if the two of them are coming here or going out to her house. I assume it's here since her computer is here.

I scroll and look at only what's important. All the messages are just people inquiring about her furniture pieces. Her notifications are all the same as well, all about her furniture. There are no notifications from anyone personal. No friends, no family, nothing that helps me. I check her search history and it's long. She seems to look up a lot of local restaurants, coffee shops and bars, antique shops, thrift stores, and a few people's names that I don't recognize. There are too many places to look through. I take out my phone and screenshot all of her search history. Maybe, just maybe, I can find a clue about her past from this search history.

I start to worry that I have been here too long. I abandon my hopes of finding the keys. They aren't here. She probably has them with her in her purse. I am not going to worry much about it. She said that they took all the stuff to the dump. What reason would she have to lie about that? She doesn't know anything about Brent or what happened in that apartment. No one does.

I race home and begin typing in the different names she was searching on Facebook. There is someone named Patricia Panchak, then after that, there is a Jay Panchak. I type his name into Facebook and it's not hard to find him. Panchak is not a common last name. A picture of a handsome guy in his mid-twenties comes up. He has light brown hair and bright eyes. Emily definitely has a type, it seems. He looks a lot like Hudson. His location says he is in Naperville, Illinois. I wonder if this is her ex-boyfriend. Why would she be searching for this guy? But that can't be right because she said she came here from Missouri. Unless she was lying.

I scroll down his page and am shocked to see all of the posts.
My prayers go out to you and your family.
I hope that you can make a quick recovery.
I miss you so much.
What a tragedy.
Jay was such a beautiful soul.

Because of Her

I notice that there are several posts directing you to a fundraiser page. I click on it and get directed to a page where you can donate money to the ongoing care for Jay Panchak. There is a short story about what happened to him. Apparently, he was home visiting his family on the winter break from his college earlier this year and had gotten into a horrible car accident that left him paralyzed and brain-damaged. According to the fundraiser page, he was in a coma for several months and now will be cared for by his mother and father. Any donations are greatly appreciated due to the high cost of his medical treatment.

I google his name and Naperville, Illinois. A few news articles come up about his car accident. I see the date of the crash. It was January 5th, which would have been right before Emily moved here to Ohio. My mind starts to whirl. There is something here, I just know it. If this was her boyfriend, she never mentioned anything about him being in a car accident. She said that he was abusive mentally.

I go back to the Facebook page. There are pictures of him in a wheelchair at a park, at an aquarium with friends and family, and many other places. He doesn't look anything like the profile photo that pops up. He has been through a lot of changes since the accident.

I scroll back month after month until before the accident. He was full of life and vibrant, with tons of photos of him at parties with lots of friends. There are a lot of photos of him and many different girls before his accident, but there is one girl that is not only in the photos before the accident but also after it. It's not Emily; it doesn't look anything like her, and this girl's name is Simone. I go to her page and read her posts. She also has a bunch of stuff posted about him and how close they were.

I scour each photo looking for Emily and don't see a single picture of her. I check all the tagged photos, and nothing there either. I check his friends list for her and her business name, and it's not listed. Damn, another brick wall. It's like everything is just on the surface. I know there is something lurking in there, I just can't get down to it.

It is getting late, and my head is killing me from all this drama over the last week. A good night's sleep will help me come up with some new ways to figure this all out. I change my clothes into my pajamas and climb into my bed.

I grab my computer and go to the fundraiser page one last time. Jay's parents' names are listed as the contacts for the fundraiser. Their phone number and address are also listed as well.

The page refreshes itself and a notification pops up showing that ten people just donated. I click on the icon; there is a list of all the names of people that have donated money. I scroll down the list. There are a lot of people who gave money to this guy. Most of the donations are small—ten or twenty dollars—and some are quite large, like five hundred dollars. I freeze when I see the name next to one of the larger donations. It's the name of the LLC that Emily bought her house with. She donated five hundred dollars to Jay's family. Why would she do that? I keep scrolling and see another large donation with the same, then another.

This is him. This is her ex-boyfriend, and they aren't from Missouri. They are from Illinois. I know it. I can feel it in my bones. Even though there are no pictures of her, he could have deleted them when they broke up. She said it was a bad breakup. That means that she was lying. She isn't from Missouri.

I go to the People Finder website and put in her name and Illinois, and several names come up with females around her age, but none that are twenty-two. I don't bother to go through them. I don't even know if that is her real name or her real age. She was probably lying about all that too. What else is she lying about?

I grab my phone and dial Hudson's number. It's 11 o'clock; they might still be at Evelyn's, but it's not too late to call him.

37

Emily

Victoria is definitely lying about something. I can't be sure if she was involved with the fire, but I will find out. She was very concerned about the fact that there were still some things from Brent's old apartment in my storage locker.

After the party I tell Hudson that I need to head to my store for just a little bit.

"It's crunch time and I need to get a few things done tonight, but you head back to your house and get into bed and wait for me. I won't be long. When I get there, I will put on something special that I bought the other day just for you."

"Oh, yeah?" His face lights up. "I will be waiting, so hurry up."

When I get to the store, I go to the storage area in the basement. All the boxes are still down here. I put the furniture to good use but never got around to throwing out the rest, and now I am glad I didn't.

When I start opening the boxes, the smell of smoke hits me hard. I understand why Brent didn't want any of it. None of this could possibly be salvageable. The first box was just a bunch of old music CDs and DVDs, and I find the balls from the pool table in there as well. The other boxes contain a lamp, some art, wine glasses, and a bunch of other random apartment items.

The last box I come to has a bunch of board games in it, and that's it. I feel defeated that there wasn't anything in here that would make her worried like she was. I know that there might have been something because of the way she responded when I told her about the boxes. I will come back tomorrow and give a more thorough look. I go to close the box when I see the silver metal spiral from a notebook sticking out of one of the board game boxes. It has been wedged inside there. I open the box and pull it out. It's a blue notebook with lined wide ruled paper inside.

The edges of it are charred from the fire, but when I open it, I can still see the writing inside. The first several pages are sentences that had been written with a pen then scratched out so violently that the paper is ripped in places. I try to read what was written underneath the scratches and tears but it's illegible. I keep flipping through the pages until I come to writing that hasn't been scratched out.

Monday August 4th

Hudson I am writing this letter that will never find its way to you. I want to put all my feelings down on paper so that I can hopefully get it out of my system. I can't keep living like this. It's tearing me up inside. The thing is, Hudson, I am in love with you, and I have been for a very long time. You are what I think of the first thing when I wake up in the morning, and the last thing before I go to bed at night. I know that you love me too. I can see it in your eyes when we are together. I just know that it's true. You date all those other girls just to get me out of your head, but I also know that you will never act on the love that you have for me because of the connections we have with the family.

Was this written by Brent? I wonder.

Did he have a thing for Hudson? Their families were connected. Maybe that's what he's writing about.

I turn the page and read the next letter. It's the same type of letter, just with slightly different variations. This one says that they should tell their family and make them understand that they will have to live with the idea of it because they are in love.

On the next page another letter says that they should run away together and never tell anyone what they are up to. Until they come back years from now and their family must accept it.

Then on the last page it says, *I am an idiot for thinking that this could ever be real between us. No one would ever accept the love that we have for each other because we are bound by family even though we are not blood related. The alcohol has made me brave to put all of this out there in the universe and helped me to finally say what I have always been thinking. Now I can let it go. I can put it all in the past. I am going to marry Brent and move with him to Los Angeles and forget about you forever. I will not come back to see you or call you. No one will ever see these letters because I am going to burn them. Love, Victoria.*

"Oh, my fucking god," I say way too loudly in the tiny storage room. My voice reverberates all over the walls, bouncing back to me.

I quickly google *322 Plum Street and fire* and click on the first article about the night the fire happened. I quickly scan the article, and there it is. The date of the fire was Monday, August 4th last year. The same night she wrote these letters.

Oh, Victoria, I think maliciously to myself. *Now I know why you hate me so badly. It's because you have a sick incestual fantasy about your brother. And it turns out you are the one who started the fire. Of course, Sloppy Victoria was too drunk to set the notebook on fire properly. You were never on some biking trip, and that scar on your arm isn't from road rash. I was right all along; it's a burn from a fire. The one you set. You are much sicker than I thought you were. I will go ahead and keep this notebook somewhere safe. I am sure it will come in handy someday soon.*

38

Victoria

Hudson finally answers after I call him three times and send a text that says *911!*

"Victoria, what's wrong?" he answers, concerned.

"I need to talk to you right now. It's an emergency. Where are you?"

"Now is not a good time, Vic. I'm in bed."

"Is Emily with you?"

"No, she had some things to take care of. She will be here later."

"Where are you?" I say in a more urgent tone.

"My house."

I hang up and grab my keys and my computer. I don't bother to change out of my pajamas. I head straight to Hudson's house.

He is waiting at the door when I get there ten minutes later. I walk right past him into his house.

"Is she here?" I ask.

"No, I told you she will be back later."

"Good, I need to talk to you in private. Emily has been lying to you, and to everyone." I am gasping for breath, trying to get my words out.

"Vic, calm down. What the hell is going on?"

"Emily is not from Missouri. She is from Illinois, somewhere around the Chicago area." I pull out my computer and show him what I have found. "She said that she left Missouri because her parents died and then she had an abusive boyfriend, right?"

"Yeah, I know. What's the point here?"

"Look at this. I am sure that this is her ex-boyfriend. His name is Jay Panchak. He got into a horrible car accident that left him paralyzed and brain-dead."

I scroll down the page and show him all the posts on his Facebook page since his accident in January.

"Again, Victoria, what's your point?"

"Look at his location. He isn't from Missouri. He's from Naperville, Illinois. I think that she has been lying about where she is from and why she left."

"Hudson?" a female voice says from right behind me. I was too absorbed in showing him what I found that I didn't hear Emily walk in.

"You need to hear this too, Emily. I know all about you now. All your lies."

"Yes, I heard what you said, Victoria."

"Do you know who this guy is, Emily?" Hudson asks her.

"Yes, I do," she says.

"See, I told you. She has been lying all along. You're not even from Missouri, are you? You lied about your ex-boyfriend being abusive. He was in an accident and maybe you were even involved somehow. I know that you are hiding from something. That's why you used an LLC and have no trail on the internet of who you are. There is also the house where she lives in, Hudson. Did you know people were murdered there?" I recite everything that I know. I can't stop now.

Hudson looks mortified. He looks to me and then to Emily.

"Wait, let's just calm down. This is a lot to take in. What is she talking about?" he asks Emily.

"First of all, that is not my ex-boyfriend. And why would you think that, Victoria?"

"Yeah, why would you think that?" Hudson mimics her.

I didn't think this all the way through before rushing over here, but if all the lies are going to be laid out on the table, then I need to come clean also. Hudson will be mad at first, but once she is long out of the picture, he will thank me.

"I did my research. You're my little brother, and from the beginning, strange things were happening that surrounded Emily. So, I went online and searched her name, but I couldn't find anything except the fact that she bought her house and rented her store with an LLC. Then I saw all the news articles related to the address she lives at. A man murdered his wife and then killed himself in the bedroom."

"What makes you think this guy was her ex-boyfriend?" Hudson asks me again.

"I was here earlier, and I saw her computer on your kitchen counter. I knew something was going on, so I had to look in it. Her Facebook page was open, and I looked at her search history. I saw the name Jay Panchak. So, I went home and looked him up."

"You snooped on my personal computer?"

Emily looks angry now, but she is not going to get away with this.

"Earlier tonight?" Hudson says, confused.

"Yes. I am sorry, Hudson, but I had to. Ask her about Jay."

"That is not my ex-boyfriend, Victoria. My ex-boyfriend's name is Mitchell, and he doesn't live in Illinois. He lives in Missouri."

"You can lie all you want, but I know for a fact that this is your ex because you donated 500 dollars several different times over the last five months to his family through their fundraiser page."

She stands there quietly, staring at me. Now I know that I have got her.

"Victoria," she speaks to me condescendingly, "I found that guy's page while I was searching for antique stores that I might be able to purchase furniture from. If you have photos of my search history, you will see that his family's antique store is also there. It's located in the same town you mentioned, Naperville. While I was looking to see if they had some pieces for sale, I noticed there was a fundraiser post for their son Jay. I clicked on his page and read about what happened to the poor guy, and I decided to donate some money to their family. That's why his name was in my search."

"You must think I am so dumb, Emily. If you don't know him or his family, then why would you donate five hundred dollars several different times? I saw it on the fundraising page. You donated it under the name of the LLC company that you made up. Also, his accident happened right before you moved here. That's not just a coincidence."

"Because you see, Victoria, unlike you, I like to use the money I got from the tragedy of my parents' deaths for good use. I would rather help other people out. Not just blow it all on alcohol, expensive apartments and cars, and fucking my husband's brother."

"You are lying, Emily, and everyone is going to see right through it!" I scream at her.

"Alright, I have heard just about enough!" Hudson screams back at me. "What in the actual fuck is going on with you, Victoria? You broke into my house, trespassed on Emily's computer, and now you're accusing her of all this bullshit! You have completely lost your mind!" Hudson is yelling loudly at me now. I have never heard him so angry in my life.

"I didn't break in. I have a key. Hudson, since she has been in your life, all this weird stuff keeps happening. She keyed my car and wrote a nasty note threatening my life, and I am pretty sure that she drugged me."

"Drugged you?" he says, exasperated.

"Halloween night, when I didn't come home. I didn't tell anyone this, but I knew that something wasn't right. You know I would never do something like that. So, I took a drug test, and it was positive for benzodiazepines, which I didn't take. Someone slipped it to me in a drink."

"Victoria, I would never *ever* do anything like that to you or anyone. I wouldn't even know what that drug is you are talking about. As for keying your car and writing a death threat, that's insane. This is absurd. Hudson is right, you have lost your mind." She turns to him. "Listen, I didn't want to tell you this before, but now that I am hearing she has been online stalking me, I think you should know she is also stalking me in person. Last week, the night that we met with her at the Irish bar, I saw her. She was pulling out of my driveway."

"That's the night that she keyed my car," I blurt out. Now I am finally getting somewhere. "She must have seen me and followed me to the market by her house; that's where I found the note on my car."

"You told Evelyn that happened at the grocery store by your new apartment, so I know that you are lying, Victoria," Hudson says.

"No, I just didn't want to tell you that I was out in Aurora that day. You lied to me about having to go to the art studio. I went there and you never showed up. Then I read about the murder at her house, and I needed to see for myself."

"You know what, I'm done. Give me back the key to my house right now and get out. You are not welcome here anymore. I have tried to help you since you have been back, but you are determined to fuck up your life once again. Emily has done nothing but try to be your friend. She didn't drug you Halloween night. If you had drugs in your system, it was because you took them yourself or the douchebag you went home with put them in your drink. How dare you accuse her. You need help, Victoria, serious help that we can't give you."

"Hudson, please listen to me. Check her driver's license. I bet Emily Lewis isn't even her real name because every time I search it online, nothing comes up."

"I was at the DMV with her, and I heard them call out her name! You have completely gone insane. No, no more listening, and I don't want to speak to you again until you get your shit together. You might choose to downward spiral and throw your whole fucking life away, but you will not take me or Emily down with you. All you do is complain about how things have been so hard because of the divorce, but ya know what? It's your own fault. You shouldn't have cheated on your husband."

"I am not leaving until you listen to me. She is dangerous," I plead with him.

"Victoria, you need to go home right now. If you push me too far, I will call the police."

Before I know it, I am standing on Hudson's front porch with the door slamming behind me. I cannot believe that he just spoke to me like that! He wouldn't even listen to me at all. Emily is obviously lying about everything. Why can't he see that?

39

Emily

Hudson rushes over and wraps his arms around me.

"I am so sorry that just happened. She is completely delusional. I am going to call my family first thing in the morning and let them know all about this. I don't want to ruin Evelyn's birthday by calling now, but we are going to have to take some drastic actions. My parents are going to need to get her some serious help."

"Hudson, I have no idea what she is talking about—death threats, vandalism, drugs? I don't understand any of that. This Jay person was honestly just someone I was trying to help."

"Stop, you don't have to explain anything. I know none of that is true."

"Actually, there is one thing that is true…" I hesitate, not sure if I should tell him about what happened at the house. But I have to. He could easily look that up online.

"Go on."

"It's about my house. There were deaths there."

"What do you mean?"

"She was right about that, but only that part. About a year and a half ago, the elderly couple that lived there died. They were tragic deaths, and the news articles portrayed it to be gruesome, so I do understand why that might have been alarming to Victoria."

I explain the history of the couple Sam and Martha, the orchards, the market, and the house to him.

"When they died, they had no one to leave it all to. No children, only a sister, and she was so distraught about what had happened, she put everything up for sale quickly. When I bought the house, I knew about the tragedy. My real estate agent told me all about it, and I looked up the news stories. The husband drowned his wife in the bathtub and then shot himself in the head. Everyone thought that he went mad, that he was suffering from dementia. They made it sound horrible. But that wasn't true.

"A few months after I moved in, I found some letters in a cabinet. The first few letters said that Martha had been sick for a long time. When they got the diagnosis that she was terminal and only had a short time left to live, they knew that it was time for them to go the way they wanted to go. They had discussed many ways to end their lives, but Martha was so sick and scared, she didn't have the strength to end her own life. The last letter was from Bill right before he took his own life. He ran her a bath and gave her extra doses of her sleeping medicine and cried while he watched her sink down into the tub and fade away. She didn't have to suffer. He said in the letter it was so heartbreaking that he wasn't even scared to do what came next. He must have hidden the letters in the cabinet before.... Well, you know the rest."

Hudson's eyes are wet with tears. "Wow, that's really heartbreaking."

"I am sorry that I never told you about it. I have never told anybody about it except his sister. That poor couple's name had been dragged through the mud for a long time. Bill's sister had a really tough time with it all. She begged me to keep it a secret."

He wraps his arms around me so tight, and I breathe him in deeply. His scent, which I have grown so accustomed to, alleviates all my worries. I sink into his arms, feeling safe the way I fit so perfectly in them.

"It's okay, I understand that completely."

"You're not mad that I didn't tell you?"

"No, not at all. It's not like you lied about it. You just weren't ready to trust in me yet. There are things that I haven't told you, but now I want to tell you everything. I want to share everything in my life with you. I had a girlfriend before I met you. Her name is Samantha. Things ended up badly between us, and I had to end it. Since then, she has been stalking me, and I even had to take out a restraining order against her."

I think about the so-called Chloe that I saw outside his house, then on the sidewalk in front of my store, and the time she came to my house. Now I know how she got to my house that day. It wasn't a coincidence at all; she must have followed me from Hudson's that night. I don't tell him any of this. I don't want to make him think I'm hiding anything. I am certainly not telling him I had already seen him a few times before we met.

"She didn't have any family or friends, so I felt kind of bad about the breakup, but she was doing so many crazy things, and honestly, I just wasn't in love with her."

"What was she doing?" I ask him.

"There were a lot of lies that she told. I kept catching her in them left and right. The last straw was when she told me that she had to leave her apartment and needed to stay with me for a while—something about her landlord selling the building—but I found out that wasn't true at all. She was living in her car. I just couldn't handle all the deceit and lying."

"Do you still see her around?"

"I haven't for a little while now. I am hoping that she has come to her senses and moved on."

"It's okay. We will deal with that together if she shows back up. We have each other now."

He stands up and tells me that he wants to check his house to see what else Victoria could have gotten into.

"I am so glad that what happened with my sister isn't scaring you off," he says to me before heading upstairs.

Victoria is so sloppy about everything. She just barged in here acting crazy with no real proof about anything. None of this would have happened if she would have just left me alone, but she can't get over her disgusting incestual feelings toward her brother. She is never going to have him. She will just have to realize that me and Hudson are going to be happy together no matter what. She can't stop it now.

I guess if she knew that Emily was short for Amelia, she might have been able to learn some things about me online, but I doubt she will be able to figure that out. I was going to tell Hudson that Emily was just a nickname, but now I will just have to change it legally to Emily. I had already thought about doing that before. I looked into it, and it's a very simple process. My mother never used my real name. I don't know why she gave it to me in the first place if she was always going to call me Emily. I started going by Amelia after she died, thinking it would change who I was, and I couldn't bear for anyone to use the nickname my mother called me. After I came here, it just seemed right to go back to Emily. After all, I could feel my mother watching over me all the time.

40

Victoria

I don't care what my brother said, I am not going to go home. I am going to do whatever I need to do to prove that this bitch is a liar. I need to act quickly. I don't know what she is capable of. She could drug Hudson or hurt him somehow. Especially now that she knows I am on to her. She swears she didn't do any of those things, but I know that she did.

I put the address to the Panchak residence that I found on the fundraiser page into my Maps app on my phone. It's about five and a half hours away from here, just outside of Chicago. If I leave now, I will arrive around 5 a.m. I can get a room and sleep a little before going to their house.

I get on the road right away. I don't stop at home to pack any personal belongings even though I still have my pajamas on. I am only going to be there a short while. I will get everything I need there.

Hudson's words were way too harsh. I cannot believe that he would talk to me like that and that he would choose Emily's side over mine. He didn't even listen to anything I had to say. I need to get to the bottom of this, and I can't stop until I do. There's a dark, ominous cloud over this whole situation. Everything in my entire being is screaming at me that something is wrong, very wrong.

I go to touch my bracelet and panic when I don't feel it on my wrist. I search around the floor of my car, trying to see if it might have fallen off. Damnit, I forgot that I gave it to my mom to take to the jeweler's. I was in such a rush to leave that I didn't even think about it. I really wish that I hadn't done that.

An hour into my drive, my phone starts ringing. The screen shows that it's Katie, so I answer.

"Vic, where are you? I am at your apartment standing out front," she says in a panicked tone.

"Why?"

"Hudson texted me and said that you were acting crazy. That you two had a big fight and that I should come check on you. What happened?"

Katie and I haven't been talking much lately. She has been spending all her time with some guy she met online. So, I explain all of the events that have taken place over the past week. From the car getting keyed and getting drugged on Halloween to finding out about Jay and everything leading right back to Emily.

"Why haven't you told me any of this?" she asks.

"The last time I tried to talk to you about her, you acted like I was just being possessive over Hudson again. But I am telling you, this is all her doing this stuff. I know it is, Katie. If you were my true friend, you would believe me."

"I want to believe you, Vic, but this is all too much."

"I know it is, and I am going to get to the bottom of it. She's dangerous, and I need to get Hudson far away from her."

I hang up the phone. I don't need another person telling me that I am wrong because I know deep in my soul that I am right.

❋

I sleep 'til ten o'clock in my hotel room before I drive over to Jay's house. I shower with the toiletries and change into the clothing I bought at the store before checking in early this morning.

The neighborhood they live in is very nice. The houses all look older, but they are large and well-maintained.

The woman that answers the door at their home is Jay's mother. I recognize her from the Facebook photos.

"Hi, Ms. Panchak?

"Yes, how can I help you?"

"My name is Brook, and I was a friend of your son Jay in high school. I hope that I am not intruding, but I have been away at college, and when I got back, I heard about the horrible accident. I wanted to come by to pay my respects and to see if I can do anything for your family. Jay and I were so close." I put on my best sad face, and she seems to believe me.

"You are not intruding at all. Would you like to come in?"

"I am not going to be any bother to you?"

"No, not at all. I would love the company. Being here with Jay all day can be very lonely sometimes. What did you say your name was again? My mind isn't what it used to be."

"Brook," I tell her. "Is it okay if I see him?"

"Of course, you can. I like to think that he can tell when he has visitors. That it somehow makes him happy."

She leads me to a room that must have been a den at one point but has now been transformed into a makeshift hospital room. There is medical equipment everywhere that must be left over from when he was in a coma. In a wheelchair facing the television is Jay. He is watching a cartoon about a dog and a cat. It is too childish for a twenty-something-year-old man.

I walk over to him. "Hi Jay, remember me? It's Brook," I ask him in a voice much too loud for this room.

"He won't be able to respond. He doesn't have the ability to understand what you are saying anymore. He can hear and acknowledge certain voices, like mine and his father's, but not other people's. He does seem to like this cartoon, though. When I put it on for him, he always seems to relax a little."

"I'm so sorry. I wasn't sure if he could communicate or not. Some of our friends said that they still come by and see him."

"Yes, he sure does have some good friends. Such good people still come around often to visit with him even though he can't communicate with them. They like to think that he will come out of this someday, and when he does, he will know that they were here."

"Will he come out of this?"

"No, he had a severe hemorrhage that affected his brain, damaging most of it."

We stand there in awkward silence for a moment. She offers me some coffee and leads me into their kitchen. She pours us two cups and we sit down at her kitchen table.

"I just want to offer my condolences. I am so sorry that this happened to your family. Jay was such a great guy. We had so much fun together in high school."

"I am sorry, I don't remember you, but like I said, my mind isn't what it used to be, and there were a lot of things that I guess I didn't know about Jay."

"My dad was really strict and didn't let me go out much."

"Well, it's always so nice to meet some of Jay's old friends. Were you friends with Simone? She comes around quite a bit. She must have really cared for him before the accident. She said that she was his girlfriend, but I didn't know her back then either."

I quickly remember Simone was the girl in a lot of his photos.

"Yes, we were close. Me, her, and our other friend Emily. We were all good friends."

"I don't think I know who Emily is either. Sorry."

I pull out my phone and bring up the pictures that were taken the weekend at my parents' cabin. I zoom in on Emily's face and show Ms. Panchak.

"This is Emily. You should know her; she hung around Jay quite a bit."

She scans the photo for a moment. I think for just a second that I see a flash of recognition in her eyes, then another moment goes by, and I see it again.

"No, sorry, I don't recognize her at all. But it's sure good to hear about how many good friends Jay had. That makes me happy."

I pull up another photo of her. "Here is another one of her. Her name is Emily Lewis."

She looks more carefully at this photo. "I know a lot of folks with the name of Lewis, but this girl isn't one of them. She sure is a pretty girl, though."

This isn't working. This lady is probably in her sixties or seventies and might be a little senile and not remember Emily.

"Would Jay recognize her?" I ask.

She furrows her brow tightly. "No, he wouldn't remember who she was at all. Like I said, he can't understand or communicate and has little to no memory left."

"Do you own an antique business?" I ask her.

"We used to before the accident, but unfortunately, we had to close the doors. Taking care of Jay is a full-time job now, and there was no time for the store anymore," she says sadly.

"I saw the fundraiser page. Do you know who the people are that send money to you?"

"We are so thankful that they have that sort of thing available. We wouldn't have been able to keep Jay here with us in the house if it weren't for the lovely people that donate money to us."

"But do you know who they are?"

"No, it's all anonymous. People from all over the world can donate."

I wish there were a way I could get her to remember Emily. I swear I saw something in her eyes when I showed her the photos, but maybe I am wrong about all of this. The family does own an antique store. Perhaps that is how she found out about what happened to Jay. It is still so strange that she would donate so much money, and not all at once but several times.

I might have to come to terms with the fact that she never knew Jay and that Emily was right and I was wrong.

I need to leave ASAP. I am getting so creeped out by being here. I can see the spokes from the back of Jay's wheelchair from the kitchen table. The dog speaking from the cartoon in the background sounds slightly devilish, and Ms. Panchak is telling a story about Jay as a child, and I am sitting here lying over and over to this woman.

"Jay was an only child, and I might have spoiled him a little too much. I thought that I had known everything about him, but there were some demons inside him that he kept well hidden."

"I am sorry to hear about all this, Ms. Panchak." I take out a pen and paper from my purse and write down my name and phone number. "Call me if you hear anything. If our friend Emily reaches out to you, let me know. I have been trying to get ahold of her to let her know about Jay."

I know it's a long shot she will call, but I am still going to keep a tiny bit of hope that I can connect Emily to this family.

I get in my car and start driving back to Cincinnati, feeling completely defeated. Looks like I must have been wrong, but only about this situation. I still think that she drugged me and keyed my car, even though I can't prove it. I still think that she is lying about her past, even though I can't find anything online about her. It all does sound crazy, I guess. Maybe I am going insane. Maybe Hudson was right about that. Everything that has happened might be catching up with me, and this is some sort of breakdown.

I'm sure that Hudson already told our parents and Evelyn how I barged in last night, accusing Emily of everything. They're probably all planning to have me committed to a hospital. I need to go home and suffer the consequences and try and get trust back with my family. Hopefully someday I will get some trust back from Hudson. That will take a lot of effort. He's surely going to stay with Emily. He took her side with no hesitation last night. I don't know how I can ever be around her knowing what I know. I'm still worried that something bad will happen to my brother, but I need to accept the truth… There's nothing I can do.

Because of her, I have lost everything—my brother, my family, and all their trust.

My phone starts ringing shortly into my drive. It's an unknown number. I don't feel like answering spam calls, so I ignore it. The ringing stops, then a minute later the same unknown number is on the cell screen again. I decide to go ahead and answer it.

"Hello, Brook? This is Patricia Panchak. Sorry to call you twice. I was just calling back to leave you a voice mail. I still get confused with how these modern electronics work."

"It's fine. What can I help you with?"

"Something was niggling at me after you left. It keeps swirling around my mind, and I think I finally put my finger on it."

"What is it?"

"It's the photo of the girl you showed me."

I perk up immediately.

"Emily?"

"Yes, that is the name that you gave me, but that name is not familiar to me. I didn't think that the girl was either at first, but the more I think about it, she looks a little like this girl that used to do some work with us when the antique shop was open. Of course, my mind just isn't what it used to be, so I might be wrong."

"What was her name?"

"It was Amelia. They don't look a whole lot alike, but there was just something so familiar to those pictures you showed me. It was something in the eyes."

"Did she know Jay?"

"Oh, I doubt it. They might have seen each other in passing, coming and going from the store, but I am fairly certain they didn't know each other personally."

"But do you think that it might be possible?"

"Amelia was such a sweet young girl, but she was very shy and quiet. She was not the type of person that Jay would have hung around with. He was always so energetic and outgoing and had a lot of pretty girls around him all the time. Not to be rude, but Amelia just wasn't that type."

"Could you give me Amelia's phone number?" I ask her, but she doesn't seem to be listening. She keeps rambling on about her son.

"Jay had his demons. Everyone else, even his father, told me there were warning signs, but I didn't want to listen. I never could believe that he was using drugs, and I still don't to this day. I guess there were a lot of things I didn't know about him. Maybe I need to come to terms with that."

"Do you know where Amelia is now?" I interrupt impatiently.

"No, I haven't seen her around for several months."

This is obviously going nowhere. "I am sorry to hear that, Ms. Panchak, but I really have to be going now."

I try to tell her gently, but now I know that she is not listening to me. It seems like she just called because she is lonely and wants to talk to someone more about her son. A son she thinks that I was close to. I will have to raise my voice to get her to hear that I need to end this call.

"He had such a large dosage in his system that night. The doctors said that if he hadn't gotten into the accident then he probably would have overdosed on that amount of drugs, but because they rushed him to the hospital after he hit that tree with his car and pumped them out of his system, they were able to save him. Only the accident left him brain-damaged anyway. I'm not sure what would've been a worse fate."

"Ms. Panchak, I know that you are having a really hard time, but I—"

"I never thought that those types of pills could be so dangerous. I have been taking Xanax occasionally for years to be able to sleep at night. I will tell you what, though, I threw those pills away as soon as I knew how bad they were. I couldn't bear to take something anymore that did this to my son."

My skin turns icy cold, and everything around me seems to move in slow motion. I can't hear what she is saying anymore. My brain is only pumping out enough blood for me to remember one thing: Xanax is a benzodiazepine, and that was the same drug that was in my system Halloween night.

"Was that what was in Jay's system?"

"Yes. Enough to overdose a man his size."

It couldn't be a coincidence that the same drug that I tested positive for was also in his system the night of the accident.

"Ms. Panchak," I say loudly into the phone, "what was Amelia's last name?"

"Lewis, the same last name as your friend."

41
Emily

Hudson's parents are still in town for one more day after Evelyn's birthday party. They were going to meet with Victoria this evening to discuss what the next steps are for her sobriety, but after Hudson called them this morning and filled them in on everything that happened last night, they have decided that they need to take her back to the cabin with them until they find a place for her to go.

Betty calls me this morning and asks me to meet her and Evelyn for breakfast. They want to talk with me about what happened last night. I really don't want to go over it all again, but I need to make sure that they believe me about all the accusations.

We meet at a little diner near the brewery. Betty knows all the staff here, and they all love her. I guess they would know her well. She probably spent a lot of time here over the years, having the brewery so close.

I am nervous to hear what she has to say but relax quickly when she profusely apologizes for Victoria once again.

"There are no excuses for what she has done. I am so thankful that she didn't do any permanent damage to you and Hudson."

I am glad to hear her say that about us. Hudson has assured me over and over that he is not upset with me, but hearing Betty say it makes me feel more secure.

"We all thought that we had helped her after she lost her parents. I just don't know where she lost her way. We should have gotten her more help back then, and we should have sent her somewhere last year after the drinking and the DUI. Now things have gotten so out of control, and I am afraid we might not be able to fix it easily," Betty says sadly.

"All this nonsense thinking that you are out to hurt our family is just beyond me. I don't know where she would be getting all these crazy delusions from." Evelyn says. "I am glad that you are taking her back with you, Mom. She needs to be close to you now."

"No one needs to apologize for what happened. I understand firsthand that losing your parents can have a long-lasting impact on your life, and Victoria obviously needs some help. You all are right to want to send her somewhere that she can be around people that will help her. I will do whatever I need to get her to understand that I am not the enemy."

"You are just a gem, Emily. We are so lucky to have you in our lives. Speaking of gems, we need to head over to the jeweler's after this. Come walk with us, it's just a few blocks from here."

We leave the restaurant and walk a few blocks to the jeweler. Betty wraps her arms inside of mine and Evelyn's on the other side. She always makes me feel like I am a part of her family. Maybe if Victoria can go away for a while, then I will have a chance to make that happen.

"We have been doing business with this jeweler ever since we bought this brewery. Bob has bought all my anniversary gifts here every year since then. It's also where Matt bought Evelyn's engagement ring."

"Are you getting another anniversary gift?" I ask Betty.

"No, not today. I am just dropping off our jewelry to get everything all polished up and cleaned. Once a year, we bring it here. They check all the rings to make sure the prongs aren't loose and the clasps on the necklaces are still in proper working order and make sure everything stays bright and shiny. Maybe someday soon we'll be coming back here for another reason." Betty winks at me. She is always winking. It's adorable.

At the jeweler, a man dripping in diamonds from his ears to his fingers greets us.

"This is Emily. She is the newest addition to our family," he greets me graciously, kissing me on both cheeks. "She is dating my son Hudson."

"This is wonderful news. When is the engagement going to happen?" he asks me, and my face must turn bright red.

Betty puts her arm around me to comfort me.

"Not quite yet, but hopefully someday soon," I reply.

Betty reaches into her purse and pulls out a blue silk bag full of jewelry and hands it over to the man. He gently pours it out onto a felt tray. I stare in shock that she is just carrying all that around in her purse. There must be fifty thousand dollars worth of jewelry in there, or maybe more. I notice that among the items is Victoria's silver charm bangle.

"Is that Victoria's?" I ask, pointing to the bracelet.

"Yes, she gave it to me last night. They polish up really nice for her. It keeps it bright and shiny. I know that's something her mother would have really loved. She can come in and get it tomorrow before we head back to the cabin. I know she would be lost without it for too long."

While Betty is explaining what she needs done with her jewels, I see Evelyn check her phone and make a startled face. She looks like something is wrong.

"Everything okay?" I ask her.

"I don't know. I just wanted to check on Victoria and…" She trails off, looking up at her mom. "It's nothing," she says and puts her phone away.

That sure did not seem like nothing, I think.

After we leave the jeweler's, we walk back to our cars to say our goodbyes.

"If I don't see you before we leave tomorrow morning then I want you to have an amazing opening day with your store. I wish I could be there for it, but Bill and I need to get back to the cabin and get things moving with Victoria."

She gives me and Evelyn both a kiss on the cheek, and I watch her drive off, feeling sad that she is leaving. I really love being around her.

"I was wondering if I could come out to your orchard and pick some apples later today?" Evelyn asks me. "I want to bake a pie for our parents before they leave. Betty will love the fact that the apples came from your orchard. She needs some cheering up right now. She is an exceptionally strong woman, but I know that all this nonsense with Victoria must be weighing heavily on her."

"Yeah, that would be totally fine. What a great idea."

"Don't tell anyone. I want it to be a surprise."

"No problem. Was everything okay earlier? You looked like something might have been wrong with Victoria."

"I didn't want to say anything in front of my mom. I know that she and my dad will be heading over to her house to get her later tonight, but I am not sure if she is going to be there. Do you know anything about Victoria leaving town?" she asks.

"No, the last thing I knew is that Hudson told her to go home last night. I know that he called her friend Katie to go over and be with her. I think she said she was heading over there."

"Hmm, that's just so strange," she says, looking down at her phone again.

"What do you mean?"

"Victoria and I have always shared our location with each other since we both got our first cell phones when we were in junior high. It was sort of a secret that we had with each other, and right now her location says that she is not in Cincinnati. The location app must be glitching or something. She wouldn't have left the state. Our parents would be furious."

"Where does it say she is?"

"Looks like somewhere called Naperville, Illinois."

42

Victoria

I drive fast while I search for Amelia Lewis and Naperville, Illinois. I start with Google, and there are a bunch of articles with that name and place that come up. I click on them one after another. A dog groomer business is the first, then a story about a wedding. I click on the wedding story and it's not the Emily I know. I scan down the page, looking for something that stands out to me, when I hear loud honking coming from directly in front of me.

I am heading right toward a semi-truck in the wrong lane. I quickly swerve my car back over into my own lane, narrowly avoiding a head-on collision. My phone clatters down onto the floor. My heart is racing in my chest, and my stomach feels like I might lose the contents of what I had for breakfast.

I pull my car over into a truck stop, grab my phone, and get out as quickly as possible. I run into the store without even locking my car. I need to calm down and focus. Killing myself in a head-on collision is not going to help Hudson at all.

I go to the cafeteria seating area, sit down, and pull the search back up. I scan down the articles until I come to one titled "Reward Increased to $50,000 for Missing Naperville Man."

The article reads that a man named Brooks Sutton, age forty-five, went missing last year on November 7th. According to his daughter Amelia Lewis, Brooks Sutton left the house at 5 p.m. on Friday afternoon and never came back home. It gives details of what he was wearing at the time he left—his height, his weight. His mother and daughter plead for any information regarding this missing person.

I type in *Brooks Sutton, Naperville* and *missing man* and read all the articles that come up about him. I pull out my computer and start typing all the information for the articles and come up with a timeline for what happened to this man.

According to investigators, he went missing on November 7th but wasn't reported missing 'til a week later by his daughter and mother because he often went away for days at a time on business trips. Cell phone towers indicated that his last known location was a hiking trail at a nature preserve called Swallow Cliff Woods in Chicago, Illinois. Upon searching the nature preserve, they were able to locate his car in the parking lot. They brought cadaver dogs to the area and asked for volunteers to help with the search. The search lasted for three days, and they finally found Brooks Sutton on November 18th. Eleven days after he went missing. He was found dead at the base of one of the cliffs from an apparent fall. After the autopsy, they determined he died from several blunt head injuries. After a short investigation, the death was ruled as an accident.

I type in both Amelia's and Brook's names to see what comes up relating to them both. A news article with his mother, Sienna Sutton, and daughter, Amelia Lewis, on November 15th pleading for anyone to come forward with any information about Brooks's disappearance. There is a video from WNG 16 News. I click on the video and see an older woman that appears to be Brooks's mother speaking in front of a camera.

"Brooks might still be alive at Swallow Cliff Woods. His only daughter and I are asking that anyone with any information please contact the police immediately. We are desperate to find Brooks safe and sound."

Standing behind Sienna is a young girl with her head bowed down. Her long brown hair cascades down each of her shoulders, concealing most of her face. This must be Amelia. I rewind the video and take several screenshots where I can see her face more clearly while it plays again and again. I zoom in on Amelia's face to see if I can tell who she might be. She has the same height as Emily, but nothing else about her resembles who I know as Emily. This girl is very overweight, and her hair is vastly different. Her posture is slumped, and she looks much younger than Emily.

I slam my hand down on the table. Every single time I get some sort of lead, it always hits a brick wall. I am so frustrated. I know that there is something here.

I google Emily and Amelia Lewis, and an article about baby names comes up. It tells me that Emily can be a nickname for Amelia. I never would have guessed that, but that's something I can go on. If only Hudson wasn't so angry with me. I could call him and ask him if this girl looks familiar or ask him if he is sure that her name is Emily Lewis. Maybe he was mistaken. Or this girl is somehow related to her.

I decide to call Ms. Panchak back. She answers right away.

"Hi, sorry to bother you again, but I am desperate to get ahold of my friend Emily. I looked up the girl you told me about, Amelia Lewis, and found that she was involved in a missing person incident. Do you know anything about that?"

"No, I was not aware that Amelia was involved in anything like that. She didn't talk much about herself. It always seemed to me that she wanted to keep her personal life private."

"You said that she did work for you? What was it that she did?"

"Well, not so much work for us; she came in and bought items from our antique store. At that time there were so many things that had been piling up over the years, and she would help me move everything around so that the customers could see them better. I also suspect that she wanted to find the hidden treasures in there as well. She was so sweet, always bringing me pastries that she baked. She was very fond of baking muffins."

Yet another coincidence. Amelia bought furniture, the same thing Emily does. This has got to be connected somehow.

"Ms. Panchak, I just texted you a picture of Amelia. Can you look at it and see that this is the same girl you are speaking about?"

I text her a screenshot of the girl from the news video and wait on hold for nearly five minutes before she comes back to the line. She might have had trouble figuring out how to do that while she was on the phone with me.

"Yes, that is Amelia," she says when she comes back.

"What makes you think that this might be the same girl as the one I am looking for?"

"It's just something about those eyes. She always seemed to be haunted by something. Not in a bad way, just that she might have been disquieted. But after looking at all the pictures that you sent me of both girls, I can be fairly certain that they are the same girl. She might have changed her appearance but women do that all the time."

I look at the photos again and don't see any resemblance between the two girls, but then again, this photo from the news report is not the best quality, and Amelia's face is half hidden by her hair. I thank Ms. Panchak and hang up again. Maybe Emily changed her appearance, and this is her. I can't imagine the girl that Hudson is dating now is the same dumpy girl in this photo, but I couldn't imagine a lot of things that have happened involving Emily.

I decide to call Hudson. He will most likely hang up on me, but it's my last chance to find out. I could show him this video, but then I would have to tell him how I came across it. He would lose his mind because I came up here to talk to the poor woman whose son had such a tragic accident. No, I can't do that yet. I need to try and get answers from Hudson. I just need to ask him two questions.

He doesn't answer when I call his number. I should have known he wouldn't.

I get back in my car and continue driving back to Cincinnati. I have to face the firing squad of Mom and Dad when I get there. It's two in the afternoon now, and I refuse to read any of the text messages or listen to the voice mails that have come from my parents, Evelyn, or Katie. Hudson has not left a single one, but I didn't think he would.

I try calling him again but no answer. I pull up our texts and voice to text him a message. I don't need another near-death experience with a semi. I need to be calm and rational and get Hudson to listen to me no matter what I have to say.

"Hudson, I know that you don't want to speak with me, but I want you to know that I am sorry. I am going to leave you and Emily alone now and go somewhere far away to get some help. I obviously do nothing but cause trouble in Cincinnati. I will let you know as soon as I am somewhere safe."

That should get his attention. I am hoping that he will believe that I am serious about not coming home and give me a call back. I just need to get him on the phone.

He calls back a half hour later.

"Vic, why are you not in Cincinnati? I called Evelyn and she said your location last showed you in Illinois?"

"I'm okay, I am just going to get some help on my own. I can't do it there in Cincinnati."

"Why, Victoria? Why can't you just let us help you? I know what I said last night was way out of line. I know that you just need some help. We are all very worried. Everyone has been trying to call you all day."

"Not you. You haven't tried to call me."

"You're right. I'm sorry. I have just been so angry after last night, but I have calmed down now. What can I do to help you?"

"I need you to do something for me, and after that, I promise that I will come back and go right into a rehabilitation program for as long as it takes to get better. I will take responsibility for everything that I have done wrong to you, Emily, Brent, our parents—everyone. I can get my life back on track finally for the last time. If you just answer two questions."

Hudson sighs loudly into the phone. "I don't know, Vic. What questions?"

"I need to know if Emily's name is actually what she says it is and if she ever had long brown hair?"

"Jesus Christ, Vic, why can't you just let this go? I already told you I heard the DMV call her name out. And why do you care about what hair color she used to have?"

"I know what you said. Look at the actual license or look in her phone or around her house. I just need those two things confirmed."

"If I do this, then you better do what you said. No more games. You come home and get help. If you don't, I can promise you that it will be a very long time before you earn my trust back again, if ever."

Hudson hangs up the phone without saying another word.

I keep driving back toward Cincinnati, waiting anxiously for Hudson to call me back. I know he will do what I asked. He just has to. If Emily isn't lying, I will keep my promise to him. I will forget about all of this and move on with my life.

It's been over an hour, and he hasn't gotten back to me. I am almost back to the city now, and I know that my mom and dad are planning on meeting me at my house later this evening, so I hope that Hudson will let me know well before then. I almost get ready to grab my phone and call him when it starts ringing.

Thank God it's him.

"Hudson, did you find anything?" I say right away.

"Yes, I did. She isn't lying about her name, Victoria."

"How do you know?"

"I searched through the things that she has here at my house, and I really don't like that I had to do that. I feel awful about it. I need to know that when this is settled, we can keep that between you and me. The only reason I did it was to get you home. She can't know that I went through her things. She would never trust me again. Do we understand each other?"

"Yes, I won't say anything to her. Did you look at her license?"

"No, she doesn't have that yet. They mail that to you a few weeks after you pass the test, but they did give her a piece of paper to use as a temporary ID until her new one comes in the mail. I remembered seeing her throw it away when we got home that day. I had to go out to my trash can and look through my old trash. I am not too happy about that, Vic, but I guess it's lucky that it was still there because, sure enough, it's her name on it. She wasn't lying. It is written clearly on there, Amelia Lewis. I guess she just goes by Emily for short. Now can you please just come home and be done with this bullshit?"

I pull my car over to the side of the road, rocks flinging up all over, bouncing off the metal, and slam on my brakes.

"Did she used to have long brown hair?"

"Yes, she did. There is a photo of her and her mother on her nightstand from when she was younger. Why does that matter? Women change their hair color all the time."

"Right, they do."

He's right. She must have changed her hair completely and lost a lot of weight. She looks dramatically different now, but none of that matters.

"So, are we good?" he asks. "You're going to come home now?"

"Yes, I am on my way back now. Is Emily going to be with you today? I want to talk to her."

"I will be seeing her later tonight. She is taking care of some things at her house. Why, you aren't going to say something crazy again, are you?"

"No, I am not going to say anything crazy to her. Like I promised you, I am coming home to make things right again."

43

Emily

As I drive home, I frantically try to think if there is any way that Victoria could figure out my past while she is up in Illinois. I can't believe she actually drove all the way up to Naperville to the Panchaks' house. She must've got their address from the fundraiser page and went up there to do more spying on me. Does this bitch have no limits? What lengths will she go to destroy me?

I know that she has talked to Patricia by now, but I don't think that she would be able to tell her anything. Victoria would say my name is Emily, and any photos she has of me would be of what I look like now. I look nothing like that pathetic girl that lived back there. Patricia would never be able to identify me as Amelia. That poor woman has been half senile since I met her, and there is certainly no way Victoria is talking to Jay. That asshole has been completely brain-dead since the accident.

I always felt so badly for Patricia after it happened. She deserved to have a much nicer child than him. That's why I sent her so much money because I wanted to help her out. She was always so nice and sweet to me. I have no idea how someone like Jay came from such a good person.

I think that everything will be okay, but after this, I will have to be more careful. If I want this to work out with Hudson and his family, I need to make sure that these types of things don't come up anymore.

Hopefully, Victoria will go off to a rehabilitation center and come back as a changed woman. Someone who isn't so dead set on screwing me over. I always have the notebook to use as collateral. Maybe I should call her and let her know that I have it? I could tell her that if she did happen to find anything out while she was up there, then I will send the notebook to the police and her family. But I don't know how to do that without making her more suspicious. Surely if she knew something by now, she would have called Hudson and everyone in her family to tattle on me.

I text Hudson as soon as I get back to my house to check in just to make sure she hasn't said anything. I need to figure out if he knows anything yet or if there's a chance he will know anything soon.

"Hey, how is it going today? Was anybody able to get ahold of Victoria?" I say, then hold my breath.

"Yeah, I just spoke with her. She left the state. Can you believe that? She said she was going to go off by herself and find help alone. I talked to her and was able to get her to calm down a little. She is on her way back to Ohio now."

"Oh my god, that's crazy. Did she say anything else?"

"Yeah, she is going to talk to you later. She promised that she is going to apologize and go straight into whatever treatment program that my parents can get her into."

"Do you think I have anything to worry about when she talks to me?"

"No, she said she is not going to act crazy anymore. She is done with all that now. She knows that she was acting crazy before."

"Oh, that's great. I'm so glad to hear that." A huge rush of relief rolls over my body that Victoria didn't find out anything. "Will I see you later tonight then?"

"Yeah, I will be there whenever you are ready for me to come over."

"Okay, I will let you know when I am finished here. I can't wait to see you."

I want him to come over right now and hold me. I'm trembling from the scare that I just had, but Evelyn will be out here to my house later to pick some apples. It's okay. I can wait until after she leaves.

"Can I tell you something?" he says.

"Yes, of course, anything."

"I love you."

I beam with excitement to hear those words from him.

"I love you too, Hudson." I take a deep breath and let all the pleasure of his words run through my body. He said it. He said I love you.

"Oh, also," he says, "I didn't know that you go by a nickname."

I feel something slam into my head and my body falls forward onto the floor. Pain rushes through my head, and my vision blurs. I try to blink away the pain and push myself up, but I can't focus. That's when I noticed that there are a few tiny, dark red droplets forming on the beige carpet in front of me. I reach my hand behind my head and when I look at it, it is smeared with the same red liquid. I am so confused about what just happened. I try to remember what I was doing just a minute ago. Was I on the phone? I think that I was talking to Hudson, but I can't remember what was happening only a minute ago. Only then do I hear someone talking in the room with me.

"You couldn't just leave well enough alone, could you. I warned you to stay away from him, but you just wouldn't listen."

I turn toward the voice to see who it is, but my vision is so blurred that I can't see very well. I can make out the silhouette of a person and I know that it's female by the sound of her voice.

She's not very tall and has darker-colored hair. I try to speak, but I can't summon my voice. The pain coming from the back of my head is hammering so hard that I can't get any words out.

"Well, unfortunately, this is just the way it is going to be. If you would have listened, this wouldn't be happening to you right now. You see, Hudson is *my* boyfriend, and you are not going to take him away from me," the female voice continues to speak.

I finally start to get a grip on reality and on what's happening here. The pain subsides in my head just enough for me to see who it is standing in my living room.

It's Chloe, or Samantha, whatever her name is. I think she just hit me with something in the back of my head.

"What the hell are you doing in my house? Why did you hit me?" I finally get the words out.

"Are you deaf? Did you not hear what I just said? I warned you to stay away from Hudson. I wrote you a note and left it for you. I saw the two of you talking out on the street in front of your store. That's when I knew I needed to keep an eye on you. I looked the Teal Lotus up online. I am not going to lie, I was very impressed with what you are doing. Maybe after you are gone, I will try picking up something like that. I am sure Hudson would like that. I knew Hudson was going to come around someday and be with me again, and I couldn't let you fuck everything up. You are such a whore. I followed you home weeks ago. You stayed at his house until the early morning, then got in an Uber to go home. Sneaking out like the fucking slut you are. I was hoping it was just a one-night stand; after all, you two didn't see each other after that for a while. But then he came to your house, and the two of you haven't spent a day apart since then. Now I need to end whatever it is that is going on between the two of you."

I notice that in her hand is a giant knife. It looks like one of my knives from the block in the kitchen. She must've gotten it before she hit me. The look in her eyes is demonic, like there is something evil that has taken over. Very much like the look I saw in her eyes the time I ran into her on the sidewalk in front of Hudson's house, only now it's directed at me. I wondered what had happened to her. Why I hadn't encountered her again after she came to my house. I knew I had caught a glimpse of her in front of my store that Friday evening weeks ago. I just couldn't be sure. And all this time I thought that the note left underneath the windshield wiper of the Teal Lotus was from Victoria. How could I be so stupid? How could I let my guard down like this?

She lunges toward me, and I grab the vase on the table next to the couch and throw it at her as hard as I can. It breaks when it comes into contact with her shoulder.

"You bitch!" I hear her scream.

I muster up the strength to run. I open the back door before she reaches me. I run as fast as I can through the orchards. I know that I can lose her here. I know them better than she does. I run down the path that I cleared before and weave in and out through the trees. My vision is still blurred, but I keep pushing on. I can hear her behind me, but my head is throbbing so hard and loud that I can't tell how close she is. She might be on the other side of the orchard, or she might be just behind me.

I stumble into the open patch where I had been tending to the apples and trip over something. I look down and see that it's a shovel. I gain some clarity at the moment that I find the shovel. I bend down and wrap my fingers around the base. It feels hard and solid between my fingertips.

"Boo!" I hear her say behind me, and then hear her maniacal laugh echoing through the trees. She is just a few feet away from me.

I grip the base of the shovel hard and swing around behind me, using every bit of strength that I have. I feel the impact reverberate throughout my entire body while I watch her body fall to the ground with a hollow thump. Blood pours out of the right side of her head, soaking into the dirt around her. Her unblinking eyes are wide, staring up at the afternoon sky. Just then, the snow starts to fall. Leaving fat snowflakes all over her blank face.

Of course, it starts to snow now.

I let out a breath that I feel like I've been holding in since she hit me inside my living room. Hudson and I won't have to worry about her anymore.

44

Emily

I try to compose myself when I get back into my house. My shirt is ripped from running through the orchard and getting scraped from the branches of the trees. I am freezing cold and the bash on my head is killing me. I go to my kitchen and wash my hair in the sink, rinsing out all the blood that has started to thicken into a crust on my head. I run my hands under the warm water, splashing it on my face over and over, watching the dirt and blood drain into the sink, and slowly pulling myself back into the moment.

How could I be so stupid all this time? I thought that note was from Victoria getting me back for keying her car. Not from Samantha. I should have been watching for her to come back to my house or my store. She already came to my house once. I let my guard down all because of Victoria.

I change out of my ripped clothing and clean up all the shards of glass from the vase that I threw at her. I go outside to look for her car. I didn't see it when I got home earlier. I would have noticed a bright red car in the driveway. I find the Honda Civic parked behind my workshop in the grass, so I wouldn't have seen it. I open the door; it's filled with all sorts of stuff, as if she's been living in her car. I think Hudson mentioned that to me at some point. I find her wallet in the glove box and look inside. Her license says her name is Samantha Mercer. In the photo she still has the honey-blonde hair she had when I first saw her. The same color that I now have.

I don't know what to do with the car right now, so I go into my workshop and grab a large canvas sheet that I use for painting and drape it over the top of the car, concealing the bright red color from showing. It will do for now until I can figure out what to do with it. I just can't process that right now.

My phone rings. It's Victoria. I must have had a concussion because I answer the phone without even thinking about it. I don't have any time to talk to her right now.

"Hello, Victoria."

45

Victoria

I get to Hudson's house a short time later. I feel awful that I'm going to have to break his poor little heart. I will tell him about Emily being Amelia and all the horrible things that she has done. He will believe now that I have proof that she is the one who drugged me and threatened me because she has done the same awful things to others in her past. She is probably responsible for what happened to her stepfather too. She is certainly guilty of what happened to Jay. I don't know if that ever was her ex-boyfriend, maybe she has some sick delusions about him, but I don't care why she did it. I will be able to tell the police what drugs were found in my system. I still have the drug test at home, not that it will be admissible in court, but it will still get the ball rolling. Once they start looking into her past, everything will start to tie itself together.

 Hudson will be okay after all this. It will be hard at first, but I'll be there for him after he finds out how badly he has been deceived. I'll help him get through all the pain and sadness. And he'll be so thankful that I went through hell and back just for him. My whole family will. They will soon understand why I've been acting so crazy. They will understand that my intuition was right about Emily the whole entire time, and there will be no rehabilitation center for me. That's for sure.

Before I go inside Hudson's house, I need to make one phone call, and I can't be any happier about it.

Emily answers the phone after one ring. "Hello, Victoria."

"Amelia, how are you?"

She pauses for a few moments before speaking. "I hear you've been on a little adventure." Her voice sounds strained, as if she already knows that this was coming.

"Yes, it was quite an exciting adventure. I learned some really important things. Things that would blow your mind."

"Like?"

"Like who you really are. I know everything now, Emily—or Amelia, whatever you want to call yourself. It doesn't matter anymore. Everything is going to come out about you now. I'm going to tell Hudson everything."

"I'll bet you don't have anything to tell Hudson."

"Oh, I sure do. I have a cute little video of you from the WNG 16 News and all the stories that come with it. The story about your stepfather, Brooks, and how he really died. The story of your ex-boyfriend Jay and his little accident. What do you think Hudson's gonna do when he learns that you were the one who drugged his sister after all, and with the same drugs that you used to try and kill your ex-boyfriend—if he even was your boyfriend? I'm sure that he won't be too happy about that. And what do you think he's going to do when he finds out that your stepfather didn't die from cancer, that he died because you pushed him off of a cliff? Now I know the police that investigated the fall called it an accident, but I'm sure once I have given them all this information that I have about you, they might just reopen that case when they know that you're connected to another suspicious incident involving Jay Panchak."

"You can't prove any of that," Emily says desperately.

"Oh, I most certainly can. I have Patricia Panchak, and I have already looked up Brooks's mother, Sienna, online. I will be giving her a call soon."

There is nothing but silence on the other end of the line, so I keep going. I want Emily to really hurt after everything she has done to me.

"What do you think Hudson is going to do when he finds out that you used to be a fat ugly pig? How did you manage to change your appearance so much anyway? I didn't even recognize it was you at first in the news video. I had to call Hudson and have him snoop through your things to find out what your real name was, and he did it willingly, with no convincing at all. Maybe he doesn't love you as much as you think he does. He found your driver's license paper in the bottom of the trash. He went through trash for me, Emily. That's how much he cares for me and not for you. If it wasn't for that, I would've never known that your real name is Amelia, and I wouldn't have been able to connect you to Illinois—and you might have gotten away with everything."

"No one will find me guilty of anything," she says as a last attempt to prove her innocence.

"You're right. In the end, after the police do their investigations, they might not be able to charge you with anything, but Hudson will never speak to you again. He hates liars. He broke up with his last girlfriend because she was a crazy, lying bitch. After everything you've done to me—keying my car, threatening to kill me, drugging me, not to mention lying to our whole entire family about your stepfather and your ex-boyfriend and where you are from—he won't ever forgive you. What do you think my mother is going to say about this? She used to be quite smitten with you, but there is no way that she will be anymore."

"Okay fine, Victoria, but I have some things that you should know also. There are things that I know about you as well."

She tries to bait me, but I am not going to fall for it.

"Oh, sorry, I don't have any more time. I'm at Hudson's house right now, getting ready to walk through his front door and tell him the entire story. So, I guess I'll say my goodbyes to you now. Hopefully the next time I see you will be behind bars."

I hang up the phone and turn it on silent. I don't want to hear the phone ringing when she tries to call back. I'm gonna need to devote all my attention to telling Hudson this story.

46

Emily

Fuck, fuck! What do I do? What do I do? My mind goes completely blank after hearing that Victoria actually does know what happened. My head is blazing with pain right now. I don't know what's happening. I start to feel so dizzy that I can't stand up anymore. I let myself fall onto the floor and lay my head down on the carpet.

My phone is still in my hand. I need to call Hudson and tell him to not listen to anything Victoria has to say. The concussion is causing so much confusion because I can't even figure out how to call him. I keep pushing buttons on my phone, but I am so lightheaded that I can't see straight.

I spend too much time trying to pull myself together enough to figure out how to use the phone, precious moments that I really need. Dammit, Samantha, why did you have to choose now of all times to come here to do this? I close my eyes to try and quell the dizziness and feel myself drift off to sleep.

When I awake, I have no idea how much time has passed. The light from outside the window is different, telling me more time than I realized has gone by. That was valuable time I could have used to save Hudson and me. I don't know what I would've said to him, but it's too late now. I'm sure that Victoria has told him everything. Now it's only a matter of time before Victoria brings the police to my house. How long will that be? It's not like she could just call them and tell them that Hudson has a crazy girlfriend, and they need to come out to my house and arrest me, so I have some time to get my things and go.

I hear something that sounds like knocking. I realize that it's coming from the front door. Someone is out front of my house. Who in the hell can it be now?

I manage to get up off the floor and get to the door to open it.

"Evelyn," I say, shocked. "What are you doing here?"

"I said I was going to stop by today and pick some apples, remember? We talked about surprising Betty by making her a pie. She will be so thrilled to know that the apples came from your orchard. You would not believe how much she really likes you. I love seeing my mom so happy when she's around you."

"Sorry, I forgot. I just don't think right now is a good time."

"Are you okay? You're as white as a ghost."

Her phone starts ringing in her purse. She pulls it out, checks the screen.

"Give me one second. I just need to deal with her."

"Victoria, you're heading back home, right? Hudson said he talked to you." Evelyn pauses for a moment while she listens to Victoria speaking. "I don't have time for this right now, Victoria," Evelyn rolls her eyes and ends the call abruptly. "That girl needs some serious help," she says to me.

"Everything is all messed up now." My voice is low and slurred, and my head is spinning so fast now that I feel like I might vomit.

"No, everything will be fine. Don't worry. As soon as Mom and Dad get Victoria back to the cabin, they will straighten everything out with her. They already have a rehab center that they want her to go to. They were working on it, making calls all day today. It will help her with her drinking problems and her mental health."

I laugh aloud. Victoria won't have to go to any rehabilitation center. No one will think she is the crazy one anymore. They will feel sorry for her and praise her for saving their family from someone like me. I will be the one put in some sort of center. Most likely prison.

"I need to run to the bathroom. I am so sorry, I have mommy bladder. Is it down this hall?" She points down the hallway, and I nod.

While she is in the bathroom, I hear her phone ding in her purse and pull it out. A text message screen pops up from Hudson.

Evelyn if you hear from Emily, don't answer her. Victoria was right.

Then, just a few seconds later, another text message from him. *She has lied about everything and is dangerous.*

Well then, I guess it's all over. That solidifies it. I shut her phone off and put it and her purse and stuff it under the counter in my kitchen where she won't see it.

Now I know that everything is lost. Victoria has completely ruined my life, and Hudson will hate me forever. If only I wouldn't have let that bitch of a mother get me to go on the news and plead for help to find her asshole of a son… I knew that video would come back to haunt me. I imagine Victoria and Brooks's mom having a conversation about me, the two of them laughing over my demise.

Even if there was some way that he could forgive me for lying about my past, he's never going to forgive me for what I have done to his sister, and once she gives that information to the police, it's only a matter of time before they get involved. When they get here, there's also the matter of Samantha. I underestimated Victoria once before, but I won't be doing that again. I need to figure out what my next move is.

Evelyn comes out of the bathroom. "I am so sorry about that. You will know what I am talking about once you pop out a few kids," she giggles. "What's wrong? You don't look so good."

"Nothing, I am just tired from getting everything ready for the store. I am going to let myself sleep for an entire day before it opens on Saturday."

My stomach wretches hearing myself say that. The store will never open on Saturday, or any other day. I will never get to see the vintage open and closed sign that Harper gave me being turned to open or see the bustle of people coming in. It was going to be my twenty-third birthday, a special present to myself that I deserved, that I worked so hard for.

"I can't imagine how tired you must be. I am so proud of you. You have inspired me to get out there and do something meaningful with my life also. I mean, being a mother is meaningful, but I can do more than just be a stay-at-home mom."

I am barely registering anything that she is saying to me. Suddenly, I feel like I'm having an epiphany. The throbbing in my head stops, and all my rage and sorrow float away. I just feel numb. I have a sudden clarity of what needs to happen next. I wonder if this is what a concussion feels like or if it's just the realization that I have lost everything. It's conceivable that it's all too much all at once, and my mind has just finally snapped. Either way, I now know what I have to do.

"Let's go pick some apples," I tell Evelyn.

We put on our coats and head outside. Evelyn doesn't even bother to check her phone or look for it. Why would she? She is as clueless as can be right now. So sweet and so innocent, and not a suspicious bone in her body. I feel bad about what I must do, but Victoria needs to pay for what she's done, and unfortunately, poor Evelyn is the one who's gonna have to suffer. This will hurt Victoria more than anything. Well, not as bad as if something happened to Hudson, but this will be the next best thing.

"Can you believe it's snowing already? It's only the beginning of November. We are so lucky that you still have some apples to pick," she says giddily.

We walk out through the path in the orchard where the apples are still growing. The same path that I ran through, away from Samantha earlier, toward the spot where her body bled out.

"This is so exciting. We all should chip in and cultivate this orchard to get it going again next year. It's just so magical and beautiful out here, especially with the snow falling."

Evelyn is happily rambling on about the orchard and how much joy it would bring the family. I look around sadly. It won't be bringing anyone in their family any joy. It will only bring pain and sadness. I look around and realize how much I am going to miss it.

"Evelyn," I interrupt her, "I want to tell you a story."

47

Victoria

I tell Hudson everything that I have learned today, everything that I have known from the beginning about Emily. I start by showing him the news video of her in Chicago, Illinois, pleading for help for her stepfather. At first, he doesn't believe that it's her in the video, but after telling him about my conversation with Jay's mother and how she can identify her as being the same person, he starts to give in. When he realizes that they have the same name, the same age, the same long brown hair, he knows that I am telling the truth. He breaks down crying, and I hold on to him tightly. I knew this was going to be hard on him. He makes me proud, though, when he pulls himself together quickly.

"I can't let this hurt me right now. We need to figure out what to do."

"Should we call the police?" I ask him.

"I still have that detective's number from when I had to take out the restraining order against that girl Samantha. I will give him a call."

"Okay. While you are doing that, I am going to call Evelyn and Mom and Dad."

I pick up my phone and call Evelyn first. I try to explain what is happening quickly, but she gets frustrated and hangs up on me.

"She is still really pissed at me. She isn't going to listen to what I have to say. You are going to have to call her yourself," I tell Hudson.

"She is probably just with the kids right now. It's around the time they all get home from school. I left a message with the detective. Hopefully he will call me back soon."

Hudson takes out his phone and sends a few messages to Evelyn.

"I'm sure she will call back when she isn't around the kids," he tells me calmly.

Hudson's face looks so sad right now, but it's okay; I am going to be there for him. I will help him get through this tough time. I go over and wrap my arms around him and give him a deep long hug. He holds me back, squeezing me tightly. We embrace like this for quite a while. It feels so good to be in his arms. When he pulls away, his eyes are wet with tears again.

"I just can't believe I never saw any of this coming. How did she fool our entire family?"

"She didn't fool me, Hudson, never once. I knew something was wrong from the moment I met her."

"I know, and I am so sorry I ever doubted you. I never ever will again, that's for sure. I am so sorry that you were caught in the middle of it all."

"Don't worry. She will pay for everything she has done to me. I still have all the evidence—the drug test and the death threat. I will spend all my time and resources making sure she gets what's coming to her."

Hudson nods his head, defeated. He grabs his phone again to make some more calls. Thankfully he has finally come to his senses. He will get over this girl in no time at all. In a month or two, she will just be a distant memory, and he and I can get back to the way things used to be.

"Vic, I just tried Evelyn's number and it went straight to voice mail."

"She probably shut off her phone after I called her. Try calling Matt."

Hudson gets Matt on the phone and puts him on speaker so we can both talk to him. We explain that Evelyn's phone is shut off and that we need to get ahold of her ASAP.

"She's not here right now. Are you sure her phone is shut off? That's not like her to do that," Matt says.

"Do you know where she went?" Hudson asks.

"She went to pick some apples. She wanted to bake a pie for Betty." We hear something crashing in the background and a bunch of laughter coming from their kids. "Listen, I got to go, I am on kid duty this afternoon."

"Okay Matt, tell her to call us as soon as you talk to her." He gets off the phone with Matt and has a worried look on his face.

"That's weird. Why would Evelyn go pick apples in November?" I ask Hudson. "It started snowing today already."

I stare at Hudson, waiting for a response, but he is silent for a long time, then his face begins to morph into something more panicked.

"What's wrong?" I ask, alarmed.

"I think that I know where she is picking apples."

"Where?" I ask impatiently.

"Emily's orchard."

48

Emily

"There have been three heartbreaks in my life, Evelyn, and when someone breaks my heart, something needs to be done about it. The worst one was the first. It was when my mother died. She wasn't always the best mother that she could be, but she loved me very much, and I loved her even more. My mother had been sick for so awfully long. The cancer treatments were an awful thing for her to go through. She ended up losing her hair, her beauty, her laughter, and eventually her life. I watched it all fade away. That's why when I found out that my stepfather Brooks was cheating on her, I had to do something about it. The whole time she was sick, he was out running around with several other women. If he hadn't been doing that, and staying home to help care for his wife, maybe she could have beaten the cancer. You could not imagine the anger that rose inside of me day after day, watching him leave the house for long periods of time, lying about where he was going. There was no way I was going to let him get away with that. He was an avid hiker. He would go hiking at the nature preserves all over the Chicago area where we lived. Did I mention that to you and your family? No, I don't think I did.

"You see, I never lived in Missouri. I am from Illinois. Born and raised. I lived there my entire life. Anyways, a few months after my mother died, I followed Brooks, just like I had been following him for several months. I figured he was probably going to one of his girlfriend's houses. I didn't know what exactly I was going to do that particular day, but that day I was really angry, like so angry that I could actually feel the blood boiling inside my body. I lost my mom, and he was out there, living his life still, being happy, while she was buried in the ground."

Evelyn stops picking apples and looks very confused. She has got to be turning over in her mind what I am telling her and trying to make sense of it all.

"Did you say that you are from Illinois?" she asks me, and I don't respond.

"That day, he didn't go to a woman's house, but instead, he went to a place called Swallow Creek Nature Preserve. It's a hiking spot close to where we lived that boasts steep hiking hills. Now, at that time I was so out of shape that I could barely walk a mile on the road, let alone hike up a steep cliff, but I was determined to follow him.

"Fate was on my side that day because he was so busy on his phone with someone that he was walking at a snail's pace and not paying attention to his surroundings. From the way that he was talking, it must've been one of his girlfriends. So, I followed him up the hill, panting and desperately trying to keep up. There were lots of other people on the trail and he was too distracted to notice I was behind him even though I was breathing like a pig so loudly and sweating profusely. Then I heard him tell the woman he was on the phone with that he loved her, and I snapped. In the beginning, I hadn't really known why I was following him up that cliff, but in that moment, I knew exactly why, and he gave me all the ammunition I needed to go through with it.

"I waited until no one was around, and I did it. I picked up a rock, and I hit him on the side of the head, and then I pushed him. I watched him fall over the side of the cliff, hitting several large rocks and tree branches on the way down until I couldn't see him anymore. Then I walked back down the trail and went home."

Evelyn's face is pure shock now. She isn't moving a single muscle in her body. She isn't even blinking. After a minute of silence between the two of us, she finally manages to get her words out.

"Emily, I…I…think that we should head back now," she stutters.

"No, Evelyn, I need to finish my story first. Now after that, Brooks's evil mother forced me to do that stupid news interview, begging for people to help us find him. If it weren't for that, your fucking sister would have never found out and none of this would be happening. His mother told me that if I didn't do it that she was going to kick me out of the house, but it didn't matter because she ended up kicking me out anyway with nothing. No money and no place to live, but the joke was on her. After they closed the investigations ruling his death an accident, Brooks's lawyer called me and told me that I was getting a $500,000 life insurance policy and that his mother wasn't entitled to any of it. I was his next of kin, so it all went to me, every penny. She was so pissed when she found out, but karma is a bitch.

"That's when I met Jay, and he could not have come along at a more perfect time. I was so sad from losing my parents. He was gorgeous and charming, and he was nice to me at first, but then I started to realize that I was nothing more to him than one of his side chicks. He would come over, he would fuck me, and then he would leave. That's all we ever did, and I thought that I was in a real relationship. I had no clue that he was just using me until I found out that he was also doing the same thing with several other girls, just like Brooks was. He told me that he loved me and that I was special, but when I confronted him that night, he told me that I was fat and ugly and that I would never be the kind of girl that he could fall in love with. He said that he was embarrassed to bring me around anyone he knew.

"Finding out that I meant nothing to him was my second heartbreak. So, the night I confronted him, I filled his drink with my mother's Xanax prescription. She had tons of that kind of stuff from when she was sick. I crushed it up so fine that he didn't even know it was in there, and he drank it. Jay never made it home that night."

"Emily, everything is going to be fine. You have Hudson now, and our family. You won't have to be heartbroken ever again," Evelyn says to me as she starts walking away from the apple trees.

"You're wrong, Evelyn!" I scream at her, and she turns back around to look at me, stunned with fear streaking across her face. "Unfortunately, Victoria knows about everything and has already told Hudson, so this will be my third heartbreak—losing him and his whole family. It's going to hurt me badly. It already does. I really did love him, you know. I didn't even want to get into a relationship with him in the first place, but he pushed and pushed and pushed until I finally gave in. Then Victoria had to put her nose where it didn't belong and mess everything up, and now, she's also going to have to be heartbroken too. Because of her, I have lost everything. I have lost Hudson, you and your sweet little girl, your parents, and the chance to have a family again."

I reach down and grab the same shovel that I used to protect myself with earlier today.

"Sorry Evelyn, but I have to do this. I was hoping that I could be a part of your family. I really did want you to be my sister."

Evelyn sees the shovel in my hand, and she tries to run away back to safety, only she gets confused and runs in the opposite direction, away from my house, towards the ravine. I take the shovel and follow closely behind her. I don't have to move quickly because she keeps running into trees and falling over. When she comes out of the orchard and sees the deep crevasse sprawled out in front of her, she stops dead in her tracks. She turns around and looks at me. Her eyes are so filled with fright that it barely even looks like sweet, kind Evelyn anymore.

"Emily, please don't do this!"

49

Victoria

"We have to call the police now!"

My voice is shrill and panicked. I pull up Evelyn's location on my phone, and it comes back saying *Location is unavailable.*

"It's fine, Vic. We don't need to worry too much about it right now. Emily doesn't know that you know anything yet, or that you have told me. I talked to her just earlier and told her that you were coming back to apologize. That you were going to go into treatment. We just need to get out there, get Evelyn away from her, and then drive to the police station and explain everything."

"No, Hudson, you don't understand!" I say hysterically.

"Understand what?"

"I already told Emily everything. I called her right before I got here and talked to you. If Evelyn is out there at her house, who knows what Emily will do to her. She is bound to be really upset with me, with all of us."

We both run out of Hudson's house as fast as we can. He takes my keys and starts driving towards Emily's house, speeding so fast in the falling snow that I worry we will slip off the road.

"How long ago did you call her and tell her?"

"I don't know, maybe an hour ago, maybe two."

"Okay, now you need to call the police. We don't have time to wait for the detective to call us back."

I call the emergency police number and explain the situation. I frantically tell the operator that there is a psychopath that might hurt our sister, and they need to send out the police right away.

"Is your sister in immediate danger?" the woman asks me.

"Yes, she is! My brother's girlfriend might hurt her. She is really mad right now and has hurt other people in the past. She might have even killed before."

I detect a note of insincerity in the woman's voice when she tells me they will send a non-emergency officer out to the residence. I try to argue with her more about the urgency of the matter, but she tells me that someone will be out there as soon as they can.

"They are going to send someone out, but they aren't taking it seriously. I don't know how long it will be, so you need to hurry, Hudson."

"Why would you do that, Victoria?" he says worriedly. "Why the hell would you call Emily and tell her before talking to me?"

"I thought that it would be okay. I was going to be with you and didn't think she could hurt us anymore, after I told you. I had no idea Evelyn was going to her house."

The half an hour it takes to get to Emily's house is brutal. Visions of her hurting Evelyn keep swirling through my mind. I keep looking over at Hudson. His face is distorted into a Hudson that I barely recognize. It's snowing harder outside now, and I am worried that the road is slippery, but I keep yelling at him to drive faster. To try to keep myself occupied by trying Evelyn's phone over and over, to no avail. I even try Emily's number and there is no answer there either.

We pull up into her driveway and see that both Evelyn's car and Emily's truck are parked there. We run into the house, yelling their names, and there is no answer. We check the workshop also, but no one is there. I follow Hudson as he runs out back towards what looks like the orchard. The trees are all overgrown and overlap each other, making it hard to see anything. Hudson yells their names over and over. I try to keep up with him, but the tree branches and bushes are scratching me, and it hurts. I hear Hudson far ahead calling out. I finally come to a clearing and see Hudson looking around at the trees, his face distorted with torment.

"This should have been where they were picking apples!" he calls out when he sees me.

I search around frantically. The snow is falling in thick chunks, making it difficult to see anything. My legs and arms are scratched up and bleeding. I'm freezing already from the cold temperatures outside. Hudson takes off running again and I follow him. We come out of the orchard, and I see him standing at the edge, looking down at something that I assume is the ravine. I finally get up next to him, trying to catch my breath. I look down into the deep crevasse squinting my eyes, trying to see what he is looking at.

"What are you looking at?" I say breathlessly.

The wind has picked up now, and I have to raise my voice so he can hear me.

"I don't know!" he yells back to me over the wind. "Can you see anything down there? Does that look like a person to you?"

Hudson is standing so close to the edge. I grab his arm so that he doesn't stumble into it.

I look down harder to try and see what he is seeing. I see something that looks like it has the shape of a person, but it's hard to make it out because it's pretty far down there and the snow is piling up. The wind blows harder, moving the freshly fallen snow around, and then I see it. Long dark hair strewn out around a human head that looks like it is covered in something dark, maybe blood. I start screaming uncontrollably. A guttural sound that I don't recognize comes out.

"No, no, no, no! Hudson, we need to get down there! It's Evelyn!"

He isn't speaking or moving; he just stands there completely still, staring at Evelyn's body. I keep screaming and start to pace back and forth, looking for a way to get down into the ravine. If I can just find a path that leads down there, then I can help Evelyn.

Hudson grabs my arms and shakes me violently.

"Victoria, you aren't going to be able to help her now!" His face is stricken with grief.

"We need to get down to her! She might still be alive!"

I try to pull away from him, but he grips my arms tighter.

"Victoria, listen to me! You can't get down there. It's too steep and slippery with the snow falling." I try to pull away, but he screams in my face, "Look! She isn't moving at all. If she fell from this height, she wouldn't still be alive."

I start to cry uncontrollably. I step away from the edge of the ravine because my legs are unsteady, and I don't trust myself not to fall down in there. Poor Evelyn, my sweet, loving sister, laying down there all alone, the freezing snow falling on top of her.

"What happened? How did she get down there?" I cry out.

Hudson bends his head down and starts crying with me.

"You know what happened. Emily is what happened."

"Do you think she pushed her over?" I say, but I already know the answer to that question. She pushed her stepfather over a cliff, so of course she would do this to Evelyn, too, just to get back at me for telling Hudson and ruining her life.

"Emily! Where are you?" Hudson screams out, his voice sounding raving mad. "How could you do this?"

"Hudson, we need to call the police again and tell them there is an emergency now! Maybe they can get down there and help her. I don't want to believe that she is dead. I just can't... I-I-I can't go through this again. I can't lose another person that I love."

All those old feelings resurfaced, the ones I had the night the police came to my door and told me that my parents wouldn't be coming home ever again. The immense pain that I felt when I heard the two officers say that they were both dead.

Hudson finally snaps out of his rage and pulls out his cell phone, and just as he dials their numbers for the emergency line, I hear something in the distance. It's faint. The wind is gusting loudly, so it's hard to make out what the sound was. Hudson must hear it, too, because he freezes and looks around wildly.

"Did you hear that?" I ask him.

"Shhhh, I think I heard someone calling my name," he says.

We both stand perfectly still until we hear it again. Louder this time.

"Hudson…"

We hear a weak female voice call out to us. We start running toward the voice when we see Evelyn sitting up against a tree near the edge of the orchard. She is covered in snow, and there is blood dripping from her head.

50

Victoria

A few grueling hours later, Hudson and I are finally allowed to go into Evelyn's hospital room and see her. They needed to sew up the large gash in her head, and the police needed to question all of us about what exactly happened today. The sight of her laying in that hospital bed, with that ugly blue gown on and her head bandaged up, made me burst into tears of joy that she was okay, but also tears of rage at what Emily has done to her. I run over and jump into her bed, throwing my arms around her weak body, burrowing my head into her.

"Hey, hey, I'm okay, Victoria. Just some stitches and some bruises," she says, comforting me when I am the one who should be comforting her.

I can't help it. I am sobbing uncontrollably into her chest while she rubs my hair.

"I thought that you were dead. Hudson and I saw a person down in the ravine and thought that it was you. I wouldn't have been able to handle that. It was too much to think that I might not ever see you again."

"You saw a person in the ravine?" Evelyn asks, confused.

Hudson walks into the room shortly after me. The doctors tried to tell us that Evelyn was only allowed one visitor at a time, but we told them that was unacceptable and wouldn't take no for an answer.

"No, we only thought it was you because we couldn't find you. It was only some branches from the trees and some rocks, but it really did look like it might be a person for a moment," he says.

"I am going to kill that bitch when they find her. I am going to make her pay for everything she has done," I say, still sobbing.

"Don't worry, Victoria, the police are out looking for her now, and they will find her. The detective assured us of that. They will take care of everything. And don't worry, Evelyn. I have been on the phone with Matt and Mom and Dad constantly over the last few hours. They are all safe back at your house with the kids. They have two officers watching the house until they find Emily."

"Detective Bryant told me that, but thanks for keeping in touch with them, especially Matt. I am sure that he is going crazy with worry right now."

"He wanted to get in the car and drive here as soon as he found out, but the police told him he needed to stay with the kids. I am sure that it was really hard to know that it was best to stay with them knowing that you were here. He calmed down when he knew that me and Victoria were going to be here the entire time."

"What happened out there, Evelyn?" I ask her.

"I really don't know. One minute I was talking with a girl that I thought was a good person, that nice girl that had been so kind, then all of a sudden, she was completely different. Angry and hateful. She told me that she killed her stepfather, and then I thought she was going to kill me. I was so scared. I tried to run away from her, and then everything went black."

Evelyn's eyes fill with horror, remembering what happened, and a tear runs down her cheek.

"It's okay. You don't have to strain yourself right now. You need to rest. We can talk about everything when you are better, after they catch Emily and she is in jail," Hudson says calmly to her.

"I still can't wrap my head around what happened. I don't understand how she could have deceived everyone the way that she did. I tried to tell Detective Bryant everything that she told me, but it's hard to remember everything she said."

Two men come in, breaking the tension in Evelyn's hospital room, a well-received interruption. One of the men is Detective Bryant, who had questioned me and Hudson earlier, and a new officer named Mays.

"Oh, thank God," I say, relieved to see them. "Do you have Emily in custody?"

The two men look timidly at each other before delivering the news to us.

"Well, Mrs. Berman, I am sorry to say that we haven't found her yet. We had several officers search the house, the workshop, her vehicle, the orchard, and the business down on Plum Street, but unfortunately, we found nothing. Don't worry, we are still looking. Her name has been flagged, so if she tries to get on a plane or rent a car, we will know about it right away. Do you know if she had another vehicle? Or if there was someone else out there when you arrived? Another car?" Detective Bryant asks Hudson.

"No, she just had that Dodge Ram truck."

"Are you sure about that? We found tire tracks in the snow indicating that another car, a much smaller one, had driven away from the residence. It looked like it was parked behind the workshop. Do you ever remember seeing a car parked back there before, or maybe just today, Mr. Berman?"

"No, never. I spent lots of time out there in the workshop with Emily and on her property, and there was never another car parked there. Plus, Victoria and I searched the whole area when we got there, and still no car," Hudson tells them.

"Hmmm, okay then," the detective says suspiciously to Hudson. "The thing is, the car was already on her property. There are no tracks leading to the house, only away from it down the driveway.

"Maybe we just didn't see another car. We were in full panic mode by the time we got there," I tell the detective.

"It doesn't seem like she took much from inside the house. Some clothing seems to be taken, makeup, most of the bathroom items... But we will still be investigating all of that." He turns his attention to Evelyn. "Now, you said that you weren't sure what she hit you in the head with. Were you able to remember anything?"

"It's hard to remember, everything was all happening so fast, and I was scared out of my mind, but I am pretty sure that it was something wooden, maybe a tool she had by the trees," Evelyn tells them.

"Wooden like a tree branch, perhaps?"

"Yeah, that could have been what it was."

"Okay, we found some branches that had your blood on them, but with the snow falling so hard, it's hard to be sure that any one of them was the weapon used, but we will keep looking and be in touch with you."

"Wait, what do you mean, be in touch with us?" I raise my voice at the detectives. "You need to find her now, like tonight. She is dangerous, and she could come back and kill one of us—or all of us. She killed her stepfather and admitted it, and she has already threatened me and tried to hurt me before. Call Sienna Sutton or Patricia Panchak, and get in touch with the detectives who investigated those cases."

"I know that you all are very worried right now, and what happened to you and your sister is very serious, but we are doing everything we can to find Amelia Lewis. We have all the information that you gave us and will be contacting the proper authorities in Illinois. In the meantime, we are going to keep guard outside of the hospital room and at your residence until we find out more."

The detectives turn to leave the room, and I can't help but get an intense sinking feeling deep in the pit of my stomach. They can't just leave us like this. Emily is still out there. She might be right outside of the hospital right now waiting for me. After all, I am the one she would most likely want to hurt. If she wanted to kill Evelyn, she would have. She only hurt her to send a message. I am the one she will be after.

I stand up and follow them out of the room, yelling at them as they walk down the hallway, "So that's it? You are just going to abandon us like this?"

"Mrs. Berman, we are not going to abandon you. We are going to keep looking until we find her."

51

Victoria

It's been a week and still no news about Emily. The detectives said that she left no trail of where she had gone and that they don't have any leads. They found nothing missing from her store, so when she left her house in Aurora, she just vanished in a car that was never on the property in the first place.

I have wracked my brain over and over and don't remember seeing any way she could have left the house. There was no other car parked there unless she had it hidden somehow. The detectives alluded a few times during my dozens of phone calls that we were perhaps somehow involved with her leaving, that we weren't telling them everything we knew. They treated us like we were accomplices in what happened to Evelyn. They don't even seem to be doing much of an investigation anymore. They said that because Evelyn had only minor injuries, they couldn't justify the nationwide search that I demanded from them. They said that they were looking into what happened in Illinois to Jay and Brooks but have not come up with any proof.

"Evelyn was the proof!" I yelled at Detective Bryant on the phone yesterday. "She told you that Emily admitted that she killed her stepfather."

Detective Bryant, with his annoyingly calm nature, told me that they can't rely on anything Evelyn said because she had a head injury and can't remember a lot of what Emily had said.

That was unfortunately true. Evelyn has not been able to remember most of what happened that day, or maybe she is blocking it out. I told her that we need to see a psychologist or maybe a hypnotist to help her recover the missing memories, but she said she just wants to forget about everything and be with her family. She had the nerve to tell me that we all need to start thinking about moving on with our lives since they haven't been able to find her, but that's bullshit. I can't just move on.

Every day is hard to get through, knowing that she is still out there. She could pop up at any time and hurt one of us again. I barely sleep. The nightmares come every single time I close my eyes. I check over my shoulder every five minutes when I leave the house. I am constantly worried that she is lurking around the corner. When I eat or drink anything, I am worried that it will be drugged with something and that I won't be able to protect my family.

Hudson hasn't been the same since that horrible day either. He is really depressed and won't even leave his house for anything, not even to go to the store. He is scared, too, that she is out there and might even still miss her a little bit. I threw out all her things so he wouldn't have to look at them and made sure there was no sign left of her at his house.

Thankfully he has me here. I haven't left his side all week, not once. I have everything we need delivered right to the front door.

Today though, I need to leave to go to the jeweler to get my bracelet and go back home to pack some more things. I tell Hudson that I will only be gone for an hour tops, and he has assured me that he will be okay while I am gone, so I feel confident that leaving will be okay.

"Hi, my name is Victoria Berman. I am here to pick up a bracelet that my mother, Betty Berman, brought in last week," I say to the lady working at the jeweler's today. I have never met her before. We usually deal with Gerard. He has been the owner here for as long as I can remember.

She looks at me with confusion and calls to a man in the back.

"Gerard, there is someone here to pick up a bracelet!"

Gerard comes to the front. "Ah, Victoria," he says cheerfully. "What can I help you with today?"

I explain to him that I am here to get my silver bangle.

"I know that I was supposed to come and get it sooner, but our family has been going through some things right now. I assume that it is ready for me?"

"Yes, your mother brought in the bracelet last Wednesday, but then it was picked up later that same day. I was told that you were going on a big trip and needed to get it back right away."

"Did you say last Wednesday?"

"Yes, I remember thinking it was strange that she was back in on the same day to retrieve the bracelet. She was lucky that I had already finished. It was all cleaned and shiny for you by the time she came back."

"No, that is not possible. My mom would not have done that without telling me, and besides, she was not available last Wednesday evening to come in. You see, we had a family emergency that day and—"

"No, it wasn't your mother who came and got it," Gerard interrupts. "It was that lovely young lady that is dating your brother, Hudson."

My heart stops beating. I try to take in a breath, and I can't. I manage to get just one word out.

"Who?"

"Your future sister-in-law, Emily."

I don't remember leaving the jeweler and I don't remember driving to my apartment. The whole way there, all I could think about is that she took my bracelet. That fucking bitch Emily went into the jeweler and stole my bracelet, and I will never see it again.

I pull up in front of my apartment building and put my head down on my steering wheel. I let the tears fall from my face, seething with grief over the loss of it. My mother gave that to me when I was so young. I have worn it almost my entire life. I don't know how to live without having it on my wrist, being able to touch it and feel the presence of my parents. It was the only thing that kept me sane at times, knowing that it was there.

I pull myself together long enough to walk into my building and head toward the elevator. The landlord—I can never remember his name—tries to stop me as I walk through the lobby. I have no time to deal with him right now. I am barely able to hold it together long enough to get my things. I can't imagine what he must want, but I am sure that it's not worth my time right now.

I walk into my living room and start to pack a bag to take back to Hudson's. I originally thought that I would just bring a few things so that I could stay there a few more days, until Hudson can get back on his feet, but now I know that I cannot be alone either. Her presence is still everywhere, especially now that I know she has my bracelet. She has ruined everything. My family is broken, and now my heart is broken.

I grab my largest suitcase instead of the bag I had intended on bringing. I don't even know what I throw into it. I just fill it with whatever seems important so that I can leave here as soon as possible and get back home to Hudson.

As I walk back through the lobby, the landlord is still there waiting for me and stops me.

"Victoria, I signed for this today. It's for you."

He hands me a manilla envelope addressed to me in red ink. The return address is my parents' cabin in Knox. That's strange. I don't remember my mom telling me that she was mailing anything to my apartment. She knows that I have been staying with Hudson.

I look up at the landlord. "Where did you get this?" I hiss at him louder than I intended to.

"It came in the mail today, certified mail. They wouldn't leave it without someone signing for it. Are you okay, Victoria? You look like you have seen a ghost."

I get to my car and open it. A gust of an awful smell fills the inside of my car. What is that? Burning smoke, maybe?

Inside the large envelope is a small stack of white copy paper and a smaller envelope with my name on it written, again in red ink. I pull out the papers and notice that the edges have been burned on each of the pages. I flip through the pages and realize with shock that these are copies from a notebook. Not just any notebook—*my* notebook, the one from that night over a year ago.

How in the hell is this possible? I set that notebook on fire, so how is it not burned to ashes? Where did this come from? I look back at the front of the larger envelope and see that it is in fact my parents' address. They couldn't have sent this. They thought that I was on a biking trip that night, and if they did somehow know, they would have said something to me a long time ago. Betty and Bob are not ones to keep these kinds of things to themselves, especially when it involves me.

I reach back inside and grab the smaller envelope and open it. Inside is a handwritten note also written in red ink.

Dear Victoria,

I hope that you are well. I know that I am. You thought that you ruined my life, and you might be taking pleasure in thinking that, but just know that you didn't. By now I am somewhere far, far away, having a way better time than you are. You tried to ruin my life and now I am going to ruin yours. I have the original notebook. Well, I should say I had the original notebook. The police should have it here in a few days, and you might have to answer for the damage you caused and for lying about it. I also mailed a copy of it to your parents' cabin. I wish I could see how upset Betty and Bob will be when they find out what you did.

I hope you like how authentic I tried to make it look, by burning the edges, and writing in red ink. Just like the color of the fire that you set in August last year. I thought that was a nice touch. I am wondering if you know that I have your bracelet yet. It's absolutely stunning and looks better on me.

So, I guess I'll say my goodbye to you now. Hopefully the next time I see you will be behind bars.

Love, Emily

The pages from the envelope and the letter slowly fall from my fingers to the floor of my car. I am too numb to move. I am immediately thrust back into that moment, the night of the fire. I can't see anything around me except the memory of red and orange flames bouncing around. I even think that I can feel the heat on my face for a moment. It starts to get hotter and hotter, so I try to pull myself back into the moment. I try to lift my hand to start my car to roll down the window, but my body won't move. I gasp for breath to cleanse out the smell of smoke that surely can't actually be real, but I realize that I am not even breathing. I start to gag and choke. I can't manage to suck in any air. It's like this nightmare will never end.

I hear the sound of knocking, and a faint sound of a man's voice calling my name. It's muffled like it's far away. All at once, my vision and my hearing come back from that horrible night long ago...

I look around and see that I am still in my car, and there is a man knocking loudly on my window, yelling at me to roll it down. I realize that it's my landlord, and he looks terrified. There are people stopped on the street staring into my car with horror stricken across their faces.

I reach over and push the button that rolls down my window.

"Jesus Christ, Victoria! Are you okay? Should I call someone?"

"Why?"

"My dear, you were screaming something awful and clawing at your face and neck. I was just about to call the police or an ambulance to get you out of the car."

I look down at my hands and see that there are a few small spots of blood under my nails.

Epilogue

I stretch out lazily on my beach chair, breathing in deeply. The salty ocean air fills my lungs and gives me a sense of calm and peace. I lift my arm up above me and twist and shake my wrist back and forth, admiring the way the sun rays reflect off the tiny charms on the silver bangle bracelet. I listen to the melodious chiming the charms make as they bounce off each other. It's like these charms were made for me, a part of my life—my history, not hers. A fit of happy laughter bursts out of me. This place is way better than Ohio. I should have just come here first. It's where I always wanted to be.

I will say that I do miss some things: I miss my house and the beautiful orchard. I miss the way it looked in the early mornings before I would start my run; that will be forever ingrained in my memories. And I miss my dear friend Harper. I know that she is doing well. According to her social media, she is blissfully happy with her new husband, but I won't miss anything else, certainly none of the members of the Berman family. They were all stuck-up fakes and liars who couldn't accept me for who I am and had to find some sort of fault in me. The Teal Lotus was going to be beautiful, but all that work wasn't leaving any room for fun. It was all work and no play.

The only thing I will take from knowing Hudson is that I am still so young and have a lot of living to do. Sure, he was fun while he lasted, and I definitely didn't mind getting out of him what I needed, but now what I need is to get out there and explore life. I shouldn't tie myself down to a life of working nonstop around the clock, killing myself at such a young age. I need to get out there and explore this world and enjoy my time here. I can start my own business anywhere when I'm finally ready.

Hudson turned out to be a traitorous asshole. He went behind my back to help his sister. Turns out he has a history of turning his back on people like that. He did the same thing to poor Samantha. After leaving that awful day in November in her little red Honda Civic, I searched through her belongings and found all sorts of information about her. I found the passwords for her bank account, which was almost empty, and her credit card, which had been maxed out, and I also found the passcode for her phone, so I was able to review all of her texts and social media, which told me a lot more about who Hudson really was. In the car here were also some journals that she would occasionally write in. I read everything that I could find about her in that car. Hudson sure has a way of finding girls that he can prey on. Young, weak girls who don't have anyone else to lean on. Samantha was caught in his treacherous web the way that I was. She was just a poor orphan who had been through several foster homes growing up, abused over and over until she ran away. She probably could have gotten her life together if she wouldn't have met Hudson.

It was too bad that I had to kill her and push her body into the ravine. Perhaps the two of us could have been friends, but after all, she did try to kill me first. I had to do what I had to do. Sometimes that's the way it goes. It's been six months and they still haven't found her body yet. By now she is either buried under the mud, rocks, and tree branches, or the animals have gotten to her, leaving her nothing but bones. I don't think anyone will be looking for her or missing her anyways, as sad as that is.

Thanks to the media frenzy about who really started that fire on Plum Street, no one seems to be looking for me. They probably don't believe a word of what Victoria said about me, especially after the family that lived on the third floor got their hands on the notebooks I sent to the police. Apparently, the little boy who was burned had lost the use of his arm because of that fire, so I don't think that Victoria will be getting off too easily for what she did, even with the fancy lawyers she has been parading around the media. It's been wildly entertaining watching the press conferences with her standing in the background looking more like a badly aging woman than the beautiful old-fashioned movie star I had seen her as before.

Everything worked out exactly the way it should have. In the end, I couldn't kill Evelyn; it wasn't her fault she has such horrible siblings, and she didn't deserve to die, even if it meant hurting Victoria and Hudson. Plus, I couldn't do that to her sweet little girl, Addison.

I still have some of my inheritance money left, thanks to my paranoia about Brooks's mother taking it from me somehow that I never kept it in a bank, and I get to live where I always wanted to be. I can honestly say that I have never been happier in my life.

I sit up on my lounge chair and begin to look around for the server to refill my cocktail when I hear a man's voice standing above me.

"Hi," he says in a deep husky tone.

I cover my eyes with one hand to see him better in the sunlight.

"Hello," I say back to him. He's tall, dark, and handsome, with tan skin and a muscular body.

"I was wondering if I might join you. It's a beautiful day today," he says coyly.

A flutter of excitement runs through my body, and I motion to the chair next to me. He sits down quickly, and I notice up close that he has the most beautiful bright blue eyes.

"My name is Robert," he says, holding out his hand.

"Nice to meet you, Robert. My name is Samantha."

Printed in Great Britain
by Amazon